House of Owls

House of Owls

A Fictional Story of Mystery, Politics,
Romance, Murder, and More

Neil Wickham

To order additional copies of this book, contact:
Xlibris
1-888-795-4274
www.Xlibris.com
Orders@Xlibris.com
808780

Acknowledgments

Writing a story is much easier when you receive help and input from many people. I would like to say thank you to all those *many people* who helped me with this book. Thank you all!

While many people helped me in many ways, I would like to say a special thank you to a few who helped a lot. Thank you very much to my niece, Sherry Hinkley, for her professionalism in making my picture look so good. Also, thank you very much to Annie Spiro and her dear, late husband, Dr. Victor Spiro, for the many very valuable suggestions that they made. I must give a very special, super thank you to Bobbi Natale and her dear husband, Elliot, for all the hard work they did in editing and reviewing my story. Not surprisingly, my biggest thank you is for my dear wife, Maggie, for her unending support and for reviewing all aspects of my story.

Thank you all!

Chapter 1
Leather Vest and Black Boots
Thursday, April 18

"Hey, Billy, how ya doin'?" said the big burly man as he barged into my office from the hallway, followed by his sidekick.

"I'm fine," I said. "How can I help you?"

The one who spoke to me was the first man through the doorway. He was a big heavy guy with unruly long dark hair and a beard that was equally unkempt. He was dressed in biker-style clothes with a black leather vest and a grubby blue denim shirt and jeans. His heavy work boots were the color of something you might find in a baby's diaper.

He was accompanied by another big burly man whose hair and beard were also long, dark, and scraggly. He was dressed in a similar grungy style with black denim jeans and jacket over a black T-shirt. His big oversized black boots came up his legs almost to his knees. Both these guys were so huge and hairy that they looked like Sasquatches that could be lurking about in a dark forest somewhere. They were both dressed in clothes that were so grungy they would probably be rejected by the Salvation Army Thrift Store.

My office was a good size at about twenty feet by twenty feet, but these two oversized goons made it seem crowded. They looked like they would be out of place anywhere in a well-organized world but were especially out of place in my office.

My office was decorated quite simply in a traditional style with vertical mahogany paneling below the wainscoting and the walls painted with a soft dusty-rose color on the upper half. The only decorations on the walls in my office were my framed MBA certificate from McMaster University and a framed bond certificate.

The bond was one that was issued by the czarist government of Russia in October 1916. The bond certificate had a face value of one thousand rubles and had twenty coupons attached, with stated values of fifty rubles each to be paid one each year for twenty years. One coupon had been clipped and cashed, and the rest were still attached to the certificate. They were never paid because after the Bolshevik revolution in October 1917, the czarist government no longer existed. Their debts were never honored by the seventy-five-year communist dictatorship or by the current so-called democratic government of Russia.

The bond certificate was given to me by one of my first clients. He told me that it would serve as a constant reminder to me and to all who saw it that it is very important to undertake thorough research for any prospective investment before you put your money on the line.

Both thugs glared at me with their dark brown eyes as Leather Vest spoke to me in an accusatory manner. "You're Billy, ain't ya? We thought ya was 'cuz we saw the name on your door that says William R. Jones V. You're sitting in this office, so we guessed you was him. Our friends told us to look for William R. Jones V that everybody calls Billy, so we must be right."

The one with the black boots was carrying a briefcase that was neat-looking and seemed to clash with the clothes they were wearing. As Black Boots opened the briefcase, which looked to be full of money, Leather Vest said, "Our friends would like to offer you some money to cancel the meeting of your "owly" group tomorrow night and break up your owly club. We've got two hundred thousand dollars here, and it's all yours if you agree."

"Yes, I'm Billy, and there is no way that I will accept your attempt to bribe me," I answered in a loud voice. "I don't know who you are. You didn't tell me who you are, and I don't accept bribes. When you come into our company's office, you're supposed to wait in the reception area until you are invited in to see someone," I said with as much authority as I could muster.

I was no shrinking violet at six feet, one inch tall and a fit 195 pounds from my almost daily workout regimen. I also recently started learning karate since I was roughed up a little in a bar at a Super Bowl party back in the early part of February. I had only advanced two levels so far, to the orange belt, and I didn't feel ready to use my new weapon just yet. My better judgment advised me that it would not be a good idea to get into a physical tussle with the two mammoths who looked like they had sledgehammers for fists.

I was a cautious and conservative MBA investment guy dressed in clothes that were not really suitable for boxing or wrestling. Since I didn't want to get into a physical battle against these two monsters, I stayed behind my three feet by six feet heavy mahogany desk with my laptop computer on top, all of which provided a small boost to my confidence. But they could still get to me quite easily if they wanted to.

There was nobody at the front desk when we came in, so we came right through looking for ya. We're here to give ya a message from our friends. They told us that you and your owly bunch are trying to change how our government works and they don't like that. We came to offer you some cash and to tell ya what our friends would like," said Leather Vest. "Do you get the message, Billy?"

Leather Vest spoke loudly and forcefully, which was quite intimidating. With his reference to my owly friends, I realized that the purpose of the visit from these two goons was an attempt to threaten my associates in the House of Owls group and me. They seemed to be strongly opposed to us moving forward with our program to develop and promote the concepts of Direct Democracy, a form of government where referenda are held for all legislation and political decisions.

"I know what you are saying, big man, but it just won't happen that way. The meetings of our group will continue because we care about Direct Democracy. We will not be stopped by what you and your frightened, fanatical little friends say or do. Get out of my office immediately, or I will phone the police and have you arrested for trespassing. Get out of here now!" I ordered.

Both Leather Vest and Black Boots seemed to get the message that I was serious about telling them to leave. My threat to phone the police seemed to frighten them a little, so they left.

I followed them out of my office at a safe distance and watched them go down the stairway and out the front door of our office building into the parking area. I went to the window at the front of the second floor, pulled the drape aside, and looked out. It was a clear and bright spring afternoon, and I could easily see the two thugs as I watched them jump into a large black pickup truck and drive away. I could see by the emblem on the tailgate that it was a Ram Big Horn 4X4 pickup truck, but I couldn't read the license plate because it was smudged over with mud and was unreadable.

I did notice that their license plate had black letters and numbers on a white background, the colors of license plates for pickup trucks in the Province of Ontario. Most other vehicles in Ontario had blue letters and numbers on a white background. Our town, Niagara-on-the-Lake, is a touristy town, and we often see cars, pickup trucks, and other vehicles with license plates from many other places especially from the New York state just across the Niagara River from here.

Chapter 2
Reflections
Thursday, April 18

As I was returning to my office and reflecting on this incident, it seemed to me that for some reason, the so-called "friends" of Leather Vest and Black Boots were strongly opposed to our new Direct Democracy movement. I guess that it might be reasonable, from their perspective, to oppose Direct Democracy. It would take away the ability of lobbyists to win friends and influence people by paying large chunks of money or giving other types of "gifts" to influence voting by elected representatives. This is the way they so often do now, just like what they tried to do with me here today.

It was only two weeks ago that we started to get organized and decided to name our new group the House of Owls. One of the reasons for the choice of that name was the onomatopoeic acronym HOO. Many organizations tend to use acronyms, and we liked the sound of this one. The other main reason was that an owl was the symbol for the ancient city-state of Athens in Greece, where the basic concepts of democracy were developed.

As I walked back from the window heading toward my office, I saw that Sally James was at her desk. Sally was a blond-haired, medium-height, medium-build, smartly dressed, fashionable lady in her early fifties. She was our highly efficient gatekeeper, receptionist, telephone operator mail clerk, stationery supplies organizer, and general helper for everything. She sat at a horseshoe-shaped reception desk, with the open side of the desk at her back toward the wall, in the front lobby on the second floor. Another one of her jobs was to direct clients and other visitors to various peoples' offices.

The reception area had a light-beige-colored, herringbone-patterned Berber carpet, and the walls were painted a light dusty rose color. The words *William R. Jones Investment Company* were in big deep-burgundy-colored letters on the wall behind Sally. I asked her how Leather Vest and Black Boots were able to get through my office. She told me that it must have been during the few moments that she had slipped out to go to the washroom.

The grand edifice that is the office building owned and occupied by the William R. Jones Investment Company was built by my grandfather, William R. Jones III, in the southeastern part of the town of Niagara-on-the-Lake. He had the foresight to think that the company's future office-space requirements would probably be much greater than the then current needs. That was why he had the building made much larger than was needed at the time it was built.

Our company's office building was two stories high. The street level was occupied by our real estate division, which manages the many company-owned properties as well as other properties managed for real estate investment clients. The street-level floor also housed a company-owned, real estate sales agency business and a modest-sized lunchroom. I had an office on the second floor, as did my father, my grandfather, and all the other investment division personnel of William R. Jones Investment Company.

Our town, Niagara-on-the-Lake, had a population of only about 18,000 but had more than 3.5 million visitors each year. Some of the younger millennials liked to refer to the name of our town by the acronym NOTL. I preferred to use the full name. NOTL sounded like it could be the name of the eighth sibling of the Von Trapp family singers to go along with Gretl and Lisl.

In viewing the geography of the Niagara Peninsula, it looks almost like a rectangle. The south shore of Lake Ontario would be the top line of the rectangle, and the north shore of Lake Erie would be the bottom line. The Niagara River, including Niagara Falls, would be the right-hand side. The vertical line of the rectangle on the east and the western side opens out into the heartland area of southwestern Ontario and the rest of Canada. Niagara-on-the-Lake is in the upper right-hand corner of the rectangle where the Niagara River flows from Lake Erie into Lake Ontario before the water continues to flow downstream through Lake Ontario to the Saint Lawrence River and eventually out through the Gulf of St. Lawrence into the North Atlantic Ocean and beyond.

Chapter 3
House of Owls
Thursday, April 18

The House of Owls was created nearly two weeks ago at a meeting on April 5. The small founding group thought that it was a good idea for North American society to begin to move forward from the current form of representative, democratic government. We all thought that it was time to advance to Direct Democracy, the form of democracy where all people vote directly on all issues rather than through their elected representatives whose opinions are often tainted and motivated by extraneous considerations, the prospects for personal gains, or both.

At the founding meeting, there were four of us from the Niagara-on-the-Lake area of Ontario and four like-minded people from the Niagara Falls area of New York state.

I, Billy Jones, was the instigator of the Canadian group that consists of my good friends Henri Renault and his wife Jeanne, Paul Browne, and myself.

I have known the Renault family for many years. They own and operate one of the 150 or so wineries in the greater Niagara region of Southern Ontario. Henri was about five feet, eleven inches tall with dark blond hair and was quite fit from working hard. He worked at the family winery all through his years of high school and university and inherited the winery when his father passed away five years ago. His wife, formerly Jeanne Boudreau, grew up on her family's vineyard next door to the Renaults. Jeanne was about five feet, six inches tall with sandy blond hair and was also very fit from working hard at the winery. Henri and Jeanne were nearly lifelong friends and became husband and wife three years ago. They own and manage the Chateau des Chutes Winery.

Paul Browne was a successful, local, independent lawyer who was very interested in the political process. Paul was six feet tall with dark hair, very lean and fit, and was always impeccably dressed. He represented both our firms, William R. Jones Investment Company and the Renault's Chateau des Chutes Winery, as well as other clients. His law firm had four other lawyers as well as himself with six support staff and was one of the few law firms based in Niagara-on-the-Lake. He had been a good friend of our family for many years.

The group of four from the Niagara Falls, New York area, included Maria Simone, her father Michael Simone, John Weldon, and his wife Samantha. Maria and Samantha became interested in Direct Democracy through their study of ancient history and their interest in politics. They were both high school history teachers working at different schools in the Niagara frontier area in New York state. They had known each other and had been good friends for many years all the way back to grade school, and they were both interested in politics as well as history.

Michael Simone joined the House of Owls because he was personally very interested in Direct Democracy and also because he wanted to support his daughter's interests. He was an experienced CPA and had a very successful private accounting practice based in Niagara Falls that covered all of the Western New York state area.

Much like Michael Simone, John Weldon joined the House of Owls group because he was personally very interested in Direct Democracy and also wanted to support his wife's, Samantha's, interest. He was a civil engineer and was a founding partner in a successful local engineering company.

I had been interested in politics since my early teens mainly because my family had always been interested in politics. Political events and ideas were a frequent source of conversation at our dinner table for as long as I can remember. My family knew that they needed to be constantly, politically alert because they knew that politicians were always looking for new ways to take more money from people with higher incomes and stronger financial positions.

The first meeting of the magnificent eight was in the boardroom at Michael Simone's office in a midsize commercial office building on Main Street in downtown Niagara Falls, New York. Michael's office occupied the whole fifth floor of the ten-story building. His accounting and bookkeeping practice needed that much space to accommodate his staff of twenty people, which included five other CPAs in addition to himself.

The eight of us first got together after Paul Browne had read an article in the *Buffalo News* about a Direct Democracy movement being organized in the western part of New York state that mentioned the name of Michael Simone. Paul followed this up by contacting Michael, which led to all of us getting together to discuss our mutual interest to see if we could somehow work together. Now both groups were working together under our chosen name of House of Owls.

At our first meeting, none of us was surprised to discover that we all had the same objectives of wanting to promote the development of Direct Democracy at all levels of government in our respective regions, in both Canada and the United States. We all knew that this would be a formidable challenge, but we thought we were ready to take it on.

We all had past experiences that showed us quite clearly how undemocratic the present system of representative democracy could be. Each of us had seen that time after time, political representatives were elected even though most of the electorate agreed with only a few of their primary policies but strongly disagreed with many of their other political ideas. The result was that most people didn't like or didn't want the legislation that was often passed.

The main problem was that in each election, the person who did not win also usually had some good policy ideas but fewer meaningful and acceptable ones than the person who was elected. As a result, many good political ideas were never brought to the table for consideration. Direct Democracy could help to solve that problem. Every citizen should have the democratic right to express their view on all issues by a referendum of all citizens on each and every issue. That was the only true democratic way.

After lengthy discussions on our objectives, about how we would organize our group, and what name to call ourselves, we chose to incorporate as a not-for-profit political organization using the name House of Owls. We did not want to be a political party, but rather a political movement that could appeal to all political parties. We decided to meet again in two weeks on Friday, April 19, at the Renault's Chateau des Chutes Winery in Niagara-on-the-Lake. We also decided to invite as many friends, acquaintances, and business associates as we could entice to join us at the meeting.

We all agreed to the name House of Owls because we wanted a name for our organization that was both distinctive and relevant. Maria and Samantha, our two history teachers, reminded us that owls had always been relevant to democracy because owls were the symbol of the ancient Grecian city-state of Athens, where democracy was first organized.

Athenian democracy developed at about 500 BC in the city-state of Athens, which was comprised of the ancient city of Athens and the surrounding territory of Attica. One of the most important elements of Athenian democracy was that it was a system of Direct Democracy wherein all citizens vote directly on all legislation and executive bills.

The word *democracy* itself is derived from the ancient Greek language. The Greek word *demos* means "people," and the Greek word *kratos* means "power." Democracy is "people power."

The owl of Athena was the very well-recognized symbol of ancient Athens. In Greek mythology, a little owl traditionally represented Athena, the virgin goddess of wisdom, after whom the city of Athens was named. The owl was also used extensively as a symbol of knowledge and wisdom for many years throughout the Western world.

All the people in our founding group were very happy to go along with the recommendation of the history teachers and use the owl as the symbol for our new group, which quickly adopted the name House of Owls and the agenda to promote Direct Democracy whenever and wherever we could.

Chapter 4
The Man
Thursday, April 18

After Leather Vest and Black Boots left Billy's office on Thursday, they drove south on the Niagara Parkway toward Niagara Falls. On the way, they flipped the switch to automatically change their license plates back to the orange-and-black New York–state ones. This would make it easier for them to get across the Rainbow Bridge and back into the United States at Niagara Falls, New York.

Once they crossed the bridge and cleared through US Customs and Immigration, they headed toward the I-90 highway going east toward their home in Albany, the New York state capital about three hundred miles from Niagara Falls. Usually, this trip would take about four and a half hours, but with a heavy foot on the gas, they made it in just under four hours this time.

Leather Vest and Black Boots knew that they should report to "The Man" as soon as they could. It was late in the afternoon when they arrived back in Albany, and they went straight to his downtown office to report on the success, or lack of it, of their meeting with Billy Jones at his office in Niagara-on-the-Lake.

The Man showed them into his office and offered them coffee, which they both accepted. His office was medium-sized and sparsely decorated but was designed for functionality rather than as a big business-executive showplace.

The showplace for his business was actually his large, well-appointed and well-equipped boardroom. It was twenty feet wide by thirty-five feet long. It had a long highly polished mahogany table and a dozen executive-style black leather chairs placed around the table. The carpet was a plush, rich-looking cappuccino color matching the color of the painted walls. The boardroom also contained a large flat-screen TV, two laptops, and numerous other gadgets, including window blinds that went up or down at the flip of a switch. The Man used his grand boardroom only for meetings with important clients.

The Man was of medium height, about five feet, nine inches tall with a slim build and short and thinning dark hair. He was well-dressed in a suit and tie, but altogether, he still looked a bit like a weasel.

After minimal small talk, he began to ask questions about various projects that his henchmen were working on. He told them, "I've had a report back from the client who bought the Mercedes 360 SL that you took from the driveway of its owner. The car is now on its way out of the country to the overseas buyer. That went well."

Leather Vest, who was often the spokesman for the dynamic duo, spoke up and told The Man, "The pharmacist in Rochester, Dr. Rajinder Singh, had continued to refuse to fill the extra prescriptions for opioid drugs that we asked him to do. Now he's sleeping with the fishes in Lake Ontario, and we don't think he will be found any time soon. Cement coffins don't float too good, do they?"

"I have some good news," said The Man. "Our former client who used to deal in making phony credit cards and selling them is back in business. He would like us to provide him with credit card data again, like we used to do. You remember, names, credit card numbers, and PIN numbers that he can use to make new phony credit cards from blanks. Do you still have those devices that you used to place into ATMs and gas pump card readers before?"

Leather Vest answered, "Ya, we still got about thirty of 'em, and we both remember how to use 'em."

"That's good," said The Man. "I don't want you to use them here in Albany. Maybe Rochester, Syracuse, or Buffalo would be better."

"Ya, we would like Rochester and Syracuse best, but we'll need to move the equipment around a little. It's too easy to get caught if ya leave 'em in one place too long," Leather Vest pointed out.

The Man asked, "Are both of you still members of the Albany branch of the Blue Cobra Club? I was thinking that you might need some extra help with some of the projects."

Leather Vest responded with "Ya, we still meet with some of the boys most days. We could get some help from our Blue Cobra friends whenever we need it."

The Man asked, "How did things go with the project in Niagara-on-the-Lake?"

Leather Vest described their short meeting with Billy Jones. He said, "We offered him the two hundred thousand dollars that you gave us to offer, but he refused it. We was very forceful in demanding that Billy cancel tomorrow night's meeting of his owly bunch and all future meetings as well. Billy said he understood the message, but he would not cancel tomorrow night's meeting or any others. Billy was very loud and pushy and said that he would call the police if we didn't leave his office right away. That's why we didn't hang around very long 'cuz we don't like talking to the cops anywhere at any time."

The Man said, "It looks like your trip to Niagara-on-the-Lake was not very successful."

Leather Vest said, "We delivered the message like ya told us, but it seems like it didn't sink in with Billy."

The Man advised them, "It looks like a stronger message might be the best answer for our next move. We will need to keep escalating our efforts each time until we are successful. The two of you should plan on going back to Niagara-on-the-Lake for the meeting of the House of Owls on Friday evening. That's tomorrow, at the Chateau des Chutes Winery. While you are there, you should keep an eye on who is there and try to figure out if there is anybody on watch in the parking area.

"When you go back to check out the meeting, you should wait until the meeting starts then go through the parking lot to write down the license plate numbers of each car. You should also make a note of where each car is from and what kind of car it is. You should bring this information back to me. It is very important that you should keep out of sight as much as possible, and you should try to not let anyone see you or know what you are doing."

The two bullyboys agreed to do as The Man told them and that they would come back to talk with him on Saturday after going to the meeting at Chateau des Chutes on Friday evening. They had their instructions and knew what they had to do for the next meeting of the House of Owls.

Although they were slovenly in many ways, the two thugs knew that it was necessary to keep relatively fit to be able to continue doing their jobs, so they decided to go to their local fitness club for a light workout.

Chapter 5
About William Rhys Jones
1897 to the Present

The William R. Jones Investment Company has a long history, and the name William R. Jones, an even longer one. It goes back to near the end of the nineteenth century in the old country.

The first William R. Jones was born in Aberfan, a small coal-mining town in the Aber Valley of Southeast Wales in Great Britain. His father was Rhys Lloyd Jones, the greengrocer of Aberfan. William the First was born in 1897, and he grew up working in his father's store starting at an early age. He was always eager to learn more about the world beyond the Aber Valley and was ready to join the Royal Welsh Fusiliers and go off to fight in World War I in 1914.

William survived the ravages of the war, saved his soldier's pay, and was ready to make his own way in the world after the end of the war in 1918. After many discussions with friends, neighbors, his parents, and other relatives, he decided he would go to Canada to build his future.

David Morgan—whom everyone called Dai Morgan, a good friend of William's and the son of a neighbor in Aberfan—had gone to a city in Canada called Toronto. According to all the letters he wrote back to his parents, he was doing quite well and enjoyed living in Canada. William the First wrote to Dai Morgan and asked if he could stay with him for a short time while he looked for a job in Toronto and got settled, if he immigrated to Toronto. After a positive reply came back from Dai,

William was ready to go. He bought a ticket for passage on Cunard's *RMS Aurania* and was in Liverpool, ready for the ship's departure in early April 1919.

The *RMS Aurania* crossed the North Atlantic and went up the Saint Lawrence River to Montreal. From there, William went by train to Toronto. When he arrived at Union Station in Toronto, William allowed himself the luxury of taking a taxi to Dai Morgan's house in the eastern part of downtown Toronto.

William's reunion with Dai was a happy one as they had always been good friends and had enjoyed each other's company back home in Aberfan. After an extended celebration that evening with good food and several bottles of beer, they both had a very comfortable and sound night's sleep. The next morning, William was eager and ready to go out and look for a job in his new country.

Dai had suggested that William might want to look for a job in a grocery store in the produce section because of all the experience he had at his father's greengrocer business back in Aberfan. William thought that was a great idea and would start his job search by looking into all the grocery stores near Dai's home.

The first two stores that William went to the next day had no openings for produce clerks. However, William was lucky and very happy when he talked to Theodore Loblaw, who was just starting out in the grocery business and wanted someone with experience to work in the produce section of his new local grocery store. That fact that he could start right away sealed the deal between them.

William was very happy about getting a job so quickly. He thought it would be a good idea if he went to see Dai at his job with Frank S. Hall and Company Stockbrokers and tell him about his good fortune. Dai had told William that his job was in the investment business and that he was a "board marker." This meant that he took the latest stock-market price changes from a ticker tape and wrote the numbers with chalk on a huge green chalkboard.

Dai thought that this was a good job because his hours were good and the work was not too difficult. He needed to arrive at work half an hour before stock trading started at ten each morning, and he could leave an hour after trading stopped at three each afternoon. The fact that the job was only five days a week, Monday to Friday, was another attractive feature. He received a good salary of twenty dollars a week and often received cash tips and investment suggestions from the stock traders who sat in the customers' room watching the stock price changes as he marked them on the chalkboard.

William sat in the customers' room with the investors who were there, watching the board, while he waited for Dai to get time off for a short lunch break. William became quite curious about the whole process of Dai marking the board and the investors shrewdly watching all the changes as they were posted.

Over lunch, William talked about his new job with Theodore Loblaw. Dai talked about his job and explained how his board marking helped the investment process. The men sitting in the customers' room would decide to buy or sell shares of various companies as the prices continued to change and were marked on the big chalkboard. Dai had not bought any stocks for himself yet even though he had received quite a few recommendations from investors in the customers' room. But he thought that he would make a purchase sometime soon.

As time went on, William became very comfortable in his new job and enjoyed what he was doing. Dai told him about how he had started to purchase stocks for himself from time to time and was quite successful with most of the trades that he had made. He suggested to William that he might want to try investing sometime to see if he could make some extra money.

Dai continued to make investment suggestions to William, and William eventually decided that he would try it. William's first investment was for only three hundred dollars to buy shares in a company that just started to drill for gold in Northern Ontario. A few weeks later, the price of the stock soared, and William quickly sold his holdings and cashed out $3,400. William had a profit of $3,100 on his investment and was quite excited about that. He thought that he could afford to risk this money in future investments since none of it was really his own money.

Dai talked with the investors in the customers' room every day, always looking for good investment ideas for himself and for William. One day, one of the most successful investors told him about Canau Mining Limited, an attractive-looking gold-mining prospect in Northern Ontario whose shares were trading at only $0.10 each. Dai talked with William about the Canau shares, and they both decided to buy as many as they could reasonably afford. William invested all his profits from the earlier trade and purchased 31,000 shares at $0.10 a share.

This proved to be an exceptionally good investment. A few weeks after they bought their shares, the price of Canau shares began to rise rapidly. The first drill hole showed good quantities of high-grade gold ore. Results from the second and third drill holes were even better, and the stock price continued in its rapidly rising trend. Several drill holes later, the stock priced had soared to a high value of $51 a share, and both Dai and William decided it was time to sell. William sold his 31,000 shares at an average price of $50.25 for a total amount of $1,557,750. This was a huge profit and an immense amount of money. Since there was no income tax on capital gains in those days, William now had a new fortune of more than $1.5 million that he could spend on anything that he wanted.

A few months earlier, William had rented a house of his own and moved out of Dai's house so that Dai could make room for his sister Dona, who wanted to immigrate to Canada. The name Dona, with one N, goes back to the name of a goddess in ancient Welsh mythology. She came to Toronto to work as one of the housekeeping staff for Toronto's wealthy Eaton family.

William began courting Dona before he made the big investment profit, and now after he had made a very large amount of money, he thought he was financially secure and could afford to think about getting married. His timing was good, and Dona agreed to marry him. They took a honeymoon trip, by sea, back to visit with both their families in Aberfan. During their travels, William pondered what he and Dona might do in the future now that they were financially comfortable.

After considering many options, they thought that they might enjoy the life of William being a gentleman farmer. They decided that they would like to move to the area near Niagara Falls because it was away from Toronto, but not too far away. After considering several properties that looked interesting, they decided to purchase three one-hundred-acre blocks of farmland near the village of Saint David's, which were planted with peach and cherry trees. The name Saint David's reminded them of the patron saint of Wales, and that had to be a good omen. They wondered if there were any other Welsh families in the area.

Saint David's wasn't named after the patron saint of Wales but was actually named after David Secord, a major in Butler's Rangers. He was a loyalist and a leader of the British military unit that fought in the War of 1812 against the Americans. David Secord was the father of his more famous daughter, Laura Secord, who made her historic walk of twenty miles through unchartered forests, avoiding American patrols on a hot summer day in 1813 to warn the British and Canadian militia forces of the impending assault by the invading American army.

William had left his job with Loblaw before they went on their honeymoon, and he and Dona were now ready to move to their new home in Saint David's. They lived in the old farmhouse while their new, grander house was being built. They also hired a farm manager to look after the farming business for them since neither of them had any experience with agriculture.

Shortly after Dai and William made their big score with the purchase of Canau mining shares, they both realized how fortunate they had been with their speculative venture, and they decided that they would be much more cautious with their money in the future. While Dai had been working as a board marker for Frank S. Hall and Company, he had read as many books as he could get his hands on about business, economics, finance, and investments, and he had become a very thoughtful and well-informed investor.

Dai did not know very many people in Toronto and had no confidence in his ability to develop a base of clients as a stockbroker with his old firm. With the investment knowledge he had gained from his job and from his extensive study, he was confident that he had the skills to be a very good investment advisor. He applied for investment advisor positions at several different banks and trust companies in the Toronto financial district. After several interviews, he was hired by the Ontario Trust Company to assist in managing investments for their estates, trusts, and personal clients.

After many meetings to discuss investments with Dai, William became very comfortable with the idea of putting a large portion of his wealth with Dai and Ontario Trust to manage. William was confident that both Dai and the trust company would be very conservative in managing his money, and he knew that was the best way for him and Dona and their long-term future.

William had his three-hundred-acre farm and several income-producing rental and real estate properties in the area. Now he also had a conservative portfolio of government of Canada bonds and blue chip stocks that Dai managed for him at Ontario Trust. He thought that this diversified approach to investing his wealth could provide sufficient financial security for him and Dona for the rest of their lives.

During the 1920s, the value of William's investments increased several times over. Toward the end of the decade, Dai and William both thought that investment markets had become very speculative and risky. William decided to sell some of his real estate holdings and all his stocks and put the money into government of Canada bonds.

Investments in carefully selected real estate and government bonds proved to be the right things to have. For most of the decade of the 1930s, the world was in a severe economic depression, but the family of William R. Jones remained financially very strong.

The second William R. Jones, or Junior, was born in June of 1922. William and Dona wanted to have more children, but it was not to be. Fortunately, Junior was a very healthy child and grew into a very healthy, strong, and intelligent young man.

When Britain declared war on Germany on September 3, 1939, Canada quickly followed suit and joined with Britain by entering the war on September 10, 1939. Junior was only seventeen at the time, but he was ready, willing, able, and eager to join up in June of 1940, right after his eighteenth birthday.

Captain William R. Jones II survived the war and returned home to Saint David's in December 1945. Junior enjoyed his life growing up on the farm but was now ready to go off to the University of Toronto to study business management.

Junior was aware that he needed to be well educated to take over the management of the family's business affairs eventually. After graduating from university, he moved back to the family homestead in Saint David's, where he resolved to learn as much as he possibly could about the family farm, the family's various real estate holdings, and the family's investments in stocks and bonds. Junior's review of the family's holdings led to some structural changes and the creation of William R. Jones Investment Company.

Junior married his high school sweetheart, Mary Davies, in January 1946, and the third William R. Jones was born ten months later. Time flashed by very quickly, and the Third, who had taken an active interest in family affairs from an early age, began to make worthwhile suggestions and valuable contributions to the business activities of William R. Jones Investment Company.

The Third was now generally known as W. R., a nickname that he had been given by fellow students while he was at university, and it continued afterward. It was quite common in those days for business leaders to be called by their initials rather than by their given names. As it happened, it also helped to differentiate the third William R. Jones from the first and the second.

W. R. met and married the love of his life, Anna Jones, while he was studying business management at the University of Western Ontario in London. When they were married, she didn't even need to change her name—only from Ms. Jones to Mrs. Jones.

The first William and his wife, Dona, both passed away within a few weeks of each other in the winter of 1967, the year of the one-hundredth birthday celebration of Canada becoming an independent nation. William the Second, no longer known as Junior, continued to manage the family business and its many components from the established homestead in Saint David's. But W. R. decided that he wanted to build a new home in the downtown area of Niagara-on-the-Lake.

After an extensive search and review, W. R. decided that the family should purchase a five-acre vacant property in the southeast part of the town and build the new family home there. This was a new area of development for the town, which was why W. R. was able to lobby for the name Saint David's Place for the name of their new street.

This proved to be a great location, so he convinced the family to buy a lot across the street for a new office building for the company. Captain Jones and W. R. had been considering moving the company's office from the countryside in Saint David's into town for some time. This seemed like the right time to make the move.

The fourth William R. Jones was born in June of 1966. He was a happy child who loved animals and birds and all living things. When the time came for him to go away to university, he was certain that he wanted to train to become a medical doctor. With some guidance from his parents, he chose to go to McMaster University in nearby Hamilton for his medical education.

After graduating from McMaster medical school, he stayed on there to intern at the McMaster hospital for his internship. Since the hospital was affiliated with the university, this was a very easy transition. During the time of his internship, William the Fourth became disenchanted with being a doctor and discussed the possibility of coming home to work with the family company. It happened.

The Fourth had been dating Megan Turner, a professor of history at McMaster University, during his medical internship. Now that he would be moving back to Niagara-on-the-Lake, he thought he would ask her to marry him. He did, and they were married.

Anna Jones, wife of W. R., passed away from pneumonia the year before William the Fourth and Megan Turner were married. Since W. R. was now living alone in the large house on Saint David's Place in Niagara-on-the-Lake, he gave his home to William the Fourth and Megan as a wedding present. They graciously accepted his present and begged him to continue living there with them. He accepted.

The William R. Jones Investment Company continued to grow and prosper. In recent years, friends and associates of both W. R. and William the Fourth asked if the company could manage their personal investments for them. From managing just a few nonfamily clients, their business continued to grow, and now the company managed over $3 billion for clients in addition to the family assets of about $1.3 billion in real estate investments and a similar amount in stocks and bonds.

Over the years, the company expanded its staff by adding an accountant, two nonfamily investment advisors, several associates, and a receptionist, who was very much a multitasking person.

In its plan for the future, the company allowed for extra office space in case there ever was a William R. Jones the Fifth. There was. William R. Jones V was born in June of 1991, the son of William R. Jones IV and Megan.

William R. Jones V was me, Billy Jones. I lived with my parents and my grandfather at no. 5 Saint David's Place in Niagara-on-the-Lake, the family homestead. Our house was a large eight-thousand-square foot dark redbrick two-story mid-Victorian structure sitting on five acres of land. Many people called our house a mansion, but we called it home.

Since we were all named William R. Jones, most people referred to my grandfather as W. R., my father as William, and me as Billy, except for me, and I referred to W. R. as Grandfather. We did need some form of differentiation so that when people mentioned the name William R. Jones, we will know which one of us was being credited or blamed for whatever it was that happened.

I was much like the previous four William R. Joneses in general appearance, attitude, and character. We were all about six feet tall, give or take an inch. We all had dark hair, except for Grandfather, who now had gray hair. We were all somewhat conservative and cautious in our nature, good at investments, and very interested in politics. Over time, we had all developed a strong understanding of moral and ethical principles that we applied to our daily living.

Chapter 6
Billy and Maria
Friday, April 19

I was at my desk in the company office at no. 10 Saint David's Place in Niagara-on-the-Lake, reflecting on many things. I was thinking about how well the company was doing under the leadership of my father and grandfather. I was also very pleased at the progress the House of Owls group was making with our Direct Democracy movement. Not the least of my thoughts was my strong attraction to Maria Simone, who I first met just two weeks ago.

My first impression of Maria was that she was a very attractive young lady of medium height, with a classic pretty face, sparkling big brown eyes, and shoulder-length dark hair so perfect that she could be in a commercial for an expensive shampoo. She also had an infectious, happy smile that was hard for anyone not to like. In our brief conversations together, it seemed to me that she was also a very intelligent person.

As my mind was wandering, my office phone rang, and I answered, "Hello, this is Billy Jones. How may I help you?"

"Hello, Billy, it's Maria Simone calling. You remember we met two weeks ago at the meeting with the House of Owls group? I'm calling to see if my father and I could get together with you for an early dinner this evening, before our meeting at seven thirty. We thought that it would be helpful if the three of us discussed some of our ideas for the agenda beforehand."

I eagerly responded with "Maria, that sounds like a great idea. Why don't we go to the Orchard Inn here in Niagara-on the-Lake? It's a very nice place, and we would be comfortable there for dinner. Why don't we meet there at, let's say, five o'clock? Getting together will give us some time to discuss the things we've planned for the meeting."

"That sounds good, Billy. If you could give me some directions, that would be helpful," she asked.

"I assume you will be coming from home. After you come off the Rainbow Bridge into Canada, you should go north along the Niagara Parkway. It goes right into downtown Niagara-on-the-Lake. From there, you can follow your GPS to get to the Orchard Inn at this address," and I recited the address from memory.

"Thanks, Billy. We should be able to find it OK. We're looking forward to seeing you at as close to five o'clock as we can make it."

As I hung up my phone from Maria's call, I found that I was silently smiling to myself at the pleasant thought of meeting with her again in a friendly, almost-private setting. Thinking more about it, I thought that I should phone the Orchard Inn to make a reservation for the three of us for dinner. I phoned and asked for a quiet, out-of-the-way table for three for five o'clock. It was done.

Chapter 7
The Dinner Meeting
Friday, April 19

I drove my red Corvette into the parking lot at the Orchard Inn, arriving at about 4:50. I wanted to be a couple of minutes early for our get-together. My Corvette was a gift to me from my parents for doing well at university and finishing my MBA in the top 10 of my class. It was also my personal transportation to use at my new job when I started working at William R. Jones Investment Company.

As I was just getting out of my car, a recent model of black Mercedes S-Class sedan pulled up beside me. It was Michael and Maria Simone. Michael parked his car, and they got out. Maria was dressed in a medium-blue-colored pantsuit with a white silk blouse. It looked very business-like but was still quite feminine. I was sure that it was a very high-fashion ensemble, but I didn't know any of those high-fashion names. Her outfit could have been from any designer from Donna Karan to Mary Quant or Betsy Ross, but I wouldn't know the difference.

Michael was dressed in a dark-blue business suit, white shirt, and tie, similar to the way I was dressed, but his suit was a little darker than mine was, and his tie was a plain light blue while mine was patterned. In physical appearance, I was slightly taller than Michael and quite a few years younger. He had basic black hair while mine was dark brown, but our physical builds were similar.

We shook hands warmly and went through the basic "hello, how are you, good to see you again" routine. After the greetings, we made our way to the entrance door of the Orchard Inn's dining room. We went in, and I told the hostess at the front desk that we had a reservation for the three of us for five o'clock. She led us to a nice, quiet table in a far corner of their main dining room where we had a good view of the whole room, but we were not too close to other tables.

She asked us if we would like black napkins instead of the white ones that were on the table. She recognized that white napkins sometimes leave very small bits of white lint on dark clothes. All three of us were wearing darker clothes. Offering this kind of choice spoke well about the high level of service at the Orchard Inn since it's usually only the highest-quality restaurants that offer the black napkin option. She gave each of us black napkins and menus to peruse and then left us.

The Orchard Inn dining room looked very attractive, with white tablecloths on all the tables, a single rose in a simple vase on each table, and matching elegant-looking chairs throughout the room.

I said to Maria and Michael, "Getting together beforehand was a very good idea. Thanks for being so thoughtful. I am very pleased to be able to reconfirm, in my own mind, that we have some very good people, like the two of you, helping to promote the cause of Direct Democracy within our House of Owls group."

Michael responded by saying "Thank you for your kind words, Billy. You may well remember that when we last met, I agreed to function as the keynote speaker for tonight's meeting."

I responded anxiously with "I hope you haven't changed your mind, Michael. I don't think anyone else is prepared to speak tonight. I think we could have as many as fifty people there, and it would not be good for us to disappoint a group of that size at our first meeting."

Michael responded, "No, Billy. I am quite ready to give a talk tonight for about half an hour. I think that's probably a long enough time for our audience. If I went on much longer, they could get very restless or even walk out."

The server came to take our orders. None of us was very hungry. So Michael and I each ordered an eight-ounce rib eye steak, accompanied by a Caesar salad, and Maria ordered a Cobb salad. I was thinking of ordering a bottle of wine to go with our meal because I saw on the wine list that they had a Cabernet Sauvignon from our friends at the Chateau des Chutes Winery. We decided to pass on the wine this time so we could keep our minds clear and alert for the meeting.

"I plan on talking about a number of things that relate to Direct Democracy. I'll include some thoughts on various subjects such as gun control, balanced budgets, why we need stronger drug laws, and why we should provide better funding for health care and our veterans.

"My thoughts are that the majority of public opinion would be in favor of all these things, but we know that there are strong groups lobbying against them for various reasons. In a society that has Direct Democracy, these things would probably have been made into new laws long before now. I will also include some comments about the results of the British referendum that resulted in Brexit and the results of the referendum on abortion in Ireland," said Michael.

"Do you have a written speech and copies to hand out to each person after the meeting?" I asked.

"No, I don't have a written speech, but I do have some notes to keep me on track. I was planning to record my talk and have it transcribed for distribution at a later date. It's a good idea to have some follow-up contact to keep our friends interested in our cause. We could email copies to all attendees in a day or so," said Michael.

"Sending out copies to everyone seems like a very good idea. We will have a table set up near the entryway in the tasting room to greet people as they come in. I plan on asking for a business card from each person or asking them to write their name, address, phone number, and email address on a blank card if they don't have a business card with them. We should have the names of everyone who attends the meeting, and having their personal information would make it easy for us to email a copy of our comments to each of them. Maria, maybe you could help me at the desk? You will probably know many of the people from your side of the border," I said.

"That sounds like a good idea. Yes, I will be happy to sit at the table with you and help with meeting people as they come in. Yes, I think I probably will know many of the people who come over from our side of the river," she replied.

After a pause in the conversation, I thought I should tell them about my experience yesterday with the two hoodlums. I proceeded to tell them the story. "Two large grungy-looking thugs came into my office demanding that I cancel tonight's meeting of the House of Owls. They also offered me a bribe of two hundred thousand dollars in cash if I would cancel the meeting. They said that their friends didn't want our owly bunch meeting tonight, or ever again, trying to change the form of our government.

"I am guessing that some lobby groups or political parties don't like the idea of Direct Democracy. They must have paid these intimidators to come to my office to harass me and bribe me. They thought I might accept their bribe and disband the House of Owls group. But I have no interest in breaking up our group, and I obviously didn't accept their bribe money."

Maria was very concerned and upset. She put her hand on my arm that was resting on the table as she asked anxiously, "What did they do? You didn't get hurt, did you?"

"Thank you for your concern. What happened was that these two big elephants barged into my office early yesterday afternoon bellowing their threats at me. After I told them I would call the police, they seemed to become nervous and left. In my mind, I think of them as Leather Vest and Black Boots because those descriptive names seemed like their most recognizable features. I don't know who they were or where they came from. The big black Ram pickup truck that they drove away in had an Ontario license plate, but it was smudged with mud and was unreadable," I answered Maria's concerns.

"I have asked an old friend of mine, Jeramiah Delvechio, if he could monitor the parking lot at the Chateau des Chutes Winery for us during our meeting tonight to check for anything unusual. Jeramiah has been known by his nickname Ram for most of his life. The name Ram is an unusual diminutive of his name, Jeramiah, but it also relates to his being born on April 5, 1991, the Chinese year of the ram and under Aries, the zodiac sign of the ram.

"He and several associates have a private investigations business, Delvechio Investigations, based in Niagara Falls. He is very smart and very good at what he does. Ram is both a lawyer and a CPA, which gives him very good credentials as a private investigator for his many corporate and government clients. Having him watch over the parking area tonight might be helpful. I hope we don't have any trouble, but you never know," I added.

The food came, and dinner was good, but conversation was limited until it was time for coffee when Michael said, "I have had a few crank calls at my office about the House of Owls and Direct Democracy. They must have read my comments in the *Niagara Gazette* or heard about it from some of my friends. I never really thought much about any trouble we might have, but as you say, you never know."

Maria added, "I have talked about Direct Democracy and the House of Owls to other teachers at my school. Some agree with us, and some don't. But the worst part is that most of them just don't care. I don't think that any of them would be as aggressive as the toughs who came to your office were."

The time for our meeting was getting closer, so I said, "I think we should be going so we can be at our meeting early and get ready to greet all the attendees. I hope they will all become new members of our House of Owls group.

"You probably remember that the Chateau des Chutes Winery, where we are going, is owned and operated by my good friends Henri and Jeanne Renault. They are both part of the start-up group for the House of Owls in Canada, and they are both very interested in the Direct Democracy movement. Michael, if it's OK with you, I will lead the way, and you can just follow me over to the winery. It's only about five minutes away," I said.

We went out to our cars, and I led the way over to the winery. The parking lot at Chateau des Chutes was quite large and covered in neatly kept crushed stone. We both found parking spots near the entryway to the retail area, and all three of us got out of our cars and were ready to go in and say hello to everybody. There were already a few cars in the parking lot, giving the impression that we could have a good turnout for our meeting.

Chapter 8
The Meeting at Chateau des Chutes Winery
Friday, April 19

As we entered the winery building, Henri and Jeanne Renault were there waiting for us and all the others to arrive.

Henri was thirty-one years of age, about five feet, eleven inches tall with a slightly muscular build, dark-blond hair, and a perpetual happy smile that could easily be the model for the ubiquitous happy face. Jeanne was thirty years of age, about five feet, seven inches tall with the same dark-blond hair as Henri and a trim figure from hard work and a selective diet. Like her husband, Henri, Jeanne liked to smile a lot. She said it was good for the soul.

They were both dressed in what appeared to be the winery's uniform of merlot-colored jeans and honey-gold-colored shirts, about the same color as their Riesling Ice Wine. The shirts had the name Chateau des Chutes Winery embroidered on the left side of the chest, just above the pocket. The pockets in their shirts looked like just a slit with the pocket pouch sewed on from the inside, unlike usual shirt pockets that are a patch of cloth sewed onto the outside.

They had everything arranged with a greeting table near the entryway and forty-eight chairs set up in six rows of eight, broken by a center aisle with four chairs on each side in each row, and there was a podium at the front for the speaker. They said they had additional chairs available if we needed them. They also had their tasting bar set up for the guests to sample and, hopefully, purchase some of their products. Henri and Jeanne were well aware that free samples often led to sales.

The space where our meeting was to be held was the area where Henri, Jeanne, or other senior staff members usually showed a short video presentation about the winery and some of the processes they use in wine making to groups of visitors. After visiting groups watched the video, they would take the visitors on a tour of the Chateau des Chutes wine-making facilities, followed by a tasting session that usually included some of their best wines.

The five of us—Henri, Jeanne, Michael, Maria, and I—thought we should briefly review our previous discussions about memberships, expenses, organizational structure for the House of Owls, who should be the leaders, and all those many start-up organizational things.

We had previously decided that we would have both a Canadian group and a US group, with Michael Simone as leader of the US team and me as leader of the Canadian team. We defined our basic objective as getting the political systems in Canada and the US to gradually move to Direct Democracy at all levels of government—municipal, provincial, or state and at the federal level. We all agreed that our initial focus should be on our local municipal governments since these would likely be the least difficult to reach and influence.

We also decided that we would ask for, but not demand, a membership fee from everyone who attended that night's meeting. We thought that a reasonable amount would be twenty-five dollars for Canadians and twenty dollars for our US members to allow for the different values of the two countries' currencies.

Our plan was to mail out the membership cards to everyone over the next two weeks. We would also be emailing out copies of Michael Simone's comments from tonight so that each person would have the opportunity to go through them again and so they could also send them on to friends, business associates, and their local politicians.

Maria and I arranged our seats at the sign-in table and got ready to meet people as they arrived. While we waited, I said to Maria, "You know, we should really get to know each other a little better. Why don't you tell me something about yourself?"

Maria said, "Sure, Billy, why not? I think you know that I am a high school history teacher in Niagara Falls. I am twenty-six years old, and I live with my father in the family home. It's just him and me since my mother passed away from cancer just over four years ago. I graduated with a major in history and politics from Syracuse University, along with my good friend Samantha Weldon, who you have met as a member of the House of Owls group.

"Samantha and I have known each other and have been good friends since our early childhood years. Although my father and I don't go to church every Sunday, we are Roman Catholics, and I believe in most of the religious ideals like the Ten Commandments and so on. You can tell by my educational background that I have a strong interest in history and politics, which is why I am happy to be a part of the House of Owls group. I haven't been going out on dates very often recently, and I don't have a regular boyfriend right now. That's my short summary. Now it's your turn, Billy. Tell me a little about yourself."

I answered with "I earned my MBA at McMaster University, just down the road from here in Hamilton. I knew that I wanted to work with our family investment company, and that's why I did the MBA program at McMaster. I had been doing odd jobs at our family company since my early teens, and I knew that I wanted to work in the investment business. As you know, investment considerations are very sensitive to political changes, so I need to keep up with all things political. I am twenty-eight years old, and I live in the family home with my parents and my grandfather. I don't date very often either, and I don't have a regular girlfriend right now. Maybe we should go out on a date sometime?"

Before we could continue about ourselves, people began to arrive, and Maria and I got very busy taking down names, collecting membership fees and business cards, and generally welcoming everyone. Maria looked after most of the people from the US, many of whom she knew, and I looked after the folks from Canada, many of whom I knew. As time passed, it looked like we would have a full house with about fifty or more people in attendance. It was now just past seven thirty and was time to get the meeting started.

I assumed the responsibility of host for the evening and went to the podium and began, "Welcome, everyone, to this first public meeting of the House of Owls, and thank you all for coming out. I would like to thank Henri and Jeanne Renault for providing this room for our meeting tonight. If you haven't already sampled some of their good wines, you may want to do so before you leave tonight. You may even want to buy a bottle or two of their products. They're very good.

"As you all know, the House of Owls is a political movement, not a political party, dedicated to the development of Direct Democracy. We think that it is more important to be a movement that can appeal to all political parties than it is to create a new political party.

"I would like to introduce the eight original founders of HOO. There are four of us from the New York state, and four of us from Ontario. Please stand and be recognized as I call your names. From New York state, Maria Simone, who was at the desk with me when you came in, her father Michael Simone, John Weldon, and his wife Samantha Weldon. From Ontario, Henri and Jeanne Renault—our friendly winemakers and our hosts for this evening—Paul Browne, and me.

"Our founding eight have agreed that we will have functioning groups on both sides of the border. Michael Simone has agreed to lead the US group, and I will be leading the Canadian group. In case I haven't met any of you, I am Billy Jones, and I live here in Niagara-on-the-Lake. Please welcome Michael Simone, who will talk to us tonight about the need to move to Direct Democracy."

Michael walked up to the podium and began, "Thank you all for coming out tonight and for showing your support for the House of Owls and Direct Democracy, and thank you again to Henri and Jeanne Renault for allowing us to use this room in your winery. It's very generous of you.

"Abraham Lincoln—our great sixteenth president of the United States—in his historic speech at Gettysburg, Pennsylvania, on November 19, 1863, during the US Civil War, said, 'That government of the people, by the people and for the people shall not perish from this earth.' We all think that he was right. Democracy is the best form of government, and we know that Direct Democracy is the best form of democratic government. President Lincoln must have had a premonition of the way of the future when he said "by the people," or maybe he had read ancient Greek history and was well aware of the basic concepts of Direct Democracy as they were developed in ancient Greece.

"The problem with representative democracy is that most of us disagree with our elected representative on too many subjects even though we voted for them as the best candidate in the election. That shortcoming needs to change, and Direct Democracy is the best possible solution to the problem. Every citizen should have the democratic right to express their view on all issues by a referendum of all citizens on each and every political issue. That's the way of the future.

"I am an American, and I am not wearing a short-sleeved shirt today even though I have the right to bare arms"—there was a slight titter from the audience—"One of the many major problems we have today in the United States is the gun lobby. Thousands of US citizens are being killed every year because there is no effective control on the ownership or possession of guns of all kinds. The National Rifle Association and other groups are heavily funded by the gun lobby so that if legislation to control guns is presented, it gets watered down into nothing or defeated. The gun lobby has been very effective at coercing many politicians to support their positions with cash payments or other benefits. Since the vast majority of Americans and Canadians are probably in favor of some form of gun control, under a Direct Democracy regime, gun controls would exist. A move to Direct Democracy is necessary to establish reasonable gun controls."

Michael continued to talk about the various hot topics that are most important to the House of Owls group and with others who care about Direct Democracy. He talked about more government funding for health care, particularly for our seniors and our veterans; about balanced budgets; and about capital punishment for serious murderers, like your Canadian guys Paul Bernardo, Dellen Millard, and Bruce McArthur with his little shop of horrors. He continued his comments, citing several more examples of things that could be and would be changed for the better in a society with Direct Democracy.

He began his closing comments with "In June of 2016, the people of Great Britain voted in a national referendum to leave the European Union. This was a total surprise to the politicians who wanted to stay in the European Union because they thought they knew what was best for the country and what the British people wanted. They were wrong, as politicians often are, and the people voted in the referendum to tell them what they really wanted. This was Direct Democracy at work.

"More recently, on May 28, 2018, Ireland held a referendum on abortion, and the people won by a wide margin. The vote was whether to overturn the currently existing ban on legal abortion in Ireland. Surprise, surprise: the vote was 66.4 percent in favor of lifting the ban. The government of Ireland did not have the courage to propose the legislation and vote on it in Parliament because the Catholic Church, the predominate church in Ireland, was strongly opposed to allowing legal abortion. Fortunately, the government was prepared to put the issue to a referendum to let the people make the decision so they could keep out of the bad books of the church. Power to the people—Direct Democracy at work.

"Whether it's called a referendum, Direct Democracy, or something else, it is the same thing—power in the hands of the people. Direct Democracy is not just a quixotic dream, as some may think. It is real. It is a form of democracy whose time has come again." Michael finished his talk and was given a solid round of extended applause by the audience.

I went up to the podium to thank Michael for his thoughtful comments, which drew another round of applause. I mentioned to the group that the wine bar was now open and that we could discuss Michael's comments and other thoughts over a glass of wine. I said that we would be sending out copies of Michael's comments by email to everyone and that they should send them on to their friends, business associates, and especially to their politicians.

Most of the people at the meeting joined Maria, Michael, and I at the wine bar, wanting to taste several of the good-quality wines that the Renaults had to offer. I noticed that many people were also walking out with packages of one or more bottles under their arms.

Chapter 9
The Parking Lot at Chateau
des Chutes Winery
Friday, April 19

While the others continued to enjoy their glass of wine, I thought that I should check outside in the parking lot to see if Ram had seen anything unusual while our meeting was in progress. I walked out the front door of the winery and looked around the parking lot to see if I could see Ram anywhere. I noticed his white BMW X5 SUV parked off in the back corner of the parking area, and I thought I should go and see if he was there. As I walked toward his SUV, I heard what sounded like painful moaning and groaning coming from that direction.

As I approached his SUV, I saw Ram sitting on the ground, dressed in jeans and a light spring jacket and looking groggy and confused. I moved quickly toward him and asked if he was OK and what had happened. His speech was slow and slurred, but he said, "I was sitting in my SUV watching these two large lumps moving about the parking lot. They appeared to be writing down the license plate numbers of all the cars parked there.

"When I stepped out of my SUV, I saw two big scraggly-looking guys. One wore a leather vest over his blue denim shirt, and the other wore a black denim jacket and jeans and had big black boots. As I went to ask them what they were doing, they responded with heavy punches to my head and body. I fell, and the Neanderthal with black boots tromped on my right ankle and ground it very hard into the crushed stone. He gave me a kick in the ribs for good measure. They took off after that in what looked like a large black Ram pickup truck. I tried to get the license plate number, but it was muddy and not readable. I think it was a New York–state plate though.

"My ribs are sore, and my ankle is swollen. But I don't think anything is broken or severely injured. The one exception is that my brand-new Black Jack cowboy boots are badly scratched and scuffed and will need a lot of remedial work. This is very upsetting because I just bought these boots a few days ago, and they cost me nearly two thousand dollars. I'll need to take them to my shoe repair guy to see if he can get them cleaned, polished, and buffed up to look half decent again. I did see their faces, and I will recognize them the next time I see them. I will get even with them one of these days."

I said to Ram, "You had better come inside, and we'll try to see if you have any unusual cuts or bruises that might need treatment." He limped along with my help, and we went inside to the men's room to look over his condition as much as we could. I said, "You should let me take you to the emergency room at the hospital just to be sure that you don't have any severe wounds that are not showing."

We came out of the men's room and looked for Henri and Jeanne to tell them I would be leaving to take Ram to the hospital emergency room. Michael and Maria Simone overheard us and rushed over to ask what happened. I told them that Ram had a run-in with the two thugs who barged into my office the previous day and I wanted to make sure that he was OK. I told Maria that I would call her tomorrow morning at home to give her an update on Ram's condition and then left.

The Niagara-on-the-Lake hospital was on the other side of town from the Chateau des Chutes Winery, but the town was not very big, so it didn't take long for us to get there. I helped Ram to the emergency room and checked him in to see the attending doctor. Ram was a low priority for the emergency room triage, but it didn't take too long since it was not a busy night. Ram was checked over carefully by the doctor and was told that he had no major problems, just a few scrapes and cuts, bruised ribs, and a swollen ankle. The doctor told us that all these should heal up in a fairly short time. Ram asked the doctor if it was OK for him to drive, and the doctor told him that it was.

As I was driving Ram back to his SUV parked at the winery, I asked him, "Did you see these toughs well enough to recognize them if you ever see them again, and did you see what they were doing in the Chateau des Chutes parking lot?"

He replied, "Yes. As I mentioned earlier when I was still quite groggy, it looked like they were probably the same two thugs that you said came into your office yesterday. They fit your descriptive names of Leather Vest and Black Boots."

"It looks like we could have some ongoing trouble with these guys. For some reason, they seem quite set on making it difficult for the House of Owls to keep going ahead with our program to develop Direct Democracy. I wonder if there is anything that we should do," I queried.

"You're right, Billy. These guys will probably continue to cause trouble for you and HOO in the future. I will check them out with some of my sources to see if I can find out if we can put actual names to the descriptive names that we're using. It would also be helpful if we could find out whom they work for. This one is on me. I owe them for tonight. I don't like getting beat up like this or getting the cuts and bruises. I need some payback," said Ram.

As we arrived back at the winery, I said to Ram, "Thanks for all your help tonight. I am very sorry that you got hurt by those guys. If you're going to try to find out who they are, you should be very careful. Who knows what these troublemakers are capable of doing?"

Ram limped to his SUV and said, "Thanks for helping me to the hospital emergency, Billy. I'll talk with you soon," and he drove away.

I knew Ram would be all right. He had always been a strong, tough guy and was able to take care of himself. In the past, Ram had used his six feet, two inches, 220-pound, strong, athletic body to play football as a linebacker both at high school and at McMaster University, where he received or gave many heavy hits and survived with everything intact. Ram was a very good athlete. In addition to football, he had also been a very accomplished Olympic-style wrestler at both high school and university. I know from my personal, short exposure to that sport that it was very demanding both physically and mentally. Ram also played several other sports that were less dangerous such as golf and tennis.

Chapter 10
Billy and Maria Go on a Date
Saturday, April 20

Even though Friday night was a tough night, I slept well and woke up fairly early on Saturday morning, knowing that I had a lot to do today. After a shower, a quick bowl of cereal, and a glass of orange juice, I thought I should phone Ram to see if he had recovered from the scrapes and bruises of last night.

When I dialed his phone, he answered, "Good morning, Billy. Thanks for checking in on me. I have recovered from most of my slight wounds, and I am reasonably mobile again."

"Glad to hear it," I said. "From the punchy way you looked last night, I thought your recovery might take a little longer. Let's keep in touch and see how things develop with those guys. If you are able to find out who they are, please let me know right away." We both hung up, knowing that we would talk to each other again very soon.

I thought I should call Maria that morning to give her an update on Ram's condition, but I didn't want to phone too early and risk waking her early, especially on a Saturday morning. We seemed to be getting along quite well, and I didn't think it wise to call too early.

My bedroom at no. 5 Saint David's Place was quite large and allowed ample space for me to have a desk, a chair, a landline telephone, a laptop computer, and a small filing cabinet, with plenty of space remaining for the usual bedroom furniture. This was my office at home that I used very often, especially in the evenings and on weekends.

I thought a lot about Maria. She was a very attractive, smart, bubbly young lady and generally good to be around. I thought that maybe now would be the right time for me to ask her to go out to dinner with me later that night so we could get to know each other better.

It was now approaching nine thirty, and I thought it might be late enough to call Maria without disturbing her sleep.

I dialed her number, and she answered with a bubbly tone, wide awake, "Hi, Billy! You're up early today. How are you doin'?"

"Good morning, Maria. I'm fine, thanks. And how are you doing today?" I asked, trying to be as gracious as I could.

"I'm good too, Billy. Thanks for asking," she replied.

I told her, "I woke up fairly early this morning, and I have been up for a little while now. I was going to phone you earlier, but I didn't want to be too early and get you out of bed. I wanted to bring you up to date about Ram and the events of last night. I phoned him this morning, and he said he was OK. I was very pleased that he was there last night to help us out, but I was very sorry that he got hurt.

"Maria, I would like to ask you out to dinner tonight to talk about Ram, the House of Owls, our meeting last night, and also so we can continue to get to know each other better."

Maria responded with "Thank you for the invitation, Billy. That sounds like a great idea. If you come over to the US side and pick me up at home, we could go to our family's favorite Italian restaurant, Trattoria Brunelli. It's over on Transit Road just a little north and east of the Buffalo Niagara International Airport. The decor is a little kitschy, but the food is excellent. Our family has been going there for years, and we have never been disappointed. Why don't I make a reservation for, let's say, seven o'clock? They know our family very well, and I'm sure they would give us a good table."

"That sounds great, Maria. I will try to be at your house by about six thirty, but I could be a few minutes early or late. You never know for sure what the traffic backup will be like at the bridge. Please excuse me if I am a little later than six thirty, but I will try really hard to be on time. I'll see you then," I said.

"Thanks for calling, Billy. I'm looking forward to our dinner tonight, and I'll see you at about six thirty," she said.

I was very happy to have arranged a date with Maria, and I was looking forward to it very much. I knew that the rest of the day would go very slowly, slower than an escargotiere of snails trying to finish a one-hundred-millimeter race until it was time for me to head for the border.

I wasn't sure what I should wear, and I thought for a while about my available wardrobe. After long deliberations, I finally chose a simple classic combination of a plain French blue shirt with a buttoned-down collar, light-gray flannel slacks, and a navy-blue blazer, but no tie. These selections seemed to be a good combination of dressy and casual.

At five thirty, I left our house, got into my red Corvette, and headed down the Niagara Parkway to the border crossing at Niagara Falls. I thought I should leave enough time in case there might be a backup at the border. As it happened, there was a slight backup, and it was nearly twenty minutes before I showed my Canadian passport to the US customs agent and answered his usual questions of "Where are you going?" and "How long will you be in the United States?" He waved me through, and I was off to Maria's. According to my GPS, the Simone home, at 2211 Springfield Drive, was about thirteen minutes travel time from here. I followed the GPS map and the directions from the soft female GPS voice, and I arrived at Maria's home in almost exactly fourteen minutes.

I got out of my car, went up to the front door, and knocked lightly. Maria opened the door with a happy "Hello, Billy. Good to see you again. I guess the traffic wasn't too bad coming over?"

The Simone home was a very attractive, antique, redbrick one-story ranch-style house in a quiet and well-kept neighborhood with many other similarly attractive houses on the street. The inside of the house also appeared to be quite attractive and well-kept.

As she led me in, Maria said, "I thought you might like to say hello to my father while you're here, before we go out to dinner."

I said, "Yes, that would be a good idea."

We went inside together to Michael's study or office at home, which was the middle one of the three bedrooms along the one side of the house and the smallest one of the three. We found him working away on some business affairs.

I said, "Hello, Michael, how are you doing today?"

Michael responded with "Hi, Billy, I'm fine. How are you, and how is your friend Ram Delvechio after the run-in with those tough guys last night?"

I answered Michael with "I'm fine, and so is Ram. I talked with him early this morning, and he said he has a few scrapes and bruises and a swollen ankle. But otherwise, he's OK. He is very upset about the episode and said that he will put a lot of personal effort into finding out who those guys are and who they work for, and he will let me know. Ram also said that this will not cost us anything. He just wants to give a little payback for what they did to him last night. He did mention again that he was quite miffed about his new, expensive Black Jack cowboy boots getting scuffed and scratched." All three of us chuckled about the boots.

Maria said, "We should be off now for our dinner reservation at Trattoria Brunelli. It's good to be on time."

Michael said, "Yes, it's good to be on time, especially when you're going to a place where the owner, Marco Brunelli, is an old friend of ours. Have a good dinner. See you later."

Maria and I left, hopped into my Corvette, and drove toward the restaurant. She knew the way and directed me there by the shortest route. We arrived and went in to the front desk, where the hostess welcomed Maria as if an old friend. She introduced me to the hostess, who guided us to our table.

As Maria had mentioned, the dining room was decorated in a style that seemed a little glitzy with many statues of Roman heroes, gods, and goddesses in recessed sconces, paintings of Tuscan hill town scenes, and a mural of a Tuscan vineyard on one wall. The floor was carpeted instead of the usual Tuscan-type, terra-cotta tiles. Carpeting is much better at absorbing the sounds of conversations and other noises. This creates a more pleasant ambience for customers. The dining room tables were well spaced, and each one was covered in a crisp, clean white tablecloth with a fancy candle in the middle.

I asked Maria if she would like a cocktail before dinner, and she said, "No, thank you, Billy. I don't drink very much, but I wouldn't mind a glass of wine to sip on before and during dinner."

"That sounds good," I said. "I think I'll do that too. I know I shouldn't drink very much because I will be driving back to Niagara-on-the-Lake after dinner. Do you prefer red wine or white?"

"I like many different types of wine, but I often prefer a red with Italian food. They have a good wine list here. Let's have a look at it."

I pointed out, "The Chianti might be a good choice. Most of the wines from the Tuscany region are pretty good. The Ruffino brand has been around for a long time and has a good reputation that has been well-earned over the years. Why don't we try that?"

When our server came with the menus, I ordered a bottle of Chianti to start and a brochette to nibble on. Our server told us that the two specials for today, which are not on the menu, were a seafood platter with shrimp, scallops, mussels, and cod and the other one was osso buco. Each of the specialties came with a side of pasta. We looked over the menu. Our server returned, and we ordered. We both ordered the daily specials. Maria ordered the seafood platter, and I ordered the osso buco.

We chatted in a very friendly way about ourselves, our jobs, some of our likes and dislikes, our continuing interest in politics—especially Direct Democracy—and how we came to be involved with the House of Owls group. Over the course of our dinner, we enjoyed each other's company and got to know each other a lot better.

Maria said, "Let me start by telling you a little bit about the background and history of the Simone family. My grandfather, Aldo Simone, immigrated to the United States from the small town of Bellano near Lake Como in northern Italy. He came over to the US in 1947, shortly after the end of WWII, when prospects for a happy and prosperous life in Italy did not seem very favorable. He was able to purchase a small market garden farm near the little village of Aloquin in the Finger Lakes region of western New York state, situated about halfway between the city of Geneva at the head of Seneca Lake on the east and Canandaigua Lake on the west.

"My grandmother was the former Maria O'Brien, from a family of Irish descent that had lived in the Geneva area for several generations. The third son of Maria and Aldo was Donato Simone, my grandfather. My father enjoyed growing up on the family farm in Aloquin, but he wanted to become an accountant. He studied economics, commerce, and business at Syracuse University and went into accounting right after he graduated. He soon started his own accounting firm based in Niagara Falls, and it has been very successful. Our current home in Niagara Falls is not very far away from his childhood home in the Finger Lakes."

Our food came. We started to eat, and I thought that I should tell Maria a few things about our family history and me. I began with "I work for the family business, William R. Jones Investment Company. I am not sure if you are aware that my full name is actually William Rhys Jones V. Everybody calls me Billy, and that's much easier. My father, William R. Jones IV, is usually called William, and my grandfather, William R. Jones III, is usually known as W. R. In his younger days, it was quite popular for executive types like him to be called by their initials. It also helps to differentiate between the three of us.

"The first William R. Jones immigrated to Canada in 1919 shortly after the end of WWI from the town of Aberfan in Wales. William's good friend David Morgan, who also emigrated from Aberfan, worked for a stockbrokerage company in Toronto. He was known as Dai Morgan since most Welsh men with the name David are called Dai. After some time in Canada, they both made a lot of money speculating on the stock market by buying low-priced shares in gold-mining companies. One of their speculations hit it very big, and the two never looked back. This was the foundation of our family company, which I now work with.

"Like you, Maria, I consider myself somewhat religious, but I am not really a religious zealot. I do go to church most Sundays with my parents and my grandfather. We go to Saint Mark's Anglican Church in Niagara-on-the-Lake. It was built in 1791 and is the oldest Anglican Church in the province of Ontario. And you already know that I am also a strong believer in Direct Democracy."

We continued to enjoy the dinner, each other's company, and our happy conversation for almost two hours. As we were finishing our coffee, we both decided that we should give the restaurant a break and leave. We left and were in my car, heading back toward Maria's home, when I said, "Thank you, Maria, for choosing such a good restaurant and for a very nice time. I really enjoyed being with you tonight. We should do this again soon."

"Thank you, Billy. I really enjoyed our time together too, and I would very much like to go out with you again," Maria responded.

I quickly spoke up with "How about dinner on Tuesday evening? Sunday is not a good day for me to get away. It's somwhat of a family day at our house, starting with breakfast at about ten, followed by church, then a light lunch, followed by afternoon discussions of family things and an early dinner at about five. You know, family duty calls. And Monday is almost always a heavy day at the office."

"Tuesday sounds very good to me, William R. Jones V. Why don't we meet at our house, and we can go out to dinner somewhere? I will think about what might be a good place for us to try. Do you have a favorite food that I might give some consideration to when I'm thinking about which restaurant to choose for us?" she said.

We were now pulling into the driveway at the Simone home, and I replied, "That's great."

Since I always try to be a gentleman, I went to the other side of the car to open the door for Maria and help her out. We walked to the front door to say good night, and before Maria turned to go inside, we kissed each other gently for several seconds. We smiled at each other, and we both said at the same time, "I'm looking forward to our dinner on Tuesday."

Maria said, "Thank you, Billy, for a nice evening."

"It was a pleasure to be with you," I said. "I am very much looking forward to seeing you on Tuesday."

As I was driving my red Corvette back toward Niagara-on-the-Lake, I was thinking and hoping that I would be seeing Maria quite often. I was feeling happy and comfortable about being with a very attractive young lady who I really cared about.

It occurred to me that since I might be crossing the border frequently, I should think about applying for a NEXUS card. The NEXUS card program was managed jointly by the Canadian Border Services Agency and by US Customs and Border Protection, a division of the US Department of Homeland Security. The program was designed to speed up border crossings for low-risk, preapproved travelers into Canada and the United States, and it was a good value at only fifty dollars for a sticker that's good for five years.

Chapter 11
Leather Vest and Black Boots, Reporting In
Saturday, April 20

After they left Niagara-on-the-Lake on Friday night, Leather Vest and Black Boots drove down the Niagara Parkway, crossed the Rainbow Bridge, went through Customs and Immigration, and headed east to their home in Albany, New York.

They knew that they were not expected to report to The Man until midmorning on Saturday, so they went straight home to their condo building. They each owned a unit in the same ten-story building in Albany, just off US 787 Highway near the junction of High Street. Their condo was in the northeastern part the city, where the Afton Bridge crossed the Hudson River. Since they both lived in the same building, going home was easy.

On Saturday morning, Leather Vest and Black Boots went to downtown Albany for their ten o'clock meeting with The Man. They arrived on schedule and were ushered into his office, and both accepted the cup of coffee that was offered by the receptionist.

After they settled in and had a little small talk, The Man asked, "How did it go last night?"

Leather Vest responded with "We did all that you asked us to do. We got to the winery just after seven thirty when the owly meeting was supposed to start, and we looked around to see if anybody was there. We didn't see nobody, so we started doing what you asked us to do—writing down the license plate number of each car, where the car was from, and what kind of car it was.

"We finished almost the whole parking lot when a guy came out of a big white SUV parked off in the corner and asked us what we was doing. We each gave him a couple of punches, and he went down nearly unconscious. We thought this would be a good time to leave, so we did. Here are the lists that we made. This is the information that you wanted us to get."

The Man said, "Good work. I will check out these lists, talk with our clients, and see what they would like us to do next. They should get back to me in a day or two, and I will be in touch with you to let you know what our next move will be."

The discussion about the House of Owls meeting was over, but there were some other issues that The Man wanted to talk about. "I have three more projects that I would like both of you guys to work on. The first one is a little complicated, but I will try to explain it to you. One of our very good clients would like to invest in a block of what he describes as 'life insurance settlements.' A life settlement is when someone owns a life insurance policy on their own life and wants to sell it into the financial market for cash today. They don't need the insurance policy anymore and would like to have some extra cash right now. The selling price for life insurance policies varies according to the age of the individual, the condition of their health, the age of the policy itself, and a number of other factors. Our client would like to purchase a block of life insurance policies that would give him a 20 percent annual rate of return on the money he invests.

"Your job is to convince the insurance agent in Rochester, Clive Bellows, that some of his clients should be encouraged to sell their policies. The price needs to be right so that our client will be able to get his desired 20 percent rate of return on his investment. Bellows, as well as some of his clients, might need a little friendly persuasion.

"The second project is a little more straightforward. Some clients of ours would like us to convince the doctors at the Downtown Medical Clinic in Syracuse to increase the number of prescriptions and the number of pills in each prescription for patients that our friends send to the clinic for opioid drugs, such as oxycodone and fentanyl. Again, both the clinic and some of the doctors might need a little friendly persuasion to do what they are told to do.

"As I have mentioned to you before, our friends send selected people to various medical clinics to get prescriptions for pain medication. When the prescription scripts have been issued, our clients' agents take these people to various 'friendly' pharmacies to get the prescriptions filled. After the prescriptions have been filled, our friends' helpers take the pills from the people that they have set up and pay each person a small amount of money for doing the job they were hired to do.

"The helpers then deliver the pills, through our client's connections, to drug dealer associates across the country. The pills are then sold to organized dealers in drug markets like New York City, Las Vegas, Los Angles, Chicago, and other major drug centers. The pills are then sold by street drug peddlers to drug addicts for high prices to make very large profits for all the players. Most cities in North America have this type of business being played out.

"One of our clients in Pittsburgh, who operates a strip club and a 'massage parlor,' would like us to supply him with two more young ladies for this business. He suggested that we might be able to seize two nineteen- or twenty-year-old students from Syracuse University. You two have done this before, so you should know what needs to be done. When you have the two young ladies, you should call me, and I will arrange for our client to meet you at the Riverside Mall here in Albany.

"The third project is straightforward and fairly easy. The Niagara Falls City Council is considering the approval of another casino. There are only eight city councilors, so you need to convince at least five of them to vote in favor of allowing the new casino. Our clients are involved with the casino, and they would like it to get the go-ahead from the city council as soon as possible. Our clients are prepared to offer up to fifty thousand dollars to each city councilor who votes in favor of the new casino. Your job is to tell each city councilor about the cash payments that are being offered and to exert some pressure on them to vote in favor of this project. So is everything clear with you guys?"

In unison, they both answered, "Ya, boss. We are OK with all those jobs."

Leather Vest and Black Boots thought that they understood all these instructions and knew they had some difficult and busy chores ahead of them, so they thought that they should get to work right away and left The Man's office to get started.

Chapter 12
More Threats Against the House of Owls
Monday, April 22

I was in my office, hard at work on Monday morning because Mondays always seemed to be the busiest day of the week for me. The investment business was very sensitive to many of the various news items that came out each day, and several important items always seemed to accumulate over the weekend when markets were closed.

"Good morning, Billy," said Jane as she walked into my office with a letter for me. As she handed it to me, she said, "You may notice that the letter is in a plain envelope and is unstamped. It was delivered by hand to our office downstairs. I asked the receptionist if she knew who it came from, but she didn't know."

As she turned to leave my office, I said "Thank you, Jane."

The letter looked very curious, addressed to Billy Jones, here at our company's office, instead of the more conventional William R. Jones.

I opened the letter and noticed that it too, was addressed to Mr. Jones and it was unsigned. The letter read:

Dear Mr. Jones

My friends visited your office last Thursday, April 17th, to make you a generous offer to disband the House of Owls group and to cease your activities toward developing Direct Democracy in the US and Canada. You refused our offer and went ahead with your meeting on Friday, as you had planned

I will give you one more chance. I am repeating the offer again today of $200,000 in cash to you if you will cease all future operations of the House of Owls group and any activities toward Direct Democracy.

If you would like to accept my offer, place an ad in the personal column of the *Buffalo News* this Saturday, April 27. Your notice, under the heading "It's a Deal," should read as follows: "I like your offer and will accept the terms and conditions." You don't need to attach your name. I will know who it's from and will act accordingly.

If you should choose not to accept the offer, your group may well face some new difficulties in the weeks and months ahead.

The letter was unsigned.

I read the letter over several times and was quite concerned about the threats. I knew, without thinking about it, that I would not accept the offer, but I was concerned about what might happen to our group in the future. For now at least, I will keep the letter to myself.

Chapter 13
The Next Step for Billy
Monday, April 22

After a regular family day on Sunday, thinking about the startling letter that I received earlier that day and a long day's work on Monday, I was relaxing at my desk in my office at home. It was early evening, and I was thinking I should give Maria a call. I had been thinking about Maria a lot since our dinner on Saturday night, and I was feeling anxiously impatient waiting for our next dinner date on Tuesday.

I called her number and was happy to hear her usual bubbly and happy "Hello, Billy," followed by "How are you? I was hoping you would call so we could chat about our dinner for tomorrow evening and things."

"Hi, Maria. Yes, we should pick a time and place for our dinner and a time for me to come and pick you up. I would suggest maybe dinner at seven. I could pick you up at, let's say, six thirty, and that should allow lots of time to get to the restaurant. You know the restaurants in the area better than I do. Is there another one that you favor?

"Yes, there is, Billy. You're probably a steak guy, so you should like the Genesee Chophouse. They have very good steaks, prime rib of beef, and many other good selections. If you could come at about six, it would be better. My father and I would like to discuss some ideas with you for the House of Owls before dinner. Is that OK with you?"

I answered in the positive with "Yes, of course, I can do that, Maria. I can be at your place by about six. Are there some new problems for HOO that I should be concerned about?"

"No, Billy. It's just that my father was reading an article in one of his business magazines about a Direct Democracy movement in the Netherlands. Apparently, they have formed a political party dedicated to Direct Democracy and have already elected some members to the Federal Parliament of the Netherlands."

"That sounds really fascinating. I thought we were ahead of everybody with our House of Owls political movement, but it seems as though we aren't. It will be very interesting to learn about when they started and how they have progressed. I'll be there tomorrow evening at six or maybe a little before if I can make it. I'm looking forward to seeing you again and Michael, too, of course."

Chapter 14
Learning about Forum voor Democratie
Tuesday, April 23

I tried to finish work as early as I could on Tuesday and was home and ready to head off to Maria's by five thirty. I arrived at the Simone residence just before six and was welcomed at the door by Maria. We hugged and kissed hello and went to Michael's home office, where a cup of coffee was ready and waiting for me.

"Hi, Billy, come on in," said Michael. "I was just thinking about this other Direct Democracy group in the Netherlands. Maria said that she told you about them. They are out there pushing for Direct Democracy, the same as what our House of Owls group is doing. Let me tell you something about them. They call their group Forum voor Democratie, in the Dutch language, or FvD for short. The name simply means 'forum for democracy' in English.

"The FvD is based in The Hague, Netherlands. As you may know, The Hague is the political capital of the Netherlands even though Amsterdam is the constitutional capital. The FvD was formed in 2016 as a think tank led by Hendrik Allard, one of the founders. The FvD morphed into a political party and actually won 1.8 percent of the popular vote and two seats in the 150-seat Dutch Parliament in the general election of March 2017. From all that I have read, they continue to gain popularity and will likely to do much better in the next election.

"One of the principal political planks of the FvD party is that they promise Direct Democracy through binding referenda for all legislation and major government decisions. This seems like the same message that we've been preaching with our House of Owls group. Maybe we can learn something from what the FvD has already done."

"That sounds very interesting, Michael. They seem to be progressing very well. Maybe we should get in touch with them to see if one of their people might come over to give a talk at our next meeting of the House of Owls," I replied.

"That's what I was thinking, Billy," said Michael. "Would you like to try to contact them to see if they might come over?"

"Sure, I'd be happy to do that. We should think about a date for our meeting and where we could have it," I said.

"Yes, I think we should have it on the New York side of the border this time since the last one was in Niagara-on-the-Lake. I'll scout out a place that might hold, let's say, one hundred people or so and let you know," replied Michel, happy to see that I agreed with his thinking.

Maria had been listening to our discussion and added her voice of approval to what we were thinking. "We have the list of people who attended the last meeting. We can send out notices to them and ask them to tell their friends, neighbors, and business associates. We should also invite all the city council members from Niagara Falls, both New York and Ontario and from Niagara-on-the Lake. We might also consider inviting selected members of the media."

I explained, "If all the local municipal politicians come, that would help fill the room. The city of Niagara Falls, New York, has eight councilors and a mayor. Niagara Falls, Ontario, has nine and a mayor. And Niagara-on-the-Lake has nine and a lord mayor. Our lord mayor designation is the only official lord mayor in Canada. The title was granted to the town by Prince Edward, Duke of Kent and Strathearn, on a royal visit to the area in the early 1800s."

Michael advised, "I'll be at a CPA conference in New York City for Thursday, Friday, and most of Saturday this week, so I won't start looking for a meeting room until I'm back in my office next week."

We all agreed that these conversations were very productive and that our plans for moving forward were very interesting. We finished our discussions full of enthusiasm for the next meeting of HOO. We were thinking that it should be in about two or three weeks. It seemed like it would be necessary for the three of us to be in regular daily contact for the next several weeks. Maria and I left to go off to what we knew would be an enjoyable dinner, and it was.

Chapter 15
Contact with the FvD
Wednesday, April 24

My workdays in the investment business were always very interesting. There were new world events happening by the hour every day that had some kind of impact on investment decisions and the investment process. That's why I enjoyed my job working with William R. Jones Investment Company. Planning events for the House of Owls group was an added bonus. I also enjoyed that very much. Between the Company and HOO, my days were full of intrigue and activity.

I had promised Michael and Maria that I would try to contact someone at the FvD in The Hague, so I thought I should do that today. On searching the internet, I was able to locate an email address for the party's headquarters in The Hague, which seemed like a good place to start. I sent an email to Mr. Hendrik Allard, the founder of the party and the leader of the party in the House of Representatives. In my email, I told Mr. Allard about the House of Owls, that we were a political movement, not a political party, and that we were just getting started in our program to promote Direct Democracy in Canada and the United States. The most important part of the email was asking Mr. Allard if someone from their group could come to our area to speak at our next meeting. Since there was a six-hour time-zone difference between The Hague and Niagara-on-the-Lake, I didn't expect a reply until at least tomorrow.

Just as I was finishing my email to Mr. Allard, my phone rang. I picked it up and said, "This is Billy Jones. How may I help you?"

The voice answered, "Hi, Billy, it's Ram. I thought I should call to give you an update on my progress so far. I haven't found out yet who your two thugs are, but I'm getting close and should have their names and addresses in a day or two. I expect that I will also be able to find out who they are and who they work for. When I get all this information, you and I will need to sit down and think about what we can do about these people. We will have to put an end to their disruptive activities somehow."

"Ram, it's good to hear from you," I responded. "You're right. We will need to deal with these guys somehow. When you get the information, please call me, and we can think about what to do next. Thanks for calling. Your help is much appreciated." We hung up, and I continued to think and wonder about what might be the next problem with these thugs.

I waited until later in the day to call Maria, after she would be home from school. I thought I should tell her about my email to the FvD and my conversation with Ram. I also wanted to keep in touch.

Chapter 16
More Work for Leather Vest
and Black Boots
Friday, April 26

It was early afternoon on Friday, a week after the HOO meeting at Niagara-on-the-Lake. Leather Vest and Black Boots had been called to come to the office of The Man. They had arrived, were ushered into his office, were seated, and were ready to receive their new orders.

The Man came in, did the usual "Hello, how are you?" took his seat behind his big executive-style desk, and was ready to discuss the new plans for his thugs. He said, "We have had good success with the information—the license plates and types of cars—that you copied down in the parking lot at the meeting of the owly bunch last week. We have been able to get names and addresses for all the people whose license plates you recorded. We needed to come up with some ideas of what we should do to make our warnings about the House of Owls a little stronger so they might pay attention.

"After a lot of thought and tossing ideas around, we decided that we should put a real scare into those people who attended the meeting. I'm going to give you the full list of names and addresses. What I would like you to do is some small physical damage to the cars of each one who attended the meeting. The name Charles Wheatley on the list should not be touched. He is one of our 'friends' that we planted at the meeting to help keep us informed. What I mean by small physical damage are things like slash a tire, break a window or headlight or taillight, or some little thing like that. You can be a bit creative if you want and come up with other things that might get the message across."

Leather Vest asked, "How much time do we get to do this?"

The Man said, "You can take up to a week or more if you need it, but the main thing is to get it done and not get caught. I've had these little business cards made that deliver the message 'No House of Owls.' That's the only writing on the card. Each time you do some damage to a car, leave one of these under the windshield wiper."

"That sounds pretty easy. We should be able to do them all in a day or two. We might want to do most of them at night after dark. I guess we'll need to go into Canada again to get at these Ontario addresses," said Leather Vest.

"Don't forget, the most important thing is to not get caught. When you put these cards under the windshield wipers, be sure not to leave your fingerprints on them. When you handle the cards, you may want to use latex gloves or your winter gloves or something like that so your fingerprints aren't left on the cards or anywhere else on the cars."

Black Boots spoke up and said, "This looks like an easy job. We'll probably be done in a few days. We'll still get our regular pay for the job, won't we?"

The Man answered, "Yes, of course, you will. Just do the job right. Don't leave any fingerprints, and don't get caught. Give me a call when you're finished, and we can decide what we need to do next."

Chapter 17
Good News from Ram
Friday, April 26

I was in my office, working away, when my phone rang, and I picked it up. The voice said, "Hi, Billy, it's Ram."

"Hi, Ram, what's new?" I asked.

"I finally have some information for you on your two favorite thugs and their boss. We need to get together sometime soon to think about what we should do next."

"That's great, Ram. Let's get together today," I said.

Ram replied with "I'm sort of tied up with business today, but how about tomorrow? It's Saturday, and we should both be off work and have more free time to toss around different ideas about what we should do next."

"That sounds great, Ram. How about two thirty at the Golden Bull Pub in the Falls? We can get a quiet corner and sip a brew or two while we discuss our problems," I suggested.

Ram and I had been to the Golden Bull many times. It was designed like an English pub and was one of the better pubs in the Niagara Falls area. We had always found it to be a very good watering hole and also a good place to meet for quiet discussions.

"That works for me, Billy. I'll see you then," said Ram, and he hung up.

I had always known that I was fortunate to have a friend like Ram, who was such a good investigator that he could find out almost anything. His training as both a lawyer and an accountant, when added together with his natural inquisitiveness and outgoing personality, combined to make him highly skilled at his job.

The three years that he worked with CSIS, the Canadian Security Intelligence Service, right after finishing his double legal and accounting education, was also a major plus for Jeramiah Delvechio. Most Canadians considered CSIS to be the Canadian equivalent of the FBI in the US. His time at CSIS was a very good, post-educational training base and gave him much better knowledge and higher skill levels to be able to start his own investigations business.

Chapter 18
Another Date for Billy and Maria
Friday, April 26

Springtime in the Niagara region is my favorite time of the year. The snow and ice and bitter cold weather were gone, and daily temperatures were edging higher day by day. The air was fresh and invigorating. The trees were turning green again, and everything was starting to grow. Spring is great!

When I last spoke with Maria by phone, we agreed that I would be at her house by about six thirty to give us lots of time to make it to our dinner reservation at seven.

Driving down the Niagara Parkway across the Rainbow Bridge into Niagara Falls, New York, and on to Maria's house was very pleasant. Not just because it was such a beautiful spring day but also as always, I was very much looking forward to seeing Maria again.

I arrived at the Simone residence, got out of my car, and tapped lightly on the door. Maria answered and invited me in with a hug that was firmer than usual and a kiss that had more passion. I hugged and kissed her right back with equal firmness and passion. She began to unbutton my shirt, and various pieces of clothing quickly fell to the floor as we edged our way to her bedroom.

We made love then talked for a while and decided that we should cancel our dinner reservation. Then we made love and talked for a while and made love and talked for a while. This was really the first time that Maria and I had been alone together in private, and it was a happy time for both of us. We knew that her father would be away until late tomorrow afternoon, so we had no need to rush anything.

Maria said, "You must be hungry, Billy. I have some homemade lasagna that I could heat up for us."

"That would be splendid, Maria. I could go for some homemade lasagna although I'm not that hungry, at least not for food."

She chuckled at my comment, jumped out of bed, put on a robe, and went to put the lasagna in the oven to warm.

I knew that I would like to stay for the night, but after a late, tasty homemade dinner, I thought that I should be heading home so Maria's nosy neighbors wouldn't start to gossip about a red Corvette sitting in her driveway all night. We kissed and hugged and promised each other that we would do this again sometime soon.

I left and drove home uneventfully. Evenings in spring were almost as pleasant as the bright and sunny afternoons.

Chapter 19
More Damage from Leather Vest and Black Boots
Saturday, April 27

I had just gotten up on Saturday morning and prepared a coddled egg and whole wheat toast for my breakfast when my cell phone rang. I answered, "Hi, it's Billy here."

The caller said, "Hi, Billy. It's Paul Browne. I thought I should call you as early as I could this morning about some trouble that we're having for our House of Owls group."

"I hope it's not too bad, Paul. What is it?" I asked.

"When I got up this morning and went out to my car, I found that both my headlights were smashed. There was a card, like a business card, tucked under my windshield wiper with nothing on it except the words *No House of Owls*. The worst part is that I have had calls from two of my friends who were at the meeting a week ago, and they both had car damage as well. Fred Mills said that his car had one of the tires slashed, and George Malinchuck said that he had both his car's taillights smashed. They both had the same notice cards tucked under their cars' windshield wipers, like the one that was on my car," said Paul.

"That sounds pretty serious. You're a lawyer, Paul. What do you think we should do about this?" I asked.

"I'm really a corporate lawyer, Billy, and this situation looks like we will need some advice from a criminal lawyer. However, it seems to me that the right thing to do now is to talk with the police to let them know about the various events we've had, such as the run-in you had at your office, the fight that your friend Ram Delvechio had in the parking lot of Chateau des Chutes Winery after our meeting a week ago, and the many incidents of car damage last night. We need to make the police aware of these things. We also need to let them know that we think we could see more of the same in the future as our group progresses. We should probably tell everyone who has had car damage to take a picture of the damage for both their insurance company and for the police."

"That's probably a very good idea to get the police involved. Taking pictures of the damage also seems like the right thing to do. Maybe the first contact with the police could come from you, followed by contact from each of your two friends Fred Mills and George Malinchuck. It looks like the thugs who I call Leather Vest and Black Boots are targeting people who attended the meeting last week. When Ram confronted them, he noticed that they seemed to be writing down license plate numbers. That was just before they knocked him out."

"That sounds like a good strategy, Billy. I'll contact the police, and I'll ask Fred and George to do the same," said Paul.

"Paul, I am meeting with Ram this afternoon at two thirty at the Golden Bull pub in the falls. If you would care to join us, your input would be welcome and helpful. Ram says he has been able to find out who these thugs are and who they work for. You might find it interesting. If you have the time, you should join us."

"It sounds like you're making good progress already, Billy. Yes, I would like to join you and Ram." Paul agreed.

"That's great, Paul. I'm sure Ram will be interested in hearing about the car damage that you and you friends suffered. I hope we don't have any more of our House of Owls friends receiving car damage. Thanks for calling, and I'll see you this afternoon," I said, and I hung up.

I had just finished the call from Paul Browne when my phone rang again. I answered as usual. "Hi, it's Billy here."

The caller said, "Hi, Billy. It's Martin Bristol here. I thought I should call to let you know that two of the tires on my car were slashed overnight last night, and there was a card, like a business card, tucked under the windshield wiper that said 'No House of Owls.' I was wondering if anyone else, who was at our meeting, has had any car damage trouble like this."

"The answer is yes. I just got off the phone with Paul Browne, my lawyer friend who is also a member of the House of Owls group. He told me that he had both the headlights smashed on his car last night and two of his friends who were at the meeting also had car damage. Fred Mills had a tire slashed, and George Malinchuck had both taillights smashed," I told him.

"That sounds pretty scary, Billy. What do you think I should do about it? Has Paul Browne given you any advice?"

"Yes, Martin. Paul suggested—and I totally agree—that any person who has suffered damage should report it to the police right away, and they should also take pictures of the damage for both their insurance company and for the police. You're the fourth person so far, Martin, and there may well be others who were at the meeting. I hope not, but there probably will be more of our House of Owls friends receiving some kind of car damage."

"Billy, I am very sorry to hear that so much damage has been done. I will definitely report my case to the police right way."

"Thanks, Martin. That will be very helpful." And we both said our goodbyes.

It was still too early for me to head off to the meeting with Paul and Ram at the Golden Bull, which was good because I wanted to chat with Maria this morning.

I phoned her number, and Maria answered in her usual bright and cheery voice. "Good morning, Billy. Thanks for calling. I wanted to say how much I enjoyed our—lasagna dinner last night. It was great. But I do have some bad news for you as well. Three people have phoned my father this morning to say that they had some damage to their cars overnight. One had smashed headlights. Another had smashed taillights, and the other had slashed tires. All three of them also said that there was a card, like a business card, stuck under their windshield wipers, and the only words on each of the cards was the same: 'No House of Owls.' These damages to personal cars are very scary."

"I really enjoyed our lasagna dinner last night too, Maria. It was great to be with you again. You're right about all these damaged cars. It's a very scary situation. I've heard from four people on this side of the border who all had car damage overnight, the same sort of things that you have heard about."

"Billy, what should we do about this?" she asked.

"Maria, one of the people over here who had car damage last night was my good friend Paul Browne. You may recall that he is a lawyer, which is why I asked him for his advice. He strongly recommended—and I agree—that each person who has had some damage should report it to the police and take pictures of the damage both for their insurance company and for the police. You should phone back each of the people who called and ask them to do that. You might also suggest to them that they should mention that some people over here have had some similar problems and that they are probably related. The police in Niagara Falls, New York, should talk with the Niagara Regional Police Service over here. They may decide to work together on this," I said, hopeful.

"That sounds like the right thing to do, Billy. I'll go ahead and call them all back and ask them to phone the police."

"Thanks, Maria. I was hoping that we could get together for dinner tonight. Maybe we should invite your father to join us so we can give him an update on all these problems. How about dinner at seven? I'll pick up both of you at about six thirty, and I will leave the reservation up to you since you know the area better."

"That sounds good, Billy. I'll see you at about six thirty."

Chapter 20
Meeting at the Golden Bull
Saturday, April 27

I left home at no. 5 Saint David's Place to go to the Golden Bull pub a little after two in the afternoon. I arrived at the parking lot and got out of my red Corvette, but before I could get to the front door, both Ram and Paul arrived. We met in the parking lot and said hello to each other. We all shook hands and went inside.

As we sat down at an out-of-the-way corner table, our server came over to ask what we would like. We each ordered one of the Golden Bull's proprietary craft brews, which were well-known to be somewhat different, special, and very good.

I gave Ram and Paul a little background on each other since I wasn't sure if they had ever met before this afternoon. Paul said, "I did meet Ram briefly the other night after the meeting at the winery, but he wasn't in very good shape to remember much."

Ram said, "Paul, it's good to meet you again. I think I will remember better this time."

"Ram, Paul phoned me earlier this morning and told me that both headlights on his car were smashed overnight and he found a small card, like a business card, under his windshield wiper with the words *No House of Owls* on it. Paul also said that two other people called him, who attended our meeting that Friday night, and had car damage.

They also had the same type of little business cards tucked under their windshield wipers.

"Our House of Owls friends across the river, in the US, have also had problems. I talked with my good friend Maria Simone from over there this morning. She told me that she had three phone calls from people who attended our Friday meeting and had car damage overnight last night and received the same little business cards that our friends over here received," I recounted my tale of woe

I continued on to say, "Paul, Ram told me this morning that he has been able to find out who these troglodytes are and who they work for. That's what you said, isn't it, Ram?"

"That's right, Billy. I have found out who they are. The name of the one that you dubbed Leather Vest is Gary Masterson. These guys all seem to like having nicknames. His is Bat. Apparently, it's because he sometimes uses a baseball bat to carry out some of his 'administrative activities' for the Scaglione Agency. The name Bat is also a reference to the legendary Bat Masterson, who you may remember was famous for many things in the American Old West in the 1870s and 1880s. At different times, he was a buffalo hunter, an army scout, a lawman, a saloonkeeper, and a gambler. He was probably best known for his friendship with Wyatt Earp in both Dodge City, Kansas, and Tombstone, Arizona. This current Bat from Albany is not a very friendly person.

"The name of the other thug, whom you labeled Black Boots, is Harold Remington. His nickname is Gunner, which is sort of obvious for someone with the last name Remington. The Remington Arms company was founded in 1816 in Ilion, New York, by Eliphalet Remington and is the oldest gunmaker in the United States. Even though Ilion is only about eighty miles west of Albany, just off the I-95, our man Harold, or Gunner, is probably not a relative. A somewhat worrisome factor is that both Bat and Gunner are in the US Army reserve and have been trained as sharpshooters.

"Both Bat and Gunner work for the Scaglione Agency based in Albany, New York. They are both called Administrative Assistants. The Scaglione Agency is owned and managed by Anthony Scaglione.

His good friends call him simply Tony The Man. For those who don't care for him very much, he is sometimes known as Scags. Most of the agency's clients and the works it carries out are related to various types of criminal activities or politicians and political lobbying.

"The Scaglione Agency's clients include politicians from various municipalities across New York state. The agency also represents some state and federal politicians—mostly in New York state, but from other jurisdictions as well. The agency even has a number of clients in Ontario and other parts of Canada.

"Most of the agency's activities are related to acting as sort of a conduit to pay politicians in cash, drugs, sexual favors, paid holiday trips, and other perks. For receiving these favors, the politicians are told how to vote. The funding for these payoffs is provided by businesses looking for favors. The clients of the other part of the Scaglione Agency's business are many and varied. They relate mainly to criminal activities of organized crime groups," Ram explained.

"Ram, are you confident that you have identified the right people?" I asked.

"Yes, Billy. I can't disclose my information sources, but I am totally confident that these are the right guys. I was able to get some pictures of them, which will confirm to you that these are the right people. You did explain that you saw them very clearly when they came into your office. Have a look at these pictures, Billy. I'm sure that you will confirm that I am on the right track," Ram replied.

"I can easily see from the pictures that you're right. If we want to try to move forward with these names—Bat, Gunner, and Tony the Man—what do you think our next steps should be?" I asked.

"The three of us should probably go and have a chat with the Niagara Regional Police Service since they cover the whole peninsula. They may have some suggestions for us," said Paul.

"I think that's a good idea," said Ram. "I know Ian Fraser, the regional police chief, and several of the detectives. We could start there and see where it leads us."

"That all makes sense," I said. "All three of us could go there right now and explain the whole situation, going back to the two thugs bursting into my office a week ago on Thursday. We can also advise them about the thugs beating up Ram on Friday night in the parking lot at the Chateau des Chutes Winery after our meeting."

"Billy, why don't I call Chief Fraser right now to see if he could be available to meet with us this afternoon?" asked Ram.

While Ram made the call to Chief Fraser, Paul and I continued to chat about the situation. After his call, Ram advised us that the chief would be available to meet with us at about four that afternoon. We all agreed that it was good and decided to hang around the Golden Bull for a little while and enjoy our brews.

The Niagara Regional Police Service station in Niagara Falls was fairly close to the Golden Bull pub. It was at 5700 Valley Way, just a block north of the Niagara General Hospital and not far from the casino. We knew that it wouldn't take us long to get there, so we stayed at the pub, enjoying our brews, and left to go to the police station at about 3:40.

Each of us drove separately and arrived at the police station right after the other. We went in, stopped at the front desk, and asked to see Chief Ian Fraser. After a quick call by the desk clerk to confirm our appointment with the chief, we were shown into his office. After we introduced ourselves and explained everything to the chief, he said he found our situation to be very disturbing. Chief Ian Fraser was a lifelong career police officer with a sturdy build and short-cut, dark but graying hair. He mentioned that he had received fifteen or sixteen phone calls today from people in the area who received some damage to their cars last night. I suggested that these people could all be people who attended our House of Owls meeting a week ago last Friday.

The chief said, "I would like to be able to confirm that, but I can't tell you the names of the people who called. It's private and confidential."

I said, "I understand your position, and it's not a problem for us. If you think it will help, I will be happy to give you a list of the names of those who attended our meeting, and you can compare the names that you have to the names on our list."

"That sounds good, Billy. That would be very helpful," he said.

"There are a couple of other points that may be of interest to you. About half the people who attended our meeting were from across the river. Earlier today, I was chatting with a good friend from over there, and she told me that many of our American friends who attended the meeting in Niagara-on-the-Lake also received car damage overnight last night. You may want to chat with John Polowski, the chief of police in Niagara Falls, New York, about this situation."

"The problem seems more widespread than I thought it was," said the chief.

"There is one more piece of information that you should know," I said. "Through his own proprietary and confidential sources, Ram, who is a private investigator, has been able to discover who the two thugs are and who they work for. As you may suspect, we have no proof of our contention that they were the ones who did all the damage to the cars last night, but we should give you the information so you can have it to check out and keep an eye out for these guys."

Ram gave Chief Fraser the information that he had about Bat, Gunner, and Tony the Man. We wound up our meeting, thanking the chief for his help, and we promised to keep in touch.

As we were leaving the police station and headed toward our cars in the parking lot, we agreed to contact one another the next day.

Chapter 21
Damaged Cars in Niagara Falls, New York
Saturday, April 27

From the police station, I drove home to no. 5 Saint David's Place. I wanted to phone Maria before I left to go to meet with her and Michael to see if there was anything new over there about the damaged cars. After I got home, I called Maria, and she answered in a tone that was a little less than her usual bubbly, happy self.

"Hi, Billy. I'm glad you called. I am a little nervous about answering the phone because we have had a lot of calls today from people who had some damage to their cars overnight last night."

"I'm sorry to hear that, Maria. Has Michael arrived back from New York City yet?

"Yes, Billy. He got home a little after three this afternoon, and he has been taking all the disturbing calls since then. Counting the calls that I took earlier, and the ones that have come in since he arrived back home, we must be up to about twenty by now. This is all quite unsettling."

"Let's just go ahead with our plans to meet at your house at about six thirty, and the three of us go out to dinner to discuss everything."

"Billy, it may be better if I make dinner here so we can discuss everything a little more privately."

"That seems like a good idea, Maria. Thanks for offering. I look forward to seeing you soon, and I am sure I will enjoy your dinner. I'll see you at six thirty, give or take a little. You never know how long it will take to get over the bridge and through Customs and Immigration."

I left home a little before six to go to see Maria and Michael. I arrived at their house, the now familiar antique redbrick, ranch-style house at 2211 Springfield Drive, just before six thirty. I saw that both Michael's Mercedes and Maria's Honda were parked in the driveway, so I parked on the street in front of their house.

When I knocked lightly on the door, Maria answered with a kiss and a hug, and we walked together into Michael's at-home office.

I said, "Hello, Michael, good to see you again. It sounds like you and your friends here in Niagara Falls, New York, have been having the same kind of troubles that we are having over on the Canadian side."

"Yes, Billy, we have. Maria and I have had more than twenty phone calls from people we know who attended the now infamous Friday night meeting of the House of Owls in Niagara-on-the-Lake. They all had some kind of damage to their cars overnight last night. I have told each one of them to report the incident and the damage to the police."

"Michael, we have also had about twenty calls from people who attended our meeting and had their cars vandalized overnight last night. We have also advised each one of them to contact the police and let them know what happened. Some of the calls that we received went to my good friend and lawyer, Paul Browne. He was the first to advise that we should definitely tell the police about everything that happened. I think this is the right thing to do."

"Maria has found this car-damage problem with our friends a little bit unnerving, and so do I," Michael said.

"I do get a little nervous about it all," said Maria. "Why don't I go and finish getting everything ready, and we can discuss the situation over a leisurely dinner?"

After Maria had left us to finish preparing dinner, I told Michael that Ram had been able to discover who our two thugs were and who they worked for. I wasn't sure if he wanted Maria to know who these troublemakers were. He said, "Yes, it's OK, Billy. She is a stronger-willed person than you might think. She hasn't been locked in a gilded cage all her life. She can handle a little adversity."

After we sat down for dinner, I explained to Maria, "Ram has been able to discover the identity of our two thugs and who they work for. The one who I have called Leather Vest is Gary Masterson, known as Bat, and the other one who I called Black Boots is Harold Remington, known as Gunner. They work as so-called Administrative Assistants for the Scaglione Agency based in Albany, New York. The agency's business is political lobbying and 'other things,' which includes a wide range of various criminal activities. It's owned and managed by one person, Anthony Scaglione, who is known as Tony the Man."

"I would think that these are the ones who did all the car vandalism last night, or at the very least, they were responsible for having it done. But I doubt very much if we have enough evidence to ask the police to bring them in for anything," Michael pointed out.

"That raises another point that I wanted to talk about," I said. "Paul, Ram, and I spent some time with Ian Fraser, chief of police for the Niagara Regional Police Service in Niagara Falls, Ontario, this afternoon. We told him all the background information about the House of Owls, the thugs barging into my office, and the troubles at our Friday night meeting at the Chateau des Chutes Winery. We also mentioned that Ram had gotten beaten up and told him about last night's car-damage events. Chief Fraser said that the station had received fifteen or sixteen phone calls about car damage last night, and he realized that we both had the same problem. The chief said that he couldn't give out the names, so I gave him a list of the Canadians who attended the Friday night meeting. He compared our list to his list, and then he said that all our names were on his list."

"Did Chief Fraser say what the police would do about all the car-damage problems?" Maria asked.

"There really isn't much they can do at this point. We don't have any solid proof that we could go to court with, but Bat, Gunner, and Tony the Man certainly seem to be the ones responsible for our problems," I pointed out.

"We should contact the police here in Niagara Falls, New York, as well to let them know about our problems," Michael added.

"Yes, we should, Michael. Chief Fraser said that he would call John Polowski, your chief of police, to compare notes. We told Chief Fraser that we knew of car-damage problems on the New York side of the border that were the same as what we had on our side. Even so, we should have a talk with Chief Polowski or maybe even go to the station and meet with him," I said.

"It's probably too late to go today. Maybe we could phone and make an appointment for tomorrow or Monday," Maria suggested.

Michael and I both agreed that this was a good plan of action. We all knew that we had to do something. We couldn't just leave everything as unfinished and unsatisfying as it was right now.

"If you are able to get a meeting with Chief Polowski, I would be happy to come with you if you think I could help," I said.

Michael said, "I should probably arrange to go to the local police by myself on behalf of the US side of the House of Owls group. It probably won't be necessary for you to join me, but if they would like to talk with you, I could give them your phone number so they could follow up at some other time if they wanted to."

"On another subject, I did send an email to Hendrik Allard, president of the FvD political party in the Netherlands. I received an email reply back from the party just today to say that they would be very pleased to send over two of their party representatives to speak at one of our meetings sometime in the next few weeks. We should get a time and place organized as quickly as we can to take advantage of their kind offer," I said.

"Yes, Billy. That sounds good. I have looked into possible locations for us, and I think the Niagara Falls Public Library would be a good spot. It's right downtown at 1425 Main Street, which will be fairly easy for you and all our Canadian friends to find. The Earl W. Brydges Auditorium at the library can hold more than one hundred people. I could book it for us if you think that location works," said Michael.

"A Friday night or Saturday night would probably be best for most people, don't you think?" asked Maria.

Michael and I both agreed, and I added, "Why don't we start by targeting Friday, May 10, at, let's say, seven thirty at the library? I will contact the FvD folks and see if that works for them. By the tone of their email, that date and time should be OK with the FvD. They sounded like their schedule was quite flexible. Let's go ahead and book the library for that time and date, and I will confirm it back to you as soon as I get confirmation from the FvD."

"My speech from the Friday night meeting has been transcribed and is ready for distribution. I will email it to you tomorrow, Billy, so you can resend it to all your Canadian friends. Maria and I will look after distribution over here," said Michael.

"The timing of that should work really well. We can send out the notes from your speech to all the people who attended the meeting and to as many others as we can think of, especially all the local politicians on both sides of the border. We could follow that up a few days later by sending out an email invitation to our next meeting with the speaker from the FvD," I said.

"Michael, you may have guessed that Maria and I care for each other a lot, so I thought it might be a good idea if you and she could come to one of our family's Sunday evening dinners sometime soon to meet my parents and my grandfather, who also lives with us," I said.

With a smile on his face, Michael replied, "I'm happy to hear that Maria has a romantic interest, Billy. You seem to be an honest and personable young man. I think you would be good for Maria, and she would be good for you."

"Thank you for your kind thoughts, Michael. I would like to suggest that one week from tomorrow might be a good time if your personal schedule is open for that date," I offered.

"Yes, Billy, that would be good for me," Michael answered. "Is that OK with your schedule, Maria?"

"Yes, that's fine with me," Maria answered.

"I will need to confirm it with my family, but I am virtually certain that it will be OK since it's more than a week away. Our Sunday dinner is usually at five thirty, so you might want to arrive at about five to meet everyone for before-dinner drinks and conversation. I think you will find that my parents and my grandfather are easy to chat with. In the distant past, the family used to dress somewhat formally for dinner, but that has not been the case for quite a long time. We usually dress in a style that you might call smart casual," I offered.

"Billy, thanks for coming over today. We needed to understand what's going on with the car-damage problems, and it's good to know who the bad guys are even if we can't do much about it at this stage. We'll get even eventually," Michael said, and Maria nodded in agreement.

Chapter 22
Sunday Is Not Always a Day of Rest
Sunday, April 28

Sunday was supposed to be a day of rest, but this Sunday, it wasn't for me. I talked with my parents and my grandfather about inviting Michael and Maria to dinner next Sunday, and all three agreed that this was a good idea and was fine with them. Then I phoned Maria to let her and Michael know that our proposed day and time for dinner with my family was confirmed. Maria did not answer, so I left a voice message on her phone.

I sent an email to the FvD office in The Hague advising of the proposed date, time, and place for our next meeting, hoping that these would all work for them.

I also phoned Ram to see if he had any more information on our thuggish friends or any additional information from police chief Fraser. He had nothing new to report.

On reflecting about recent events, the thought occurred to me that we might have had a spy or even more than one spy in our midst at our Friday night meeting on April 19 at the winery. One way to check that out would be to check with the police to see if anybody on our list did not receive any car damage on Friday night.

I phoned for Chief Ian Fraser, and luckily, he was in. I explained my idea to him and asked, "Could you tell me if there are any names on my list that did not phone you to complain about car damage last Friday night?"

"Yes, Billy, there are several names that did not call in. One, of course, is yourself. The others are Henri and Jeanne Renault, Waldemar Falchuk, and Curtis Westfield," he reported.

"That's very helpful, Chief Fraser. I know the Renaults very well, and I am certain that they wouldn't be spies. But the other two are possible candidates. I'll phone both Waldemar Falchuk and Curtis Westfield to see if I can learn anything from them. Thank you for your help," I said, and we both hung up.

I thought I should phone Maria and Michael again to let them know about this latest ploy I was undertaking and to ask them to do the same on the New York side of the border.

I dialed her number, and Maria answered in her usual bubbly and happy voice. "Hello, Billy. How are you? I just came in from grocery shopping. I see you left a message earlier. What's up?"

"Maria, I wanted to let you know that my parents and my grandfather are happy to invite you and Michael to join us for dinner next Sunday. They're looking forward to it very much," I said.

"That's great, Billy. My father and I are also looking forward to joining you all for dinner. I think you suggested that we should be there at about five for the dinner at five thirty, didn't you?" she reconfirmed.

"Maria, the other reason I phoned was to tell you about a little ploy that I have thought about. On some reflection, I think that it is possible that we may have had one or more spies attending our Friday night meeting and passing information on to the Scaglione Agency. I phoned police chief Ian Fraser to ask him to check his list of people who phoned in about car damage on Friday night, April 26, and compare his list to my list of Canadians who attended our meeting at the winery on April 19. There were two names on the list that did not phone in and may not have had any car damage. My plan is to phone each of them and try to determine from our conversation if they might be spies. It would be very helpful if you and Michael could go through the same process on your side of the border," I explained.

"That seems like a good plan, Billy, but I think I will ask my father to do it. He is much better at that kind of thing than I am, and he will probably get better results," she said.

"That should be good, Maria. If Michael would like to chat with me before he goes ahead with the plan, please ask him to call so that we can exchange ideas," I added.

We said our goodbyes, and we both hung up.

There's no time like the present to get the job done, so I thought I would go ahead right now and phone the two people. The names, addresses, phone numbers, and email addresses were on the lists that Maria and I had made at the meeting.

Using the phone number from the list, I phoned Curtis Westfield. The phone rang several times, and then a voice message came on the line and said that this number was not in service. *That seems odd*, I thought. It was just over a week ago that he gave out this number. I thought it might be worthwhile to try to send an email to him to see if the email address might be real. I sent a short note to the email address, and it immediately bounced back as nonexistent. It looks more and more like Curtis Westfield could be an informer.

To continue my investigation, I phoned the number for Waldemar Falchuk. Someone answered with an inquisitive hello.

"This is Billy Jones calling," I said. "You may remember me from the meeting of the House of Owls group at the Chateau des Chutes Winery on Friday evening, April 19."

"Yes, Billy. I do remember you and the meeting. What can I do for you today?" he asked.

"Mr. Falchuk—"

He cut me off. "Please call me Wally," he interjected.

"Thank you, Wally," I said. "I'm calling to let you know that some of the people who attended the House of Owls meeting on Friday night, April 19, had some damage done to their cars overnight on Friday, April 26. I am following up with others who attended the meeting to see if they had any car damage that night. Did you?"

"It's funny that you should ask, Billy. My wife and I were away on Friday and Saturday night and just came home a short while ago to find the taillights in my car have been smashed and a little card, like a business card, under the windshield wiper that had 'No House of Owls' printed on it and nothing else. We took my wife's car when we went away, so my car was sitting in our driveway, exposed to anyone."

"Unfortunately, you are not alone, Wally. Most of the House of Owls members had similar experiences on Friday night. You should take a photo of the damage for your insurance company and for the police. Also, you should phone the police and tell them what happened. The other members have already done that, so it won't be much of a surprise to the police," I explained.

Wally thanked me for my call and the information and said that he would take pictures and call the police as I suggested.

I thought that I should call Ram again to explain to him my little ploy and the results so far. I dialed his number, and he answered.

"Hello, Billy, what's up? Do you have something new to tell me about the car-damage problems?" he asked.

"That's a good guess, Ram. Yes, I do. I came up with the idea that we might possibly have one or more spies in our House of Owls membership group, and it looks like I might have guessed right. My plan was to phone Chief Fraser to see if any of the names on our membership list that I gave him did not call the police to report car damage on Friday night. He gave me two names—Waldemar Falchuk and Curtis Westfield. When I talked with Wally Falchuk a few minutes ago, he explained that he was away Friday and Saturday night and just now returned home to see his car damaged. I don't think he's the culprit.

"I called the phone number for Curtis Westfield, which he gave to us when Maria and I collected names and addresses at the Friday night meeting. After several rings of his phone, a voice message came on the line that said this number is not in service. Since that was just over a week ago, I suspect that this was a phony number. I also tried the email address that he gave, and it didn't work either," I explained to Ram.

"There's certainly something fishy about this guy. You may well be right that he is an informer for somebody, probably the Scaglione Agency," said Ram. "I don't think there is anything that we can do about him right now, Billy. We don't know who he really is, and we don't have any valid contact information for him. He may think that we haven't discovered his clandestine attendance and is getting away with his spying. He may well show up again at the next meeting."

"You're right, Ram. We should just wait him out. Thanks again for your help," I said, and we both hung up.

Chapter 23
Preparing for the Next House
of Owls Meeting
Monday, April 29

Monday was usually a busy day at the office, and this Monday was no exception. I also had a fair amount of work to do this week for the House of Owls group. I needed to keep focused and active to ensure that I could get everything done on a timely basis and in the right way.

I received the email from Michael Simone with the copy of his speech attached, as he promised. I saved the attachment on the hard drive on my laptop computer and sent an email to each of the Canadian members of the House of Owls with a copy of Michael's speech attached. I used the list of names that Maria and I had made at the meeting on April 19. Not surprisingly, the email to Curtis Westfield bounced back right away again.

I thought it would be a good idea for me to speak with someone at the FvD office in The Hague to discuss the arrangements for their representatives to come and speak at our next meeting of the House of Owls on May 10. Because of the six-hour time difference, I needed to call them fairly early in the morning, my time, so that I could catch them while there was still someone in their office before they all left for the day. Their receptionist answered. I told her who I was and why

I had called, and she put me through to another person who answered in English.

"Hello, this is Wim Vanderdonk. How may I help you today?"

I responded with "Hello, Wim. This is Billy Jones from Niagara-on-the Lake in Canada. I'm calling today to follow up on our recent email exchange. As you probably know, I sent an email to the FvD office asking if someone from your party could come to speak at the next meeting of our House of Owls group. Our group is dedicated in trying to establish Direct Democracy in both Canada and the United States at all levels of government in both countries."

"Yes, Billy, I am aware of the contact we have had with you. Our party president, Hendrik Allard, has asked two of us to come to America to speak at your meeting as you have requested. The two people who will be coming to your meeting will be Lars Hogeboom and me. Either one or both of us could speak about how the FvD has developed and explain its political policies."

"That sounds great, Wim. The meeting is planned for Friday, May 10, at the library at 1425 Main Street in Niagara Falls, New York, in the Earl W. Brydges Auditorium. The auditorium is like a small theater that will hold a little over one hundred people. We hope to start at 7:30 p.m. and finish by around 9:00 p.m. to 9:30 p.m. I will send you this information by email so you will be able to print out hard copies for Lars and yourself," I said.

"Thanks, Billy. That seems pretty straightforward. We will fly on KLM Royal Dutch Airlines from The Hague to arrive at New York City at about noon your time. We can take a connecting flight from there to arrive at the Buffalo Niagara International Airport by about 2:30 p.m. on Friday. This should get us into Niagara Falls with lots of time for your meeting. I understand there is a Brockton Inn hotel just across Genesee Street from the airport. We are quite familiar with the international chain of Brockton Inns, and we like them. We have them in the Netherlands at Schiphol, in Amsterdam, and at Rotterdam, in The Hague Airport, which serves both The Hague and Rotterdam. We plan on staying there on Friday night after the meeting and flying back home on Saturday. We will arrange our own bookings to ensure that we can be certain of our own schedule, if that's all right with you. By the way, my personal email address here at the office is wvanderdonk@ fvd.nl. You can reach me there anytime," he said.

"Wim, you could phone either Michael Simone or me after you arrive and are settled in at your hotel. We will pick you up, and we can all go out for dinner before the meeting. I will put both our phone numbers in an email to you as a follow-up to this conversation.

"Wim, thank you very much for all the support from the FvD and to you and Lars for agreeing to come over. That seems to cover everything. We all look forward to meeting both you and Lars and to hearing more about the FvD and its success," I said, and we both said goodbye for now.

I phoned Michael at his office to let him know that I thought it would be a good idea for us to get together this evening to review recent developments and to go over our plans for the upcoming meeting at the library in Niagara Falls, New York, on May 10. He agreed that we should meet to discuss several things and suggested that we could meet at his home at about seven. I agreed and looked forward to the meeting with Michael and Maria.

Chapter 24
Billy Meets with Michael and Maria
Monday, April 29

Over the past few weeks, I had found that I cared more and more for Maria. I had several romantic interests in my earlier years, but my care for Maria was different and a lot more serious. Whenever I was driving alone, I frequently found that the "Maria" song from the great old Stephen Sondheim musical, *West Side Story*, was buzzing through my mind even though I didn't sing very well.

I came through the border crossing without much delay, even though I had not yet received the NEXUS card that I had applied for, and continued on to the Simone residence in Niagara Falls. I parked my car in front of their house, went to the door, tapped lightly, and was greeted by Maria with a warm and friendly kiss and a hug, as was now becoming customary whenever we met.

"Hi, Billy, it's great to see you again," she said. "Let's go into my father's at-home office, and we can discuss the latest developments with the House of Owls in more comfort."

"It's great to see you again too, Maria," I said. "Yes, there are some things that the three of us need to talk about to keep our House of Owls group moving forward."

We walked together to Michael's office, and he greeted me with "Hey, Billy, thanks for coming over again."

"Thanks, Michael," I responded. "It's always good for me to come over to visit with you and Maria. I wanted to let you know that I have completed the arrangements with the folks at FvD in The Hague to come over to speak at our meeting on May 10. The two people who will be coming over are Wim Vanderdonk and Lars Hogeboom. They are both part of the founding group of the FvD and have complete understanding and full knowledge of the party's policies and principles. Wim is one of the two FvD members elected to the Dutch Parliament along with the party president Hendrik Allard in the last election."

"That sounds good, Billy. It should be a very interesting meeting for all of us," said Michael.

"When I spoke with Wim Vanderdonk by phone earlier today, he told me that they would be making their own travel arrangements. They will be flying from The Hague to New York City by KLM Royal Dutch Airlines and taking a connecting flight to our Buffalo Niagara International Airport. They are scheduled to arrive there at about two thirty in the afternoon. They have booked rooms at the Brockton Inn, just across the street from the entry road to the airport. I suggested that the three of us would pick them up at their hotel and go for dinner before the meeting at the library at seven thirty."

"That seems like a good arrangement, Billy. Why don't you plan on driving to our house, and we can take my car? Your Corvette is a little on the small side for five people," Michael suggested. "If you could be here by about three thirty, we could pick them up at their hotel at about four and make our dinner reservation for four thirty. That should give us plenty of time to eat and chat before going to our meeting at seven thirty."

"That seems like an excellent arrangement, Michael," I said. "I'll send an email to Wim Vanderdonk at FvD and ask him to phone you here after they arrive at their hotel and are settled in, and you can let them know what our plans are. About dinner, Maria and I really enjoyed the Niagara Chophouse when we went there a short while ago. Why don't we try that restaurant again?"

"That schedule should work fine for all of us," Maria added.

"Michael, thank you for preparing the transcript of your speech and for sending it to me by email attachment. I have forwarded it on to all the Canadian names on the list that Maria and I prepared at the April 19 meeting. You said that you and Maria would send it to all the American names on our list," I said.

"Yes, Billy. I did that earlier today," said Maria.

"In another area of business for the House of Owls group, I have done some minor sleuthing that has been a little bit productive. I had a talk with the Niagara Falls, Ontario, chief of police Ian Fraser to see if any of the names on my list did not call in to the police to report car damage. One of the two names that were on my list that Chief Fraser told me were not on his list was out of town for the weekend, but the other one appears to have been a spy in our midst. The name, phone number, and email address that he gave were all fictitious. The name on our list was Curtis Westfield. When I dialed the phone number that he gave, I was answered by the operator who said the number was not in service, and when I sent an email to him with the copy of your speech attached, it immediately bounced back."

"That certainly sounds like we could have had some kind of a phony person at our meeting," said Maria. "My father and I went through the same process with the American list, but we didn't find any names of people who we thought might be spies."

"I plan on sending out invitations for our meeting on May 10 to all the people who came to our meeting on April 19. I feel confident that all those who came out last time would like to come and hear the FvD success story. I also thought it would be a good time to expand our coverage to include some of the politicians in our area.

"My plan is to send a copy of Michael's speech, along with an invitation to the May 10 meeting, to my good friend Nigel Bromley, the lord mayor of Niagara-on-the-Lake, and to the mayor of Niagara Falls, Ontario. I also plan on sending invitations to each of our local representatives from our provincial and federal governments. I will suggest to the mayors that they could bring along with them any city councilors who might be interested, and for the provincial and federal representatives, any associates who might be interested. We should try to get one hundred people or more for the meeting," I explained.

"We will do the same thing for the US members on our list, and we should also follow your plan of reaching out to our local politicians and state and federal representatives," Maria added.

"Michael, you did such a good job with recording and transcribing your speech from the last meeting. It would be very helpful if you could do that again for the FvD speeches," I suggested.

"Yes, Billy. I can arrange to do that," agreed Michael.

"Those are the points that I wanted to discuss, and I think our getting together has been very productive," I said. "Michael, Maria, did either of you have any other points that we should talk about?"

"No, Billy, we've covered the important things, but if anything else comes up in the next day or so, we will call you," said Michael. "Both of us are really looking forward to joining you at your family dinner on Sunday."

I would have liked to stay in Niagara Falls and go out to dinner somewhere with Maria, but we both had homework to do that night. So we parted, and I headed the Corvette back toward the border crossing and home to the Jones house.

Driving home was nearly as pleasant as driving over to see Maria and Michael, except I missed the blissful expectation of being with Maria that I had on the way over.

Mulling things over in my mind as I drove along, I realized just how much I was looking forward to the upcoming meeting with the two men from the Netherlands and learning more about how they had succeeded, as well as they have, in promoting the concepts of Direct Democracy in their country.

Chapter 25
Bat and Gunner Receive a Little Payback
Monday, April 29

Ram was acting on his own when he thought that a little payback might be in order. He drove to Albany on Sunday afternoon and booked into a motel on the western edge of the city. He spent some time to familiarize himself with the condo building where Bat and Gunner lived. After some scrutiny, he became confident that he could gain entry to the underground parking garage, where their personal vehicles were parked.

In Albany, as in most cities, the quietest time of the night was usually between three and five in the morning. Ram left his motel room just after 4:00 a.m., and as expected, the streets of the city were mostly empty and very quiet. He drove his BMW X5 SUV toward the area where the condo was located, which Bat and Gunner called home. He parked about three blocks away, casually walked to the building, and as expected, was able to quickly gain access to the underground parking area.

He knew that Bat's vehicle was a black Ram pickup truck and Gunner's was a dark gray Lincoln MKX SUV. He also knew the license plate numbers of both vehicles. He found the Ram pickup, verified the license plate number, and then proceeded to slash all four tires and smash both taillights and both headlights. After he finished with Bat's pickup truck, he looked around and saw Gunner's Lincoln SUV close by. He then proceeded to give it the same treatment he had given the pickup truck. With each vehicle, he left a small business card–sized note that had on it the words "You should not play with fire. You might get burned" and nothing else.

After his little escapade in the underground parking garage, Ram went back to his motel and had a pleasant sleep. He woke up just after 10:00 a.m., had some breakfast, and then leisurely drove back to Canada.

Later that morning, Bat and Gunner took a taxi over to the office of the Scaglione Agency. They wanted to talk with Tony the Man. They were in luck. He was in. He invited them into his office, offered them coffee, which they both agreed to, and asked them why they were there that day when he had not been expecting them.

Bat, the usual spokesman for the two, explained, "We came to your office in a taxi today because my pickup was badly damaged last night while it sat in our underground parking, and whoever did the damage did the same to Gunner's SUV. All four of my tires were slashed, and both my taillights and headlights were smashed. Gunner's SUV had the same damage. Our underground parking garage was a mess in our two areas and looked like a major traffic accident had happened. We did not report the damages to the police because we didn't think it would be a very good idea. We wanted to talk with you about it first. We are not sure who did it, but we both thought that it might be something to do with the owly bunch trying to get even for the damage that we did to their cars."

They asked The Man if the company would pay their repair costs since the damage was probably business related. The Man thought about it then agreed that the company would pay.

He said, "Just get your truck and your SUV fixed up, pay the repair bills, and then bring them to me. The company will reimburse you both for the full amounts."

Bat and Gunner were happy with that. They both said, "Thank you," to The Man and left.

With the damage to their personal vehicles, Bat and Gunner both realized that their efforts to scare off the House of Owls people, from their push to promote Direct Democracy, had not been very successful. They also realized that they would probably be given more jobs to deliver new warnings to the owly people in the near future.

Chapter 26
A Busy Week for Billy
Monday, April 29

Since we had gotten to know each other very well, Maria and I tried to keep in touch at least once a day by phone, and we tried to get together at least three or four times a week.

On Tuesday, April 30, I emailed out the invitations to our House of Owls meeting on Friday, May 10, to all the Canadians who attended our earlier meeting on April 19. I was very comfortable with the feeling that we were continuing to make good progress with the House of Owl group.

I also sent emails with copies of Michael's speech and an invitation to our next meeting to my good friend Nigel Bromley (the lord mayor of Niagara-on-the-Lake) and Mario Cavatelli (the mayor of Niagara Falls, Ontario). In each case, I also asked them to invite their city councilors as well, hoping that at least a few of them would join and come to our meeting.

Chapter 27
Lunch with the Lord Mayor
Wednesday, May 1

On Wednesday morning, May 1, Nigel Bromley called me at my office and asked if we could meet for lunch either that day or the next day. I agreed to meet him for lunch at the Orchard Inn at noon.

I had known Nigel for many years as a good friend. He was born and grew up in Niagara-on-the-Lake and was a true lover of our town. For his postsecondary education, he went to the University of Toronto, followed by his legal training at Osgoode Law School, which was right near the university.

After finishing near the top of his class at law school, he had many offers from major firms in Toronto and elsewhere, but he wanted to come back to our town. He was fortunate and was able to get a job as a junior prosecutor right here in Niagara-on-the-Lake. Later, he ran for the town council, and when the former lord mayor decided to retire, Nigel decided to run for the position He campaigned very hard and won that election. He had been a very popular lord mayor and was now looking forward to a possible second term. He was only thirty years of age. He loved his job, and was one of the most eligible bachelors in the area.

I wasn't sure if the purpose of our meeting that day was for the lord mayor to talk about his support for our cause or to tell me not to bother him about it. The fact that he phoned me back so quickly after I sent the email made me wonder if there was something that he wanted me to do for him. I wondered what it could be.

I arrived at the Orchard Inn just before noon, went inside, and saw the lord mayor in the lobby waiting for me. I went over to him and said, "Hello, Nigel. Good to see you again. I am told the correct, formal way to address you is 'the Right Worshipful, the Lord Mayor of Niagara-on-the-Lake.'" In jest, I greeted him formally and smiled.

Nigel was a tall man, about six feet, two inches in height with dark, well-groomed hair and a trim and fit-looking build. He broke into a big grin and said, "Hi, Billy. Good to see you again too." Responding to my jest, he chuckled and said, "Please call me Nigel. It's much easier."

"Let's take a seat at our table, and we can chat in more relaxed comfort," I said.

When the server came, I suggested, "I think we should have a glass of wine with our lunch. My good friends Henri and Jeanne Renault, make a very good Cabernet Sauvignon, and I think they have it available here. I would like to have a glass of that. Will you join me?" I asked.

"I will, Billy. That sounds good," he said. "Billy, I was very interested in the email that you sent me yesterday with the information about the House of Owls group and Michael Simone's speech. I didn't realize that we had a group right here in our area that was promoting Direct Democracy as strongly as your group is. It's a concept that I have often thought about. I agree that it is a very good idea. In any political jurisdiction, *the people* should have the right to vote for things that the majority of them want and the right to reject the things that the majority of them don't want."

"Our group has been at it for only a short while, but we are making steady progress," I said. "We were very fortunate to find out that we have some more advanced kindred souls in the Netherlands—the FvD party. They already have a solid organizational structure and two members elected to the Dutch Parliament.

"The other part of the email that I sent to you was an invitation to our meeting on May 10 in Niagara Falls, New York, where we will have two members of the FvD from the Netherlands speak about the formation of their group and their success as a political party. We are taking a little different route. Our choice is not to be a political party but rather be a political movement that we hope could eventually appeal to all parties. We think we can build faster and stronger this way," I said.

"That's like music to my ears. I really like what your group is doing, and yes, I will be at your meeting on May 10. I will also try to convince several of our councilors to join me. I know that some of them will be interested and some won't," he said.

When our server returned, we both ordered a steak sandwich, medium, with a small garden salad, and then continued our discussion.

"Billy, our town has a situation right now that should be put to a referendum for the residents of Niagara-on-the-Lake. We could put Direct Democracy to work right away. We have a developer who wants to build a large, new project on the shore of Lake Ontario in the northeastern part of our town. It would include single-family houses, multiunit town houses, and mid-rise condominiums. This is all very good, but most of the people in Niagara-on-the-Lake don't want it. They would like to keep the town at a modest size and retain the quaintness that it has had for a long time," Nigel explained. "We would like to retain our catchphrase as the Loveliest Town in Canada."

"I agree with you, Nigel. How can the House of Owls and I help you with this situation?" I asked.

"We need to get the media on our side and help them in any way we can to get the message out to all the residents of Niagara-on-the-Lake. If you could send a copy of your group's basic objectives and a copy of Michael's speech to all the media outlets over the next day or two, that would be very helpful. If you followed that up by sending out the notice of your meeting with the speakers from the FvD, then that should get their attention, and some of them may even attend your meeting. This could get them on our side," he said.

"Yes, Nigel. I can do that. It is indeed something that fits right in with our group's objectives," I said.

"At the same time, I will send out a notice to the media about the plans for this massive development and make it clear that I am personally opposed to it. I am ready to accept the judgment of the people of Niagara-on-the-Lake by holding a referendum on the project to let the people decide by a majority vote. This decision is too important to be made by the town politicians alone. It needs to be a decision made by all the residents of Niagara-on-the-Lake through a referendum," Nigel stated firmly.

"I was wondering, Nigel, if it might be worthwhile for me or someone from our House of Owls group to come and speak to our town council at one of the upcoming meetings," I asked.

"That would be very good, Billy. I will try to get you on our agenda for one of the next few meetings if possible. We meet every Tuesday and Thursday, usually starting at nine a.m. I will let you know as soon as I can get you added to an agenda," he said.

"As you know, I do have a full-time job with our family business, William R. Jones Investment Company, and I can't always get away for other things. But I can usually adjust my work schedule to allow for important outside meetings," I said.

"Thank you, Billy, for offering your valuable time. I feel confident that we can make good progress for your House of Owls group and for the people of Niagara-on-the-Lake against the proposed, big, new development project," he said.

We finished our very tasty lunch and our business for that day, and we both left to go back to work.

Chapter 28
Billy Gets Things Done
Thursday, May 2

Late Thursday morning, the lord mayor called me at my office to let me know that he had arranged a spot for me on the agenda for the town council meeting next Tuesday, May 7, to speak about our House of Owls group and Direct Democracy in general. I was very pleased with this quick result, and I thought I should pass the good word around to the other members of our group. So I sent out emails to all the members to let them know. I was certain that some of them would want to come and sit in the gallery while I was speaking to try to get a read on how well the concepts of Direct Democracy were being received by the members of the Niagara-on-the-Lake town council.

After a hard day's work at the office and supper at home, I thought I should phone Maria and Michael to let them know about my success with our lord mayor and my opportunity to speak at our town council meeting next Tuesday.

I phoned the Simone home, and Maria answered in her seemingly perpetual cheery voice. "Hi, Billy, I was hoping you would call tonight."

"Hi, Maria," I said. "I'm always looking for an excuse to call you as often as I can, and I have a really good excuse this time. Could you put me on your speaker phone and ask Michael to listen in?"

"Yes, I can, Billy. I'll turn on the speaker so that all of us can talk and listen. Please wait a minute while I go to his office and get him to join us. Please hold-," she said. After a short time, Maria spoke again, "Go ahead, Billy, I'm with my father now."

"Thanks, Maria," I said. "I would like to tell both of you about my good fortune today. I had a call this morning from Nigel Bromley, the lord mayor of Niagara-on-the-Lake. He was responding to the email that I sent him with a copy of Michael's speech attached and an invitation to our meeting on May 10 in Niagara Falls, New York. We arranged to have a lunch meeting, and we talked about many things.

"The basic point is that he is strongly in favor of Direct Democracy and would like to force a referendum of all the residents of Niagara-on-the-Lake on a real estate development project. He is personally opposed to the project, but some of his town councilors are trying to push it through. He believes that the majority of the people of the town do not want this project to go ahead, and he thinks that a referendum would resolve the issue.

"I volunteered to speak about Direct Democracy at one of the town council meetings, and he was able to arrange for me to do that at their meeting next Tuesday. He is looking for help from our House of Owls group in convincing the council to put the issue to a referendum. Naturally, I was happy to oblige and agreed. This could be a good opening for our group to gather support and publicity for our cause in our community here."

"That sounds really great, Billy," said Michael. "I will try to make it to your council meeting. It should be very interesting."

"I do have some commitments for that time, but I think I will be able to juggle things around so that I can make it to the meeting to hear your speech," said Maria.

"I have left my father's office, and I'm on the line alone now, Billy. I wanted to let you know that he and some friends are going to a hockey playoff game in Buffalo tomorrow night. The Buffalo Sabres are playing the New York Islanders. If you would like to come over, we could watch the game on television and eat popcorn and stuff."

"I'll be there. When would be a good time?" I asked. "How about sometime between six thirty and seven?"

"That seems very good, Billy," Maria said. "I'll see you then. Bye for now."

Chapter 29
Hockey Night in Buffalo
Friday, May 3

Friday was a busy day for me at the office, but I was looking forward to the weekend—Friday evening with Maria and Sunday dinner at our home with Maria and Michael meeting my family.

As six o'clock in the evening approached, I left home, drove my red Corvette toward the border crossing at Niagara Falls, and headed to Maria's house on the other side.

I knocked at the door and went in when Maria opened it, and we had a long, deep kiss and a firm hug as we worked our way toward her bedroom.

Much later, we decided to watch the rest of the hockey game on TV as the third period was about to start. The lower level of the Simone home was not at all like a basement. It was very well finished. On one side, there was a large four-seater beige leather sofa and two matching leather reclining chairs all lined up facing the big screen TV. The other side of the large, open lower level was set up as a games room with a card table and four chairs, with a billiard table off to the side. At the back of the room, there was a guest bedroom with an adjacent four-piece bathroom. The front part of the lower level was closed off and used for storage—the furnace, a hot water heater, a large freezer, and other things were kept there.

Maria had prepared a pitcher of sangria and some sandwiches, which we both enjoyed very much as we snuggled together and watched the rest of the hockey game.

When the game was over, it was still early, but I thought I should head back home. We were both sorry to part, but we knew we would see each other again very soon—Sunday for dinner at the Jones house in Niagara-on-the-Lake.

Chapter 30
Saturday, Another Day of Work for Billy
Saturday, May 4

At the Jones house, Saturday was usually a better day of rest than Sunday. That was true for most weeks, but this week, Saturday was going to be busy because I needed to get several things done.

The first thing I wanted to do was to talk with Ram to see if he had found any more information about our two favorite thugs, Bat and Gunner.

I dialed his cell phone number, and he answered, "Hi, Billy. What's new? I was thinking I should give you a call to see how things are progressing with your House of Owls group, but you beat me to it."

"Hi, Ram. Thanks for thinking about us. It's your group, too, now that you're a member," I answered. "My good news today is that I have been able to arrange to speak about the House of Owls and Direct Democracy to the next meeting of our Niagara-on-the-Lake town council, which is next Tuesday. Our lord mayor and my good friend, Nigel Bromley, has a problem with some of his council members who want to go ahead with a major real estate development project on the waterfront in the northeast part of Niagara-on-the-Lake. He is personally opposed to it, so he would like to convince the council to put it to a referendum of all the residents of our town. He is confident that a referendum would vote against the project."

"That's very interesting, Billy. I would like to go to that meeting if possible. I would like to see for myself how the council reacts to the idea of a referendum," said Ram.

"I will speak with Nigel to ask him to reserve a seat for you in the gallery. You will probably be seated with my parents, my grandfather, and me. Paul Browne, Michael Simone, and Maria Simone will also be there if they can make it, along with some other members of the House of Owls group. I have sent out an email about me speaking at the town council meeting to all the Canadian members of the House of Owls group who attended our meeting on April 19," I replied.

"Thanks, Billy. Now that I am part of HOO, I should take more interest in what the group is doing. I was planning to attend the meeting on May 10 across the river. It will be very interesting to hear the two FvD members from the Netherlands and to chat with them about how they have progressed," Ram added.

"Ram, I'm glad to see you're gaining interest in our Direct Democracy group. We may well need your help again along the way, like we did at the Chateau des Chutes meeting," I responded.

It was just a few minutes after I hung up with Ram that my phone rang, and I answered, "Good afternoon. It's Billy here."

"Hi, Billy. I was hoping I would catch you at home. It's Nigel Bromley, your friendly lord mayor calling. I just wanted to touch base with you about our town council meeting next Tuesday. The meeting will start at nine a.m., and the proposed development project will be the first item on the agenda. The council members will have a short discussion on the project, and then I will call on you to speak. I am not certain how much time you will need, but I have allotted half an hour for you. There may also be some time for questions if needed."

"Thanks for calling and letting me know the schedule for Tuesday, Nigel," I replied. "I'll be ready, and I look forward to seeing you at the meeting. My family and several close friends from the House of Owls group would like to attend to observe the council's reactions to my comments. Is it possible to reserve some seats in the gallery for them? I expect that my parents and my grandfather will be there and so do my very good friends Ram Delvechio, Paul Browne, and Michael and Maria Simone. There could be a few others as well."

"Yes, Billy. We will reserve ten seats in the front row of the gallery for you and your family and friends," he confirmed.

When our conversation was completed, we both said our "Goodbye, see you on Tuesday" and hung up.

I spent the rest of my Saturday making notes for my speech and talking with Maria on the phone about many things and letting her know about the timing of Tuesday's meeting so she could pass it on to Michael. I also told her that all my family and friends would have seats in the front row of the gallery to watch me speak from a podium on the main floor.

Later in the day, I also chatted with my parents and my grandfather about the meeting, the nine a.m. start, and that our reserved seats would be in the front row of the gallery.

Chapter 31
More Jobs for Bat and Gunner
Saturday, May 4

Tony the Man had given Gary Masterson and Harold Remington, or Bat and Gunner, several new jobs to work on and thought that he needed to call them in for a meeting to review their progress with the various projects they had in hand. The three of them had a long history of working together.

Tony the Man grew up as a member of a middle-class family living in Albany. His father was a long-standing and successful Albany lawyer who had a keen interest in politics. He never ran for elected office himself but was well-known as a skillful backroom player. Tony earned his law degree at Columbia University in New York City after previously earning a BA in political science at the University of Buffalo. Tony joined his father's law firm right out of law school and quickly learned how to play the political games required to satisfy the needs of the firm's clients. He also learned how to help shady businessmen with their problems, which was another part of his father's business. Tony continued to operate and expand the business after his father retired to Florida several years ago.

Gary Masterson and Harold Remington had been each other's best friends since their early years in grade school. They both seemed to have the same criminal slant to their ways of thinking and were involved in petty crimes of various types at a very young age. The criminal tendencies and petty criminal activities of Gary and Harold earned them some time in juvenile detention centers, short-term stints in jail over the years, and their nicknames Bat and Gunner.

About five years ago, they met Tony the Man, who, while he was acting as their lawyer, represented them in a case where they were both charged with a series of bank robberies. Tony was able to negotiate a reduced jail sentence for them, which they easily served. For Bat and Gunner, spending time in jail was about as difficult as having their socks on the wrong feet. It was during this time that they got to know The Man, and when they were released from jail, they both went to work for the Scaglione Agency as "Administrative Assistants."

On this day, Saturday, May 4, Bat and Gunner arrived at the company office at around midafternoon, as requested by Tony, and were immediately shown into his personal office.

"Thanks for coming in," he said as Bat and Gunner took their seats across the desk from him. "I thought it was time that we did a review and update on some of our projects.

"Let's start with the insurance agent in Rochester, Clive Bellows. He has had very little success so far at getting his clients to accept the prices he has offered to buy their life insurance policies. He could use a little help at persuading them. You should go to Rochester and see how you might be able to help him. Our client who wants to purchase the life insurance settlements is getting a little impatient at waiting too long for these to be put in place.

"The Downtown Medical Clinic in Syracuse and the doctors there have started to issue more prescriptions for oxycodone and fentanyl, but they are moving ahead very slowly. You should visit them and give them a little encouragement to speed up the process.

"The third new project that I told you about last time was the Niagara Falls City Council vote on accepting the proposal for a new casino in their city. The council has not yet brought it to a vote, but there seems to be enough number of councilors in favor of the project that it should get approved. However, we might need to take some more action on this one at some time in the future if things seem like they are not moving along the way they should."

The Man finished his comments on those projects and added, "There is another situation that the two of you should take care of. I am sure you both remember the damage to your personal vehicles recently. I believe that it was done by someone from the House of Owls group or someone acting for them. They seem to be very difficult people to persuade that they should stop doing what they are doing, so they will need a little more persuasion. It would be appropriate to do some major damage to the cars of both Billy Jones, the leader of the group in Canada, and his friend Jeramiah Delvechio, who is called Ram. I would suggest that you might do something in the middle of the night between three and five on Sunday night. I will leave the specifics and the details up to the two of you to decide."

The Man was finished with his projects update review, so Bat and Gunner left his office to begin their program of updating their activities for the different jobs.

Chapter 32
Dinner with the Joneses
Sunday, May 5

I was up and about earlier than usual that Sunday morning, feeling a little bit anxious about Maria and Michael meeting my family and joining us for dinner in the afternoon.

The four of us in my family—Grandfather, Mother, Father, and I—went to the eleven-o'-clock morning service at Saint Mark's Anglican Church here in Niagara-on-the-Lake as we usually did. Also, as usual, we came home to a light lunch because we always had a large dinner on Sunday. I knew that dinner, especially today, would not be very light. My mother customarily hired in a cook for Sunday dinner, but this week, Francoise came in early to get a head start on our special dinner. Since she was in so early, she also made a light lunch for us.

Sunday afternoon went very slowly for me because I was so eager to have everybody together socializing and enjoying one another's company. The magic hour of five o'clock could not come soon enough for me, but it was now quickly approaching.

Michael and Maria arrived just a few minutes before five as I had expected they would. When they came and tapped on the door, I was there to greet them and let them in. "Hello, good afternoon, and thank you both for coming," I offered.

Maria responded with a light kiss and Michael with a firm handshake. Maria said, "Thank you for inviting us, Billy. We have been looking forward to meeting your family."

Michael handed me a package that contained two bottles of wine to give to my parents. Later, I found out that both bottles were the same—Cabernet Sauvignon from the Chateau des Chutes Winery.

Both Maria and Michael were dressed in a very smart casual style, as I had suggested, because I knew that was how all the Jones family would be dressed for dinner, including me. As we came into the living room, which my grandfather called the parlor, my parents and my grandfather rose from their seats to meet Maria and Michael.

The living room or parlor had dark hardwood floors, a fireplace at one end, and three light-beige leather sofas arranged in a U shape with the fireplace at the open end of the U. Both the front of the fireplace and the mantel were made of white Carrara marble. There was a Persian area rug under the large coffee table that was in the middle, extending almost to the edge of each of the sofas. The coffee table could be reached by those of us seated on any of the three sofas.

I introduced them, "Maria and Michael, this is my mother Megan, my father William, and my grandfather William, whom we call W. R. In the Jones family, there have been five William R. Joneses, and it has always been a minor problem differentiating one from another. That's why we usually refer to my grandfather as W. R., my father a William, and me as Billy."

My mother, who was always the leader with social grace, asked us all to come in and have a seat, so we all did as we were directed. Maria and I sat on the sofa at the bottom of the U, my mother and my grandfather were on the left side, and my father and Michael were on the right-hand side.

My mother spoke up, "Please call me Megan so we can keep our conversations on an informal and casual basis. Did you have a nice trip over? Were they very busy at the bridge and customs gates today?"

Maria was the first to speak up. "Thank you for asking—Megan. Our trip over went quite smoothly. The traffic on the Rainbow Bridge was fairly light. And when we arrived at the customs gates on the

Canadian side, we were only the third car in line, so we didn't have too long to wait. My father is a patient driver and doesn't get rattled very easily, so the short waiting time was not a problem."

My mother spoke up again and suggested, "We should probably all have a drink before dinner. I sometimes like a martini in the James Bond style—you know, shaken, not stirred. Except he usually preferred vodka rather than gin, but I prefer gin. The shaking brings out the flavor in the juniper berries for a better-tasting drink. Would anyone like to join me in having a gin martini?"

Maria said, "A gin martini sounds good to me."

Before anyone else could reply, my father spoke up with "I have a bottle of a new and different single malt scotch that I would like to try if anyone would like to join me. I have had the fifteen-year-old Laphroaig in the past, which is a very good single malt Scotch, but a friend of mine suggested that I might like to try the fifteen-year-old Octomore single malt whiskey. It's from the Bruichladdich Distillery, which is also on the Isle of Islay, the same as the Laphroaig distillery. Islay is a smallish island in the southeast part of the Inner Hebrides islands off the southwest coast of Scotland. The Octomore is said to have the strongest peat smoke flavor of any Scotch whiskey anywhere."

Michael, my grandfather, and I all said yes to the Scotch.

My mother went to prepare the drinks, and Maria offered to help her. Off they went, leaving the four men to chat on their own.

Michael opened the conversation with "You have a very comfortable home here. Has it been in your family very long?"

My grandfather responded with "Thank you, Michael, for your kind thoughts. Yes, it has been in the family for quite some time. I arranged to have the house built in 1967 for my parents and for my wife Anna and me. Before that, the family had lived in the country out in Saint David's just a few miles west of here. As Billy may have mentioned to you, my grandfather—that would be William the First—immigrated to Toronto from Wales in 1919. He made a fairly large amount of money speculating in Canadian gold-mining shares and bought a large farm in Saint David's. All the later Williams, right down to Billy, have been good stewards of his windfall good fortune, and we have increased his original capital many times over. Thanks to William the First and the continuing good stewardship of all the other four Williams, our family is financially very comfortable today."

The drinks arrived, and my mother offered a toast. "Thank you, Michael and Maria, for joining us at our Sunday dinner."

We all took a sip of our drinks, and everyone expressed their satisfaction. My father was right. The Octomore Scotch had a very heavy peat-smoke flavor, but the fifteen years of aging smoothed it out a little. For those who liked Scotch, it was very good, but for those who were not traditionally Scotch drinkers, not so much.

"I have been in the accounting business all my working years, and it has been fairly good to me," said Michael. "When I first started out, I worked for the local office of the international accounting firm PricewaterhouseCoopers in Niagara Falls. After five years with PwC, I decided that I could do more of what I wanted to do if I had my own business. I went out on my own and started small, but the business has grown to be much larger and very active. My office now includes five other CPAs and a total staff of twenty, plus me."

Maria thought that it could be her turn to talk and began with "As you may have guessed, I have lived in Niagara Falls all my life except for the four years that I was away at university in Syracuse. My major at university was history, and I am now a high school history teacher at Saint Joseph's High School in Niagara Falls. Megan, Billy mentioned to me that you were once a history professor at McMaster University in Hamilton and that you are currently an associate professor at Brock University in Saint Catharines. You probably enjoy the study of history as much as I do or maybe even more. Are you a specialist in any period of history?"

Megan replied, "Yes, Maria, I have specialized in ancient Greek and Roman history. It's a time in history that I find really fascinating. We all have so much that we can learn from those ancient societies, but you and Billy already know that from your work with the House of Owls group. Direct Democracy is not the only thing we can benefit from and learn from the ancients. There were many intelligent and wise people in the ancient Greek and Roman societies."

My father spoke up and said, "One of the ways that we have found to help people relax and break the ice in conversation is to have everyone tell a funny riddle. Some people seem quite surprised that riddles are very popular, but they are. Who would like to go first?"

Michael volunteered. "You're right, William. Riddles can be a lot of fun. I have one for us. Why do some Americans like to play bridge? No guesses? OK, the answer is 'so they can bid no Trump.' I heard that one at a client meeting recently."

"That's a good one, Michael." I chuckled along with everyone else in the room. I said, "Here's another one. What do intellectual owls say? The answer is 'whooom,' or if you are part of the House of Owls group, it should be 'hoom.'"

"I heard one of the students at Saint Mary's school, where I teach, telling this one last week," said Maria. "Why do nuns wash their clothes so often? The answer is 'They don't like dirty habits.'"

"I guess we all have riddles that we remember for different reasons," William offered. "One of my old favorites is, 'Which golf club should you use if your golf ball lands on a tree branch?' The answer is 'a tree iron,' of course."

Megan said, "I guess it's probably my turn now. "If you are holding a bee in your hand what is in your eye? The answer is beauty, because beauty is in the eye of the bee holder." The others all groaned and chuckled.

"I guess we have saved the best for the last." Said W. R. with a large grin. "I think all of you have been to San Francisco at some time or other, or at least you know about Lombard Street and how it zigzags down a steep hill in a residential area. The riddle is 'If Lombard is the second most crooked street in the USA, what's first?' All of us investment-types know that the answer is 'Wall Street.'"

Everyone had a good laugh at this one.

Francoise came into the room and announced that dinner was ready and asked us all to come to the dining room, and we did.

My mother played her usual leadership role and led us all in to dinner. "We decided on a fairly traditional menu for today," my mother explained. "We thought that nearly everyone would like prime rib of roast beef with roast potatoes and fresh, newly grown Canadian asparagus, accompanied by a fresh garden salad. So that's what we decided to go with for today. Please enjoy!"

Time was passing. Everyone was enjoying their food, and light conversation continued. Maria and my mother talked about history—their favorite subject—politics, and other things. Michael, my father, and my grandfather talked about business, investments, income taxes, and other things. I tried to stay out of it all and just nodded my head up and down when I thought I should agree and from side to side when I thought I should disagree.

My mother wanted to broaden the conversation to be more inclusive and asked me the question, "Billy, how are things going with the House of Owl group?"

I answered by saying "I think we are making good progress. We had our first big meeting at the Chateau des Chutes Winery on Friday, April 19, with fifty-one people attending. Michael was the keynote speaker that night and did a very good job of delivering the Direct Democracy message. I think that I have sent a copy of his speech by email attachment to each of you, Mother, Father, and Grandfather. You should all read it. His comments are quite interesting."

"It was after that meeting that Billy's good friend Jeramiah Delvechio was roughed up by the two toughs who have been giving our group a hard time for the past several weeks," Maria pointed out.

"I will be speaking about our House of Owls group and Direct Democracy to the Niagara-on-the-Lake town council meeting next Tuesday morning at nine thirty, as I mentioned to everybody earlier. I am very pleased that all of you have said you will come to back me up with moral support. I expect that several others from the House of Owls group will also be there. Paul Browne, Henri and Jeanne Renault, and Ram Delvechio have all said they will try to make it," I explained.

Dinner was disappearing quite rapidly from everyone's plate, a testament to my mother's good food choices and Francoise's good cooking skills. A second helping was offered all around, but there were no takers as everyone was quite satiated.

"I hope everyone saved a little room for dessert? Francoise has made one of Billy's favorites, elderberry pie. Elderberries are not that common in this area, but we are able to get them sometimes. When they are available, we take advantage of it and store some extras by freezing them or making preserves," my mother explained.

The elderberry pie, with or without the French vanilla ice cream, was served and was very good. This had long been one of my favorite desserts, and everyone else seemed to enjoy it as well.

When dessert was finished and the dessert dishes cleared away, coffee and tea were offered around along with the pièce de résistance: Canadian Niagara ice wine. Many of the wineries in the greater Niagara region had added ice wine to the other selections of wine that they produced, and with great success. Canadian Niagara ice wines became well recognized internationally and even won the Grand Prix d'Honneur at Vinexpo in France several times.

"Billy may have talked to you about the new political party in the Netherlands called Forum voor Democratie, or FvD, that is pushing hard for Direct Democracy in that country. They already have two members elected to the Dutch Parliament even though the party has only existed for a few years. They expect to elect quite a few more at the next election. Billy has arranged for two of the FvD party members to come and speak to our meeting on May 10. It should be very interesting, and you should all come over to the meeting if you have time," said Michael.

My father responded with "Thank you for reminding us, Michael. Billy did tell us about the meeting and we are all planning on going. You're right. It should be very interesting to hear what the people from the FvD have to say."

Maria spoke up and said, "Time is getting on, and we all will be going to work tomorrow. So it's probably time for us to say farewell for now and head back home. My father and I have really enjoyed this evening, the extra special dinner you prepared, and most of all, your pleasant company. Thank you all for inviting us. It's been great."

Michael added, "You must come over to our home sometime soon so we can reciprocate. Maria is a very good cook. Her mother taught her well, and she enjoys preparing special dinners for special occasions and for special people like all of you."

My mother responded, "I will speak for all of us and say that we also enjoyed our dinner, and we thank you for coming over. Billy has talked about both of you for some time now, and we all agreed that we should get together. Thanks again for joining us."

Michael and Maria got up to leave amid hugs and handshakes all around. Maria had become extra special to me, and we had a quick kiss as she was leaving.

Chapter 33
Bat and Gunner Do More Dirty Work
Sunday Night and Monday, May 5 and May 6

Bat and Gunner were geared up to cause a lot of trouble overnight on Sunday. They came to Niagara Falls, Ontario, on Saturday afternoon and booked rooms at the Fallsview Casino Resort Hotel for three consecutive nights. They thought that by staying over until Tuesday morning, their return to the US would not appear to be related in any way to the damage that they had planned for overnight Sunday.

Tony the Man had supplied them with addresses for both Billy Jones and Jeramiah Delvechio. The plan was to attach C-4 plastic explosives to the gas tanks of each of their cars and set a timing device for the explosives to blow up each car at 2:00 a.m. on Monday.

Bat and Gunner left their hotel in Niagara Falls, Ontario, at about 1:00 a.m. and headed for Niagara-on-the-Lake to do their dirty work. Billy's car was easy. It was parked in the driveway at the Jones residence at no. 5 Saint David's Place. They quickly attached the explosives and the timing device set for 2:00 a.m. and left.

Jeramiah Delvechio lived in the residential section of the posh Queenston Gardens Hotel and Suites, an upscale hotel in the old village of Queenston. The village of Queenston was now part of greater Niagara-on-the-Lake, having merged with other villages in the Niagara region in 1970. All the villages—Glendale, Homer, McNab, Queenston, Saint David's, Virgil, the township of Niagara, and the old village of

Niagara-on-the-Lake—had merged to form the new town of Niagara-on-the-Lake. The Queenston Gardens Hotel was on River Street, with a good view of the Niagara River from the upper floors. The parking garage for residents of the hotel was indoors and underground, but unfortunately, it was easily accessible by nearly anyone.

Bat and Gunner had no trouble gaining access to the hotel's underground parking. They quickly located the BMW X5 SUV that belonged to Jeramiah Delvechio, attached the C-4 plastic explosives, set the timing device for 2:00 a.m., and left. They headed back to their hotel in Niagara Falls and had a good night's sleep while they waited for news of their exploits to come out on Monday.

Chapter 34
Things Go Boom in the Night
Monday, May 6

I had gone to bed at about ten thirty on Sunday night. That was earlier than usual for me. But I was tired, and I knew that I had a lot of work to do on Monday. I was in the midst of a very pleasant dream, enjoying dinner and pleasant conversation with Maria at Trattoria Brunelli in Niagara Falls, her favorite Italian restaurant. In my dream, I heard a loud, explosive bang, and I wondered if it was happening in my dream or if it was actually real. I woke up, destroying my dream, got out of bed, and went to my bedroom window to see if anything was going on outside. There was.

I could see fire and smoke in our driveway coming from what used to be my red Corvette, which was parked there. I quickly dressed in jeans, a sweatshirt, and sneakers to go downstairs and outside to see what was going on. I picked up my cell phone on the way in case I might need it for something. I did. It looked like my car had been through some kind of explosion. Pieces of the car were spread around everywhere, and the fire coming from what was left of my car was still blazing. This looked like real trouble.

Picking up my cell phone on the way out proved to be a good idea. I dialed 911. I told the emergency operator who I was, that my car had been blown up, and was still on fire, sitting in our driveway at no. 5 Saint David's Place. I asked him to please send police and firefighters right away but not bother with an ambulance because no one was injured. I quickly hung up before he could ask any more questions.

I stood outside in front of our house watching my car burn. Both my parents and my grandfather were now outside with me, asking what happened. I told them, "I don't know. But I have called 911, and the police and firemen should be here very soon." I added, "It looks like an explosion of some kind has destroyed my car."

The police and firemen both arrived very quickly. The police officers came over to me, and the sergeant introduced his partner and himself, "Hello, I am Detective Donald Forsythe, and this is my partner, Officer Myron Brooks. Don and Myron, if you like. Please tell me who you are, why you are here, where you live, and what happened here."

I told him, "I'm Billy Jones. I live here with my parents and my grandfather, the three people standing over there. I don't know what happened here, but it looks like my car has been through an explosion. I was asleep in my bedroom upstairs and was awakened by a very loud, explosive bang. I quickly got dressed, came out to see what happened, and this fire, smoke, and debris are what I found."

Detective Forsythe said, "I'll phone in for a forensics team to come out and examine the scene to see if they can find out what happened. As you suggest, it does look like some kind of explosion. This pile of burning rubble looks like it might have been a Corvette. Was it yours, Mr. Jones?"

"Please call me Billy. Yes, it was a red Corvette, and it was mine. It was a gift from my parents for graduating from McMaster University in the top 10 ranking of my MBA class."

"At a quick look, it appears as though your car may have been blown up by an explosive material such as dynamite or C-4 plastic explosive set to ignite from a timing device. Do you recall what time you heard the loud bang?" questioned Detective Forsythe.

"Yes, I remember looking at my wristwatch as I got out of bed, and it was one minute after two this morning," I said.

Detective Forsythe's shoulder microphone beeped, and a voice said, "We have another car explosion over at the Queenston Gardens Hotel in the underground parking garage. It looks like the vehicle was a BMW

SUV of some kind. It's very hard to tell with all the damage that's happened. Our talks with people at the hotel indicate that it happened at about two this morning. How is it going with the situation over there?"

"Our situation seems a lot like yours," said Detective Forsythe. "We're over at no. 5 Saint David's Place, where a car looks like it has been blown up, possibly from something like dynamite or C-4 plastic set off by a timing device. Billy Jones, the man who lives here, tells me that the car was his red Corvette."

I asked the question, "Detective Forsythe, can you tell me anything about the other car explosion that I heard from your shoulder mic?"

"Billy, we have not yet found out who the car belongs to, but we are checking it out and should know shortly. Other than that, the situation over there looks much like what we have here, a car explosion at about two this morning from causes yet to be determined. We will keep you informed as we progress because of the similarities between the two situations," said Detective Forsythe.

A voice came over the mic on Detective Forsythe's shoulder again. "We can confirm that the car that was blown up was a BMW SUV, as previously guessed, and it was parked in the underground parking garage at the hotel in an area reserved for full-time residents. The reserved parking nameplate on the wall in front of the car's parking slot was J. Delvechio. One of the police officers has gone to the front desk of the hotel to see if they can locate this person."

Before detective Forsythe could answer back, I said to him, "Mr. J. Delvechio is a very good friend of mine. His name is Jeramiah, but most people call him by his nickname, Ram. Since it's both Ram and me who have been targeted with these explosions, I am fairly certain that I know who is responsible."

"How do you know that, Billy?" asked Detective Forsythe with a puzzled look. "Whatever the reason is, tell me what you think and why," he requested.

I went through the litany of the two thugs visiting my office, their punching out Ram, and their doing damage to the cars of our House of Owls members. I told Detective Forsythe that we knew what they looked like because I had seen them for several minutes when they came to my office and Ram had seen them for a minute or so when they beat him up in the parking lot at the Chateau des Chutes Winery.

I explained to Detective Forsythe that Ram was an experienced and highly professional private investigator with his own private investigations company. Through his personal connections and some diligent searching, he was able to find out the names of these two guys, where they live, and whom they work for.

"OK, Billy. From your explanation, you could be right. Can you give me the names and addresses so that we can at least follow up on your thoughts?" asked the detective.

"Yes, of course," I volunteered. "The two guys are Gary Masterson, whose nickname is Bat, and Harold Remington, whose nickname, not surprisingly, is Gunner. They both live in the same condo building in Albany, New York, and they both work as Administrative Assistants for the Scaglione Agency, which is also based in Albany and is managed by Anthony Scaglione, known as Tony the Man. The business of the Scaglione Agency is political lobbying for various politicians at all levels in both the US and Canada. Another part of their business is strong-arming and coercing individuals and businesses into doing various things that the agency's clients want to them to do. Most of their other activities you would probably consider to be criminal or, at the very least, shady.

"Except for the two explosions tonight, Ram and I have already given all this information to your chief of police, Ian Fraser, more than a week ago. There should be a record of it at the station. The same night that many of our friends' cars were damaged here in Niagara-on-the-Lake, our friends in the House of Owls group in Niagara Falls, New York, also had many of their cars damaged. It seems quite clear that whoever these culprits are, they are targeting the members of the House of Owls group, trying to send us a message of some kind."

"Thanks for all that information, Billy. Obviously, we can't go to Albany and check out these guys, so we'll need to work through channels to see what we can do. Maybe Chief Fraser has already started the process with the Albany police. I'll check with him later today.

"We'll continue our investigations here and at the Queenston Gardens Hotel, just in case the incidents that you have told me about are not related to tonight's car explosions. But you're probably right. It seems like they could be related," said Detective Forsythe.

"Do you know if the police have been able to contact Ram Delvechio yet?" I asked.

"Yes, Billy. They were able to reach him in his suite. He is now with the police, reviewing his car damage," replied the detective.

"I was thinking that I should give him a call, if that's all right with you." I asked.

"Yes, that's OK with us, Billy. Go ahead," the detective said.

I called Ram on my cell phone, and he answered right away. After a short discussion, we agreed to meet in the all-night coffee shop at his hotel as soon as I could get there.

I asked my father if I could borrow his Lincoln MKX for a little while to go over to talk with Ram. I explained to him that Ram had had his car blown up, too, at about the same time as mine.

I drove over to the hotel, parked the car, located the all-night coffee shop, and saw Ram sitting there with cup of coffee in front of him and an unhappy scowl on his face.

After we both said hello, neither of us followed with the usual "How are you?" I asked Ram, "Do you think your car is salvageable? I know that mine is definitely not."

In a disgusted voice, Ram said, "No, Billy, my car is in about a thousand pieces, and I'm sure that even someone who is good at jigsaw puzzles would have a lot of trouble putting it back together even if they could find them all."

After I ordered a cup of coffee, I said to Ram, "Is there any doubt about who did this damage to our cars?"

Ram replied with "No, Billy, I don't think so. I don't know how far these guys are willing go to deliver their message, and I'm not sure what we can do about it. I talked with the police here and gave them the litany of past actions by these guys, who they are, where they live, and whom they work for. But there is not much our police can do against thugs who live in another country. I'll give it some thought and see if I can come up with anything."

"I went through the same explanations with Detective Forsythe about my car. He was very sympathetic, but he didn't think there was much they could do. He did offer to go through channels to advise the Albany police about who we thought the perpetrators were, but it's difficult for local police to deal outside of the country," I said.

"It seems like Direct Democracy is something that some politicians or maybe some large businesses are afraid of, and they don't want it to happen. That must be their motivation for paying the Scaglione Agency for these continuing attacks on our House of Owls group members and our meetings," I reflected.

We finished our coffees and were ready to call it a night. As we were saying our goodbyes, I said, "I hope to see you at the Niagara-on-the-Lake town council meeting on Tuesday morning."

"Yes, Billy, I'll be there," Ram said as we parted ways. Then he added, "Eventually, we'll get even with these guys."

Chapter 35
What's Next?
Monday, May 6

After I left Ram and the coffee shop, I went straight home and went to bed, hoping to get a little sleep before the night was over. Even though I was up half the night and was suffering from a high level of anxiety, I was able to get a few hours of worthwhile sleep. However, the time to go to work this morning did seem to come earlier than usual.

My mind was working well even though my body was tired. It was a good thing that most of us who work in an office environment didn't have much of a physical challenge and can function well as long as our minds are awake and alert. That was me that day.

About midmorning, I thought that I should contact some of the other House of Owls members to let them know about our not-very-friendly opposition. The first person I called was Michael Simone. I told him the story and asked him to pass it along to our other members on his side of the border. I also assured him that Ram and I were fine and had no personal, physical wounds this time. It was just that both our cars no longer existed.

I also phoned Paul Browne and Henri and Jeanne Renault to let them know about our problems of last night and to ask if they had any ideas about what we should be doing now. They all expressed their concerns but had no new ideas about what to do. Paul Browne wanted to make sure that Niagara Regional Police were fully up to date with everything, and I assured him that they were.

The day went by quickly as I had a lot of work to do, which was usually the case on Mondays for some reason or other. After I arrived home from work, I thought that I should phone Maria and explain everything to her.

When Maria answered her phone, her voice seemed to have a nervousness about it that wasn't usually there. She answered the phone with "Hello, Billy. Are you all right? My father told me about the trouble that you and Ram went through last night. It seems a little frightening. Are you both OK?"

"Yes, Maria, we're both fine, but our cars are total wrecks. When the cars were blown up at about two in the morning, we were both in our beds, sleeping. Ram lives in a luxury suite at the Queenston Gardens Hotel, and his car was blown up in the underground parking garage there. My car was blown up in our driveway. We were both a long way from the explosions when they happened, so we had no physical injuries," I said.

"Billy, you are still going ahead with your speech tomorrow morning, aren't you?" Maria asked.

"Yes, I certainly will, Maria," I said with conviction. "I would not like our troublemaking, thuggish opposition to think that they can scare me off so easily. Maria, I hope that both you and your father are still planning to come to the Niagara-on-the-Lake town council meeting tomorrow morning to hear my talk. Paul Browne and Henri and Jeanne Renault from the House of Owls group are all planning to attend, as well as my parents and my grandfather."

"Of course, we will be there, Billy," Maria said. "We are both very eager to support both you and our House of Owls group."

"Thank you for your vote of confidence, Maria. We could get some very positive publicity from this event for our group, and hopefully, we will be able to help out our town council at the same time," I said.

We both said our goodbyes for now and our see-you-tomorrows and hung up. I was hoping that Maria wasn't too upset over last night's strange happenings. I knew that she was a very sensitive person.

Chapter 36
Meeting with the Niagara-on-the-Lake Town Council
Tuesday, May 7

I was awake fairly early on Tuesday morning, feeling somewhat apprehensive about giving my talk later this morning to the town council. But I did feel that I was ready. I had never really had much trouble with public speaking, but I wanted to be sure that I made a very good impression at this meeting on behalf of our House of Owls group and for Direct Democracy.

My parents and my grandfather were also up and about, waiting for me and the right time to leave for the meeting. I needed to rely on my father for transportation this morning since I hadn't yet replaced my one thousand–piece Corvette. My family all agreed that we should be there a little early and decided that we should leave at about eight thirty.

Our departure time arrived. We loaded into my father's Lincoln MKX and headed west. Our home was on the east side of town, and the Niagara-on-the-Lake town hall was on the west side at 1593 Four Mile Creek Road, just south of the Niagara Stone Road in the former village of Virgil, which was now part of the greater town of Niagara-on-the-Lake.

As we arrived at the parking lot, I noticed that some of our House of Owls friends were already there and others were pulling into the parking lot at the same time as we arrived. Michael and Maria Simone,

Henri and Jeanne Renault, Paul Browne, Ram Delvechio, my parents, my grandfather, and I all met and greeted one another and headed into the town hall as one group.

We were shown into the front-row seats in the gallery that were reserved for us, and I was told that when the time came for me to speak, I would be invited down to the main floor for my presentation. The council meeting was already in session, having started at nine. I was on the agenda for ten o'clock.

As my time approached, an usher came to invite me down to the main area where the council was sitting. I stood off to one side as the lord mayor introduced me to the members of the council and for the benefit of other people in the gallery.

I began my comments with salutations. "The Right Worshipful, The Lord Mayor Nigel Bromley, council members, ladies and gentlemen. Thank you for inviting me here today. I am always grateful to have the opportunity to talk to anyone about Direct Democracy and our House of Owls group. We are dedicated to promoting the concepts of Direct Democracy or referenda for all government legislation at the municipal, provincial, and federal levels.

"My name is William R. Jones V. I am called Billy by almost everyone. My family, the previous four William R. Joneses, have lived in the Niagara-on-the-Lake area since 1919, and we are proud to live in 'the prettiest town in Canada.' I am the leader of the Canadian group of the House of Owls, and my friend Michael Simone from Niagara Falls, New York, who is here with us in the gallery today, is the leader of the US group.

"The House of Owls was created just over a month ago at a meeting on April 5 by a small group of people who thought that it was a good idea for North American society to move forward from the current form of representative, democratic governments and advance to Direct Democracy. It a form of democracy where all people vote directly on all issues rather than through their elected representatives whose political opinions and actions are sometimes tainted and motivated by extraneous considerations instead of only by the real issues at hand.

"Our purpose here today is to try to convince the council that they should hold a municipal referendum on the issue of the proposed major new development for the northeast lake-shore area of Niagara-on-the-Lake. All of us in the House of Owls group, as well as many others, are of the opinion that because the proposed development will have some effect on all the people in our town, it should be decided by a majority vote of all the people in our town. A referendum covering all the residents in Niagara-on-the-Lake is the only fair and reasonable way to know for certain what the majority really want.

"The problem with representative democracy is that most of us disagree with our elected representative on too many of the issues that they support even though we may generally agree with their overall political positions. This shortcoming needs to be addressed and Direct Democracy is the way to solve this problem. Every citizen should have the democratic right to express their view on all issues by a referendum of all citizen on each and every political issue. At some time in the future, that's the way it will be. Why not start now?

"I know that Lord Mayor Bromley, my family, and I are opposed to this new development, but we have all agreed that if a referendum of all the people of our town shows that a majority is in favor, then we would also support the project. We believe in the true democratic process—Direct Democracy.

"I strongly urge all of you on the council to vote to hold a referendum on this proposed new development and on any other legislation that this council may be considering that will affect all the people in our community.

"Thank you, Lord Mayor and councilors, for giving me the time and opportunity to speak to you about my favorite subject, our House of Owls group and Direct Democracy."

As I finished and returned to the gallery, the council members and the visitors in the gallery all applauded my comments. But it seemed like the applause from the small gallery was much louder than the applause from the council. These were my friends.

As the council returned to other business, we all decided (that's Direct Democracy at work) to leave and go over to the Orchard Inn for an early lunch. As a group, Paul Browne, Henri and Jeanne Renault, Ram, Michael, Maria, my parents, and my grandfather all complimented me on my speech and how well they thought it was received by the council. It was good to have supportive friends and family.

As we were parting, Ram took me aside to say that he couldn't join us for lunch today because he had some business out of town that he needed to attend to and he needed to leave right away. He said he would be back in two or three days and we could chat then about dealing with the bad guys.

Chapter 37
Ram Visits Albany Again
Wednesday, May 8

When Ram left Billy and the others after the meeting with the town counci he was heading to the border and off toward Albany, New York. He was driving his shiny, new white Jeep Grand Cherokee Overland with the powerful Hemi V8 engine that was ready for him at the Jeep dealer on early Tuesday morning. This new vehicle replaced his two-year-old BMW X5 SUV, which had been blown up into a zillion pieces of scrap metal in the explosion on Sunday night–Monday morning.

One of the safety precautions that Ram took was to park his new Jeep at a safe spot for casino parking at the Niagara Falls casino on the US side and take a taxi to the nearest car rental office. He wanted to avoid having a vehicle with an Ontario license plate seen wandering around Albany late at night. He got his rented car and was off to Albany.

With the knowledge he had gained from his two years with CSIS and with his experience as a private investigator, Ram had no difficulty locating a supplier and purchasing the materials that he wanted for the job that he was going to undertake in Albany. He knew that he had to make these purchases after he crossed the border because he didn't want to have any trouble with US Customs and Immigration.

Over the years, Ram's philosophical nature led him to accept the old talion law of like for like or an eye for an eye, as an appropriate form of retributive justice. The teaching of *an eye for an eye* is very old.

It appears in the book of Exodus in the Old Testament of the Bible and was even practiced long before biblical times in other ancient cultures. This old-fashioned law was very appealing to Ram. His thoughts were *eventually we will get even.*

Ram's driving time to Albany was about five hours, leaving him lots of time for a snack and some coffee before he could start his chores at about one in the morning. As the hands on the clock spun around to his chosen hour, Ram started out to go and do the jobs that he came for. He quickly completed the tasks and was back on the road to home.

He arrived back at his hotel at about seven in the morning and rested. He was up and about around noon and turned on the television to a Buffalo station to see if there was any news about events in Albany.

There was. CNN had reporters at two different sites. The reporter at the ten-story condo on High Street just off highway US-787 had reported that two vehicles in its underground parking area had been blown up at about two that morning. The other CNN reporter was at another site across the Hudson River on Farm Road where a Jaguar and the entire garage attached to Mr. Anthony Scaglione's house were both blown up at about two that morning too.

All three locations had small crayon drawings on the walls that depicted the talion law, *i-4-i.* The three explosions all seemed to be retributions for something, all the reporters speculated.

Some of the reporters were asking a lot of questions because they had heard of unsavory past exploits of Mr. Scaglione. Also, when they checked with the local police, they learned that both Mr. Masterson and Mr. Remington had police records with long lists of petty criminal offenses from the past.

A relaxed and smiling Ram Delvechio consumed the CNN news information as if it were some delicious comfort food, like a large, tender New York steak or a bowl of ice cream. He thought again, *Someday we'll get even.*

Chapter 38
The News from Albany Spreads
Wednesday, May 8

I was in my office on Wednesday morning, working hard and being very industrious at trying to make up for the time I was away at the Niagara-on-the-Lake town council meeting the previous day. When my phone rang, I noticed on the caller ID that it was Paul Browne, I answered, "Good morning, Paul. It's always good to hear from you. What's up?"

"Billy, I don't know if you have heard any news yet today, but I have been watching CNN on TV. They are showing that there were three explosions in Albany last night. Three cars were blown up. Two were in the same condo and belonged to Gary Masterson and Harold Remington. The third one was at the home of a person named Anthony Scaglione, who had his garage wiped out as well as his car. These Albany people sound like the same ones who have been giving us a hard time. Do you know if any of our people had anything to do with this?" Paul asked.

"Paul, this is the first that I have heard about anything in Albany. I haven't taken time to watch any TV news yet today. Thank you for bring me up to date with this news. Did the CNN reporters mention if anyone was hurt or not?" I asked.

"It appears that there were no people injured in the explosions, which is a good thing," Paul answered.

"I don't know if any of our people from HOO were involved with this, but we do have over one hundred members now. And it is possible that someone might be aggressively vengeful enough to do this. I will look into it and see what I can find out. I am sure that the Scaglione Agency has many enemies, and any one of them might consider some kind of physical action against them.

"On another subject, Paul, I hope you are planning on coming out to our meeting on Friday night at the library in Niagara Falls, New York, to listen to the two FvD members from the Netherlands tell us about their experiences with Direct Democracy," I asked.

"Thanks for reminding me, Billy. I was aware of the meeting, and I do plan on being there. About the news, if you are talking with any of the HOO members about Friday's meeting or about the news from Albany, you might want to remind them that our group cannot afford to be involved in this type of thing. HOO is just starting out, and we don't really need any bad publicity like this at this stage of our group's development. This kind of activity could create some very negative publicity for the House of Owls group. But that's not the only thing. It could also be very dangerous as well as being very much illegal," Paul reminded me.

"Paul, I appreciate your comments, and I understand the severe implications of these kind of actions. I will talk with a few of our members to see if they know anything about the events in Albany. Paul, thank you for calling me with the news and for reminding me about the possible dangers of being involved in these types of activities," I said.

"Let me know if you learn anything, Billy. I'll see you on Friday at the meeting," Paul said. Then we both hung up.

After receiving the news from Paul Browne, I thought I should give Ram a call since he usually knew what's going on in the darker side of the world.

I called him, and he answered, "Hello, Billy. I thought I might be hearing from you today. I have been watching the TV news on CNN about the explosions in Albany. Someone has done us a big favor by giving these guys a little taste of their own medicine."

"Ram, I was just on the phone with Paul Browne. As you may recall, he is a member of our House f Owls group, and he is also a very good lawyer. He reminded me that no one from our group should be involved in these kinds of activities even though they might be well deserved," I pointed out.

Ram pivoted away from the question in a very political style and said, "You're right, Billy. We shouldn't be involved in this kind of activity. But these guys only got what they deserved. It's hard for me to feel sorry for them."

"Ram, I hope you are planning to come out to our House of Owls meeting on Friday night to listen to the two FvD members from the Netherlands talk to us about their experiences with Direct Democracy," I reminded him.

"Yes, Billy. I'll be there. I have been looking forward to it. They should be quite interesting," he replied.

We both said, "See you on Friday night," and hung up.

The rest of the day went by very quickly with my continuing thoughts about the explosions in Albany and working hard at the office. I thought I should wait until early evening to call Maria at home after her day at school and I would be able to chat with both her and Michael at the same time about the Albany situation.

My plans were changed. Michael had heard about Albany and called me right after lunch to chat about the news. We went through discussions similar to my chats with Paul Browne and Ram, with a similar result. I suggested that I would like to come over to his house early this evening to review all this with both Maria and him. I mentioned we also needed to finalize our plans for the House of Owls meeting on Friday night. We agreed to meet at six o'clock and go out for dinner to talk about everything.

Chapter 39
Reviewing the Damage in Albany
Wednesday, May 8

Tony the Man called for a meeting with his Administrative Assistants, Bat and Gunner, in his office for one o'clock that afternoon. The Albany taxi companies had more business than usual today because of the extra transportation needs of Tony, Bat, and Gunner.

Bat and Gunner arrived at the office on time and were immediately ushered into Tony's office by the receptionist. They were wearing their usual grungy clothes, and it was hard to know if they wore the same clothes all the time or if they had several copies of the same dumpster salvaged–looking outfits. Tony was his usual self, well-dressed and neat-looking in a suit, shirt, and tie.

The discussion began with The Man acknowledging the difficulties that they all had the previous night and wondering what they should do about it. His next comment was "I hope that you guys didn't leave your new sharpshooter rifles in your cars overnight. You know that you will need them to carry out the plans we have for the owly meeting in Niagara Falls on Friday night."

Bat replied for both of them, "No, we always take our rifles up to our condos. We think they're a lot safer that way. The underground parking in our condo building gets broken in quite often. We also like to clean the rifles regularly so that they are always in good working order and ready to use anytime. We go to target practice at the gun club at least once a week to keep sharp, and we clean the rifles after each practice."

"That's good! Both of you better take some time today to get new vehicles. I guess there's not much left of your old ones. You will need to be in full operation by Friday. As we discussed in the past, after the owly meeting on Friday night is over, you will fire two shots each at the exit door as people are coming out. You should try not to hit anyone, but if you do, it won't matter too much. We really would not like to cause an international incident with the two guys from the FvD in the Netherlands. But we do need to do get even a little and give these owly guys a real scare," said Tony the Man.

The meeting was over, and Bat and Gunner left his office to go looking for new vehicles.

Chapter 40
Maria, Michael, and Billy
Go Out to Dinner
Wednesday, May 8

I worked until about five thirty on Wednesday afternoon, borrowed my father's car again, and headed off to the Rainbow Bridge to go across the river and to meet with Maria and Michael at their house. I arrived, parked in their driveway, got out of the car, and went to knock on the front door. As I was about to tap, Maria opened the door, followed with a hug and a kiss and "Hi, Billy, come on in." We went through to Michael's at-home office, and we were ready for some serious discussions about things that had been happening.

Because of the relatively early hour, we were all still dressed in our everyday work clothes. I was wearing my usual investment-guy uniform of navy-blue suit with a white shirt and a light-blue patterned tie. Michael was wearing his usual accountant-guy uniform, which was similar to mine. And Maria was looking great in navy-blue slacks, a blue-and-white patterned shirt, and a white cashmere cardigan. If I knew anything about women's fashion, and I don't, I probably would have been able to recite the haute couture labels for each piece of Maria's smart-looking outfit.

Michael said, "Hi, Billy, come on in. We should chat about the Albany situation a little bit before we go out for dinner."

"You're right, Michael," I said. "I first heard about the three car explosions in Albany this morning when Paul Browne phoned to tell me about them. He said that he first saw the news on CNN early this morning. Paul asked me if I thought that any of our HOO members might have done this, and I told him that I didn't know."

Maria said, "This sounds like the same kind of thing that happened to you and Ram. Do you know if Ram might do something like this?"

"I don't know if Ram did this or not," I said. "I talked with Ram after Paul called me, and we discussed the Albany situation. When I asked him if he was involved, he gave an evasive answer, so I still don't know for certain if Ram was involved or not."

"Billy, I know that retribution can sometimes seem like the right thing to do, but it is often not very wise," said Michael.

"You're right, of course, Michael. In case you are concerned that I was involved, I definitely was not," I said.

"Neither of us thought that you were, Billy, but we are pleased to hear you say so definitively," said Maria.

"We should head out for dinner now," said Michael. "I'll drive, Billy, if that's OK with you. I have booked us a table at Trattoria Brunelli. We have been there many times, and I know the quickest and easiest route to get there."

At the restaurant, we each ordered a glass of wine, a salad, and main course and discussed our plans for Friday night. We knew that Wim Vanderdonk and Lars Hogeboom, the two men from FvD, would be arriving at the Buffalo Niagara International Airport at about two on Friday afternoon and would be staying at the Brockton Inn across the street from the airport.

Our plan was that I would come to the Simone house at about 4:00 p.m. and the three of us would go together to pick up our two guests at their hotel and go to an early dinner at the Genesee Chophouse. We wanted to have an early dinner because we thought that we should be at the library by seven at the latest to have everything well organized and ready to start the meeting on time at seven thirty.

I told Michael and Maria that I would reconfirm all this information with our friends from the Netherlands by phone the next morning. It was a good idea to phone early in the day since they were six hours ahead of us. Their nine-to-five day would be finished by eleven in the morning our time.

We all agreed that this was a good plan, and we relaxed and enjoyed our dinner.

Chapter 41
Waiting for a Big Day
Thursday, May 9

Waiting for something important often creates a lot of anxiety. I was suffering some anxiety all day on Thursday.

At about nine thirty in the morning, I phoned the FvD office in The Hague, the Netherlands, and asked for Lars Hogeboom. Lars was in and available. We reviewed all the details of the trip to Niagara Falls for Lars and his associate, Wim Vanderdonk, and I was pleased to learn that nothing had changed from my previous understanding of the arrangements. We concluded our discussions, and I said, "OK, Lars, that's sounds great. We will see you at about four on Friday afternoon." And we both ended the call by saying "See you then."

After reviewing things with Lars, I thought that I should phone Michael and let him know that the plans that we discussed yesterday were in line with the program of events that Lars and Wim had expected.

Michael said, "Thanks for the update, Billy. We seem to be very well prepared. Since the meeting is in the US, I thought that it would be appropriate for me to introduce Lars and Wim. Hopefully, I will get to know them a little better during our dinner together."

"I agree, Michael," I said. "I have asked Lars to email me a short bio on each of them, and I will forward it on to you after I receive it. There will probably be more people at the meeting from your side of the border than from over here, but I expect we will be well represented. If anything important comes up between now and tomorrow afternoon, please let me know."

"Thanks, Billy. I will. But I don't expect any problems. I'll see you tomorrow," Michael said, and we both hung up.

On Thursday afternoon, I phoned the other lead members of the Canadian group of the House of Owls to make sure that they would all be coming to the meeting in Niagara Falls, New York, tomorrow evening. Henri and Jeanne Renault and Paul Browne all said that they had been looking forward to the meeting and would be there.

I phoned for Ram and connected to his cell phone. He told me that he would be at the meeting and would be driving his new white Jeep Grand Cherokee Overland, which he seemed very proud of. I asked him if there was any recent news about the events in Albany, and he said that he had not heard anything.

Ram's mention of his new Jeep reminded me that I should be able to pick up my new red Corvette from the dealer tomorrow morning. Even though I was not happy about the reason for it, I was very pleased to be getting a new red Corvette.

Chapter 42
The Day for the Meeting with the FvD
Friday, May 10

Getting a new car is an exciting time for most people even though the process of buying a new car and the anxiety of haggling over the price are not much fun. Today was my day to get my new red Corvette.

I picked up my new car from the dealer at about nine thirty on Friday morning, and I looked forward to driving over to see Maria and Michael that afternoon.

Before the highly anticipated events of that afternoon and that evening, I needed to spend some part of the day working. An investment advisor's work was never done. Each day, I needed to review large volumes of financial information, statistics, and other information as situations change quite rapidly almost by the minute. Today was a good day to do all the review things, but not much else. The day seemed to pass very slowly—as my grandfather would say, "Slower than the flow of molasses in January."

If we planned on being on time to pick up Wim Vanderdonk and Lars Hogeboom at their hotel at four that afternoon, Maria, Michael, and I would need to leave the Simone residence by about 3:30. Since I now had my NEXUS card, the time that it would take for me to get through the border would be much less than before, and it would also be reasonably predictable. I should be able to get to their place in about twenty minutes. I left my office at three, allowing myself half an hour and hoping that I could be slightly early, and I was.

I arrived at the Simone home at three twenty-five and parked my car off to one side of the driveway to allow Michael to get his car out easily later. As I tapped on the door, it opened. Maria came out and gave me a hug and a kiss. Michael followed close behind, and the three of us drove off in Michael's Mercedes to the Brockton Inn to meet with our two visitors from the Netherlands.

As we drove, Michael said, "I called over to the hotel, Billy, to make sure that our visitors had arrived OK and are ready to go out for an early dinner. They said they were fine and were looking forward to meeting us for dinner and everyone else later on."

Michael and Maria stayed in the car in the hotel's circular driveway while I went in to collect our visitors. They were already sitting in the hotel lobby and came over to introduce themselves to me when I asked the desk clerk to ring their rooms for me.

I said, "Hello, I'm Billy Jones. Michael and Maria Simone are waiting for us in his car out front. Thank you both so much for coming over for our meeting. It's a very important milestone for us to have you talk to our group and all our friends who are joining us tonight."

The taller of the two said, "Hello, Billy, I'm Wim Vanderdonk. You and I spoke on the phone and exchanged emails several times."

Wim looked almost like the near-perfect North American stereotype of a Dutch person. He was tall, about six feet, two inches, with thinning dark-blond hair and appeared to be relatively healthy and physically fit.

"This is my associate, Lars Hogeboom," Wim said. "I am one of the two FvD members of the Dutch Parliament, along with our house leader, Hendrik Allard. Lars is the president of the FvD party."

Lars looked a lot like Wim, but he was a little bit shorter, maybe six feet, even with the same thinning dark-blond hair and equally healthy and fit-looking appearance.

I said, "Nice to meet you, Lars. Let's go out, and you can meet Michael and Maria Simone. Maria is Michael's daughter and a special friend of mine."

As we came out the front door of the hotel, Maria and Michael got out of the car and came over to meet our guests. After salutations and handshakes, we all got into Michael's car and were off for dinner at the Genesee Chophouse.

Dinner was great, as expected, and friendly conversation flowed freely as we all got to know one another better. Time passed quickly. It was now just past six thirty, so we all thought we should finish our coffees and get over to the library for the meeting.

Chapter 43
The Meeting at the Library in Niagara Falls, New York
Friday, May 10

Michael drove our group—Wim Vanderdonk, Lars Hogeboom, Maria Simone, himself, and me—over to the library on Main Street. As we arrived at the parking lot in the back of the library, we could see that a few guests had already arrived and others were coming into the parking lot at the same time as we were. Michael parked his car. We all got out and walked toward the back door of the library. Along the way, we said hello and good evening to several others who were heading in the same direction.

Once we were inside the library, Maria and I saw the table near the entryway that had been set up for our group. The two of us sat at the table again to get organized, just as we had at the previous meeting, and to take the names, addresses, phone numbers, and email addresses from everyone as they arrived. We were quickly organized and ready.

The plan was that I would look after the Canadians and Maria would look after most of those from the US who attended, but I would help her out with the US folks, if needed, since there would probably be quite a few more from the US than from Canada.

After the hands on the clock passed seven, the parade of people arriving was steadily increasing for both Maria and I. Nigel Bromley, the lord mayor of Niagara-on-the-Lake, arrived early because he wanted to have an opportunity to speak with our two featured guests before the meeting. Mario Cavatelli, the mayor of Niagara Falls, Ontario, arrived with Nigel. I introduced him to Maria since she had not met him before. Among the many other Canadians who came to our desk was Mitesh Partook, a newspaper reporter from Niagara Falls, Ontario. Maria and I were both very pleased to see the press represented at our meeting. He asked us who would be best for him to chat with while he waited for the meeting to start, so we directed him to Michael and our two visitors from the Netherlands.

Among the more notable Americans to arrive early were John Polowski, the chief of police from Niagara Falls, New York, and Bruce Benson, the mayor of Niagara Falls, New York. Some of the mayor's political rivals claimed that his initials, BB, were an indication of his brainpower. Chief Polowski suggested to me that he wanted to attend our meeting for two reasons: to learn more about Direct Democracy and to be on hand in case we had any trouble from outsiders.

All the members of our founding leadership group had arrived. Henri and Jeanne Renault and Paul Browne from Canada were there, as well as Ram and my family. The other two members of the American founding group, Maria's friend Samantha Weldon and her husband John had also arrived.

The Earl W. Brydges Auditorium at the library had a seating capacity of 110 and was filling up rapidly as our planned starting time of seven thirty approached. As there were no more guests standing in line to check in with Maria and me, it seemed like a good time to get things started. So we did.

Michael went to the speaker's podium at the front, welcomed everyone, thanked them for coming, and introduced our two guests from the Netherlands who were seated in the front row. He also introduced the three mayors in attendance, the chief of police, and the other seven founding members of the House of Owls.

Wim Vanderdonk was the first speaker for the night. "Good evening, everyone, Lord Mayor Bromley, Mayor Benson, Mayor Cavatelli, Chief Polowski, and ladies and gentlemen. Thank you all for coming here tonight to hear our story of success with Direct Democracy in the Netherlands. We are very proud of our accomplishments thus far, and we are very confident that we will be able to continue to advance the concepts of Direct Democracy in the Netherlands in the future. We are also very proud of the House of Owls group and what they have accomplished for Direct Democracy thus far with their fledgling group here in America and Canada.

"I am a member of the Forum voor Democratie or FvD political party of the Netherlands. As you might imagine, the English translation of our party's name is simply 'freedom for democracy.' Our party was first formed in 2015 and had two members elected to the 150-member Dutch Parliament in the election held in March 2016. We expect to elect a much larger number of members at the next election in 2020. I am one of the two elected members, along with my associate Hendrik Allard, who is the founder of our party and the leader of our party in Parliament.

"All of you here tonight readily accept and know that democracy is the best form of government in the world today. Direct Democracy, where everyone has the right to vote by referenda on all issues, is clearly the best form of democracy. No self-appointed leader of any country should have the right to force the people of a country to accept anything that the majority of them do not want. No president, kaiser, king, czar, sultan, dictator, or other despot should have the inalienable right to make the rules of law for their country without the approval of the majority of the people in their country. Direct Democracy is the best way for all people, and one day will be readily accepted as the right way and the best way for all democratic countries."

Wim continued for some time to highlight some of the current political issues that could be best resolved by Direct Democracy referenda. He talked about Brexit in the UK, the abortion issue in Ireland, the gun control issue in both Canada and the US, the legalization of marijuana and problems with other drugs, limiting immigration, improving health care, better financial support for veterans, and several other issues of the day.

"Voting is one of the most important things we do in any democracy. Your English word *idiot* is derived from the ancient Greek word *idios*, which described a person in Greek society who was selfish, ignored political debates, and did not vote. My message to you is, don't be an *idios*. Vote on every issue."

Wim's closing comments began with "Direct Democracy is the most important plank in the FvD political platform, but a close second is the issue of balanced budgets and inflation. I will call on my associate, Lars Hogeboom, to speak about this very important subject."

As Lars came up to the podium, Wim's speech was loudly applauded by everyone. Lars began his comments by saying "Good evening, everyone. Again, thank you all for coming to hear about the two most important FvD party policies.

"I am an economist, and as you all know, if you laid all the world's economists end to end, they couldn't reach a conclusion. [pause for laughter] As an economist, balanced budgets and inflation are subjects that have always been very important to me. Your first thought might be the question, What has one got to do with the other? Although all economists do not agree, it is deficit spending by national governments and printing money to cover the deficit that is the basic cause of inflation.

"*Inflation* is not just a fancy word that financial people talk about. It is a very real and important consideration for everybody. For example, consider that when we talk about the stock market, we often hear of stock splits. When a public company decides to split its shares on a two-for-one basis, each shareholder ends up with twice as many shares, but each share is worth only half as much as it was before.

"A country's currency works the same way. If your government gave each of you one new dollar today for each dollar that you now have, the purchasing power of those dollars to buy goods and services would be half as much as it was before. Your governments and ours are doing this right now, but only a little bit at a time. However, after a number of years, the result is the same.

"The Federal Reserve in the US and the Bank of Canada, the central banking agents of your two countries, both target 2 percent as the acceptable rate of annual inflation. Even if the central bankers are able to hold inflation at that low number of 2 percent a year, the purchasing power of your respective dollars will be cut in half in just thirty-five years. Even worse, if inflation should rise to an average of 5 percent a year, it would take only fifteen years for the value of the dollar to be cut in half.

"The winners in an inflationary environment are those who borrow large amounts of money because the dollars they use to pay back their borrowings are worth much less than the dollars they borrowed. On the other hand, the losers in an inflationary environment are those people who scrimped and saved their money and saw the purchasing power of their money decline dramatically. Saving money should be a good thing, not a bad thing. Inflation is a pernicious evil, and the only level of inflation that should be acceptable is *zero*.

"Inflation is created because governments don't have the will to balance their budgets by matching the money that they spend with the amount of money they are prepared to collect in tax revenue. That is basically dishonest. If a government wants to spend a certain amount of money, it should have the honesty and integrity to raise enough money in taxes to cover their planned expenditures. The problem here is that if a government increased taxes by too much, the people would revolt, in some way, against them. And they are well aware of that. Just think of the yellow vests in France, for one instance.

"A rising rate of inflation often leads to hyperinflation and disaster. After WWI, Germany suffered one of the world's worst recent experiences of hyperinflation. The main cause, as might be expected, was that the German Weimar government printed banknotes to pay for their debts without collecting enough in taxes from their citizens to pay for their spending. That's deficit spending run amok, and it led to disaster for Germany's currency because inflation continued to accelerate into hyperinflation. That's the way it usually happens.

"Here are two simple examples of the effects of hyperinflation in Germany. In December 1918, shortly after the end of WWI, the price of one egg was fifty pfennigs or one-half of one mark, the main German currency. Due to hyperinflation, the price of one egg rose to 201 billion marks by November 1923. Similarly, the price of a kilogram of butter rose for 2.70 marks in 1913 to 6 billion marks by November 1923. This is what disaster looks like, and you don't want that in the US or Canada. We don't want that in the Netherlands either.

"A more recent example of hyperinflation is in Zimbabwe. When Zimbabwe first gained independence in 1980, the Zimbabwean dollar was valued at about one to one with the US dollar, but not for long. The deficit spending of the Zimbabwean government began slowly but accelerated rapidly after 1990 and soon reached hyperinflation. At its worst point, it required 10×30 zeros in Z$ to buy one US$. At its peak, the value of the Z$ was being cut in half every day.

"Hyperinflation is not just a story of ancient history. It is actually happening today in Venezuela. The leaders of the government of Venezuela have mismanaged and looted the country for many years. This has led to Venezuela continuing to increase budget deficits every year and the country continuing to print ever-increasing amounts of money to cover the shortages. As a result, Venezuela has been experiencing hyperinflation, and the country is in shambles. As an indication of how bad it is, let me tell you this. For example, from 2012 to 2018, the bolivar, the Venezuelan currency, plunged in value by 6,470,000 percent. What makes that even worse is that Venezuela had been experiencing high inflation or hyperinflation for many years before this period.

"No one in the Netherlands, the US, Canada, or anywhere else really wants to go into a hyperinflation situation. However, many governments seem quite unconcerned about inflation and continue to run ever-increasing budget deficits that could eventually lead to accelerating inflation and to the disastrous effects of hyperinflation.

"The FvD party has two basic policies in its political platform: Direct Democracy and dealing with balanced budgets and cutting inflation. This would lead to a strong domestic currency and a strong domestic economy. All of you here tonight may well agree with these objectives, but it is important that the underlying values of both policies should be spread all around the world and eventually adopted by as many people and by as many governments as possible.

"Thank you all for coming to hear our message and for your attention to our comments."

Michael went up to the podium as the audience was applauding the speech by Lars. He thanked both Lars and Wim for coming over from the Netherlands to talk to us about the success of the FvD and the primary objectives of their party, Direct Democracy, and balanced budgets by national governments. He added that both Lars and Wim would be staying around for a short while to have a coffee and chat with anyone who might like to ask them a question or to just say hello. Michael added that a copy of the two speeches from tonight would be transcribed and sent to everyone by email within a week or so. He thanked everyone for coming, and the meeting was adjourned.

As expected, everyone stayed around for a little while to chat in small groups with one another and with the visiting guests. All the members of the House of Owls were keenly interested in discussing Direct Democracy with our guests and were also very interested in learning more about the very negative effect of inflation.

The auditorium became a little stuffy, so several people thought they would step out the back door for a little fresh air while they continued their discussions.

Chapter 44
After the Meeting
Friday, May 10

Bat and Gunner had been ready and waiting for nearly an hour for the meeting to end and for people to come out the back door of the library. They knew that everyone would be coming out the back door because it led right onto the parking lot where they had all parked.

They had chosen their spot with great care at the south end of a large elementary school about 150 yards away, directly across from the library's back door but hidden from view by several small trees and shrubs. They wanted to be able to get a clear shot at the back door with their sniper rifles without being seen by anyone from the library. They also wanted to have a good chance at a quick and clean getaway after the shooting. Their chosen location by the school provided a quick exit through the school's short laneway to get them heading south on Eleventh Street and only a few blocks from the highway.

Both Bat and Gunner had spent much of the past week getting ready for this event. They both made sure that their new SP-50 sharpshooter rifles were clean and functioning smoothly. The SP-50 rifle was a new model from the Straight Path Rifle Company of Detroit, Michigan, which had become available just two years ago. The powerful .50 caliber rifle, with a high-powered telescopic sight, was designed for hunting and for military use.

The caliber of a rifle is the diameter of the rifle bore, usually measured as a decimal fraction of an inch, or in some cases, it was simply measured in millimeters. Hence, a 50-caliber rifle has a barrel with an inside diameter of 0.50 or half an inch. The bullets that can be fired by the rifle need to be a tiny fraction smaller than the rifle bore so they can pass through it when the gun is fired. The implication is that the bullets that the SP-50 takes are quite large and very deadly.

As four people slowly worked their way out the back door of the library from the meeting, four shots were fired in rapid succession. All four people went down from the gunshots. After firing two shots each, Bat and Gunner quickly jumped into the black Ram pickup truck and drove away in a hurry with all the truck's lights still turned off.

The black Ram pickup truck went out the school's short laneway, heading south on 11th Street to Pine Avenue, which is also called number 62 highway. On 62, they headed east to the I-190, north on I-190, and then onto I-90, heading east toward Albany and home.

They knew that it would have been shorter and more direct to go north on 11th Street out of the school laneway instead of south, but it would have taken them right past the police station only two blocks away from the library. They knew they would be very uncomfortable being that close to the police station, and they didn't think it was a good thing for them to do.

Chapter 45
After the Shooting
Friday, May 10

Wim Vanderdonk from the FvD; Bruce Benson, the mayor of Niagara Falls, New York; Mitesh Partook, a journalist from Niagara Falls, Ontario; and Ram Delvechio each thought they would like to get some fresh air after the meeting and decided to step out the back door of the library and continue their chat outside. As the four of them came through the door, four gunshots were fired. *Bang, bang, bang, bang.* And all four men went down.

Ram was stunned that someone had shot at him and put a bullet right through the left shoulder of his new Harris Tweed jacket, which also creased the upper part of his left arm. He was even more stunned when he looked at the other three men who all seemed to be very dead. Ram yelled for help and immediately heard several people running out toward him. He looked at his left shoulder and noticed that his jacket was starting to turn red as some blood oozed out of the wound. He was also starting to feel some pain in his left shoulder.

Michael Simone, Chief John Polowski, and I were standing together in a small group in the auditorium when we heard a yell for help from just outside the back door. All three of us moved very quickly. Chief Polowski was the first one through the door, followed by Michael, and then by me.

With a quick look around, the chief saw three bodies lying motionless on the ground and Ram sitting on the deck, wincing in pain but still moving. "Mr. Delvechio, are you all right? What happened?" asked Chief Polowski.

"We have been shot by a sniper," said Ram. "It looked like it came from straight out there, but I can't be sure. You had better call for several ambulances and police squad cars right away."

Chief Polowski immediately called his police station and told them that there had been a shooting at the back of the library at 1425 Main Street. He also told them that he needed at least three ambulances and several police squad cars over at the library as fast as they could get them there. He bellowed, "Immediately would be almost soon enough. Four people have been shot, and some of them could be critical."

As the chief leaned over to examine the motionless bodies a little more closely, he asked, "Mr. Delvechio, can you tell me a little more about what happened here? It looks like all three of these people are dead, but we will wait for the paramedics to have a look."

Ram responded with "Chief, the four of us were standing in a small group in the auditorium and thought it was a little stuffy, so we decided to step out here to the deck for some fresh air. As we came through the door, I heard four gunshots, and we all went down. It sounded like the shots came from straight out there in the area of those small trees and shrubs behind that building, which looks like it might be a school. That's all I know. I didn't see any vehicles out there or anyone leaving that area. They must have snuck away quickly and quietly. Oh, by the way, please call me Ram. Everyone else does."

As Ram was finishing his comments, the sound of many sirens was rapidly getting louder and louder. Both the police cars and the ambulances were getting closer and closer. Both Michael Simone and I were standing there, flabbergasted and trying to think of what could have happened here. The chief came over to us and asked both of us to go back inside to tell all the people not to leave the auditorium until after the police and paramedics have sorted out the situation outside. Michael and I did as we were told.

Three ambulances and four police cars arrived very fast, and all of the first responders went right to work. The paramedics confirmed to the chief that the three men were dead, and they said they would take Ram to the hospital right away for treatment.

The first police squad car that arrived had two officers, as usual, who were sent to the area that Ram had indicated to look for any evidence of a vehicle, tire tracks, footprints, discarded brass casings from bullets, broken small branches in the trees or shrubs, or anything else that might be useful in the investigation.

One of the other three squads stayed with the chief at the site, and the other two were sent out to look for clues—one to the north and the other to the south, with the same instructions as the chief had given to the first car. They were told to look for anything that might be helpful.

When Michael and I went back into the auditorium, we told everyone that they would need to stay inside while Chief Polowski finished directing the outside activities for the ambulances and his police squad cars. We also told them that three men had been shot and were dead and Ram Delvechio was wounded and on his way to the hospital to be patched up.

The ambulances were gone now—one to the hospital with Ram and the other two went to the morgue with the three dead people. The teams of police investigators were deployed to search for clues to the north, south, and east. The three-story library building would have blocked any possible shot coming from the west, so there was no need to search in that direction.

As the chief came back inside, Michael said, "Chief, you may want some help with this situation from higher-level police agencies. The people who were murdered here tonight were very high-profile individuals. Wim Vanderdonk was a member of the Dutch government, Mitesh Partook was a Canadian journalist, and you know Mayor Bruce Benson very well. He was very popular here in the Falls, and there will be a lot of questions. You should really give serious consideration to getting some help from higher up the chain!"

"I have already thought of that, Michael, and of course, you're right," he responded. "I'll call Howard Kendrick over at the New York

State Police right now and explain the situation to him. We can let him decide if we should go beyond his jurisdiction or not, to the FBI and maybe even to the CIA with this situation."

I added to Michael's comments, "Chief, Lars Hogeboom is extremely upset over the death of his associate and would like to call over to the Netherlands to let his people know what happened here. He has suggested that the Netherlands may want to get their international investigators involved in the situation."

"That's probably a good idea, Billy," said Chief Polowski. "I know a little bit about the police services in the Netherlands, and they are reputed to be very good. Their National Police Services Agency has a division called the Royal and Diplomatic Protection Service, which could be the best point of contact to start with. This division provides security to the king and other members of the Dutch Royal House and many others including government ministers, ambassadors, and domestic and foreign dignitaries. Would you like me to contact them, or would Lars Hogeboom prefer to do it himself?"

"Lars said that he would like to call himself," I said. "He has changed his plans a little and will be staying here for a few more days than he had originally planned until we all have a better idea of how all this happened and what is being done about it. He is staying at the Brockton Inn over by the airport and will make himself available if you need him for anything."

"Thanks, Billy. I should talk with Lars before he leaves," said the chief. "We will be having a major case review meeting with all parties within the next day or two, and he will probably want to be there, possibly with someone from the Dutch police service."

"Chief, I think that all these people would like to leave and go home now if that's OK with you. We have a list of the names, addresses, phone numbers, and email addresses of everybody who attended this meeting here tonight. I will make sure you get a copy of the list as soon as I can. However, I don't think that anyone at the meeting had anything to do with the shootings," said Michael.

"You're probably right, Michael. We should let everyone go now. It has been a very difficult evening," said the chief. "But I would like a copy of the list in case I might need it for something."

New York State Police Detective Howard Kendrick arrived, and the chief told him the whole story of the evening. Detective Kendrick was medium height with an athletic build and a shiny, clean-shaven head. He looked like Mr. Clean, except he wore a dark suit and tie instead of being all dressed in white like the advertising icon, and he had eyebrows like the Mona Lisa—none at all.

After explaining everything to Detective Kendrick, the chief asked if it was OK to let everyone go home now since it was very unlikely that anyone in the auditorium was involved with the shooting. Detective Kendrick agreed, and everyone began to file out, looking like Napoleon's battered and defeated army retreating from Moscow back to Paris in the winter of 1812.

Michael and I finally had a chance to go and talk with Maria, who had been standing off to one side with her good friend Samantha Weldon and her husband, John. Both Maria and Samantha looked as white as ghosts as we approached. Maria spoke up, "Billy, my father and I didn't see what happened. I heard that three people are dead and that Ram got shot too. Did all that really happen right here tonight?"

"Yes, Maria. Wim Vanderdonk, Mitesh Partook, and Mayor Bruce Benson were all shot and killed here tonight. Ram was very lucky. He has a wound on his left shoulder, but it doesn't look like it's very serious. Right now, he's at the hospital being treated. We are all very sorry that these shootings happened and for the three people who were murdered and their families. Tonight was not a good night for the House of Owls. Somebody seems out to get us and put our group out of business," I explained.

Maria, Michael, and I decided that we should go now and take Lars Hogeboom back to his hotel. As we were leaving Lars at his hotel, I told him that I would call him the next day with an update on everything that I could learn about by then.

As we drove back to the Simone home, Michael and I agreed that we should get together the next day to get an update from Chief Polowski and see if he had any new information on our situation.

When I left Michael and Maria, I went to the hospital emergency room to see how Ram was doing. As I entered the emergency room, I saw him sitting quietly off to one side. I went over to Ram and asked, "How are you doing? Are you all patched up and ready to go home?"

"Yes, Billy. I think I have had enough of this place for a while, but I was waiting to get a ride back to my car that I left in the library parking lot. The doctor said it would be better if I didn't drive tonight, but I think I can make it home OK."

"I think you should listen to the doctor, Ram," I said. "I can drive you home tonight and bring you back tomorrow or Sunday after you've had a chance to recover a little from your gunshot wound."

Ram agreed, and we went out to my car and headed back to Niagara-on-the-Lake. On the way home, we discussed who might have done the shooting at the library tonight, and we both knew, without too much thought, that there was only one answer.

Ram pointed out, "Billy, we need to do something about the Scaglione Agency and the thugs they hire to give us a hard time. It looks like they won't be backing off any time soon, so we'll probably have more trouble with them in the future. We could do without that. Eventually, we'll need to get even."

Chapter 46
Following Up on Friday Night
Saturday, May 11

Saturday was not a usual workday for me, but I knew that I would be very busy that day. I had many phone calls to make and many places to go for face-to-face meetings.

I wasn't sure who I should phone first, but I eventually decided to choose Chief Polowski as the best place to start to see if anything new had developed overnight. The chief was in and took my call.

He said, "Good morning, Billy. I guess you know that last night's shootings at the library is the number 1 news item today, and all the news hounds are out looking for more information."

"I didn't know that," I told the chief. "But I'm not too surprised. It isn't every day your city gets a triple homicide with your mayor and two other high-profile people getting shot and killed."

"As you suggested might happen, Billy, this situation has rapidly escalated to the upper levels of the policing ladder. Some of the area politicians are also speaking out with tough comments.

"I have scheduled a meeting at my office for tomorrow at two in the afternoon. There could be a fairly large group attending. The FBI, the CIA, and the New York State Police will be represented. There will probably also be someone from the Dutch police and maybe someone from CSIS, the Canadian group. Your House of Owls group should be represented by at least you and Michael Simone and anyone else that you would like to bring along."

"That does sound like a large group, but I guess you need to cover all the bases," I said. "I should bring along Ram Delvechio since he is really the only eyewitness, and I will ask Paul Browne to come with us as well since he is a lawyer, and we might need him to protect us from all the police heavyweights. I will be talking with Ram later this morning and ask him about bringing someone from CSIS. Ram worked at CSIS for three years before he started his own private investigations business, so he should know who to contact."

"That sounds good, Billy," said the chief. "It seems like your House of Owls group will be well represented."

"Have you spoken to Lars Hogeboom yet this morning?" I asked. "He probably has contacted the authorities in the Netherlands to get someone to come over here to get involved in the investigation. If you haven't called him yet, please let me do it."

The chief said that it was OK for me to call Lars, and then we both said goodbye with "See you tomorrow at two o'clock."

My next call of the day was to Ram. He picked up his phone on the second ring and answered, "Hi, Billy. What's new today so far?"

"Ram, I was just talking with Chief Polowski, and he told me that he has scheduled a meeting with everybody at two o'clock tomorrow afternoon," I said. "I think we should try to get someone from CSIS to join us at the meeting to help support the Canadian position in all this. The chief said there would probably be people at the meeting from the FBI, the CIA, the New York State Police, and possibly someone from the Dutch police as well."

"That sounds like a good idea, Billy," said Ram. "I know quite a few people there, and I am sure that we can get someone to join us, given the circumstances. I will call the Toronto office and let you know who will be joining us."

"Ram, if you could drive tomorrow, that would be great," I said. "As you know, my Corvette is too small, and there will probably be four of us from this side going over to the meeting. Paul Browne and I could meet you and the CSIS representative at your place, and we could all go together from there."

"That seems like a good plan, Billy," said Ram. "Why don't we all meet here at, let's say, one fifteen to give us lots of time to get across the river for the meeting at two?"

"That's great, Ram," I said. "I'll see you then." And we both said goodbye and hung up.

The next name on my call list that day was Paul Browne. I dialed, and he answered quickly.

"Hello, Billy, how are things progressing?" he asked.

"Good morning, Paul. Things are progressing well. I have talked with both Chief Polowski and Ram Delvechio so far this morning about last night's events and what will happen going forward. The chief has planned a meeting with all the police agencies and the leaders of our House of Owls group at his office for tomorrow at two o'clock in the afternoon. I would like you to be there with our Canadian group, if you can?" I asked.

"I can do that, Billy. This is a major situation, and you may need all the help you can get," Paul said.

"Thank you, Paul," I said. "The plan is that the four of us from the Canadian side should meet at the Queenston Gardens Hotel, where Ram has a residential suite, and go together in one car from there. Ram has offered to drive so you could leave your car there. If we meet at Ram's at one fifteen, it should give us enough time."

"I will see you tomorrow at the Queenston Gardens Hotel at one fifteen," Paul said in closing, and we disconnected.

My next call was to the Brockton Inn for Lars Hogeboom. The switchboard put me through to his room, and he answered with a simple "Hello, good morning."

I responded with "Hello, and good morning to you too, Lars. It's Billy Jones. I thought I should get in touch with you this morning to see if you have recovered from the dreadful events of last night."

"Yes and no," he said. "As you will appreciate, I was extremely upset by the shootings last night, especially with the shooting death of my good friend and long-standing political associate, Wim Vanderdonk. I phoned back to the Netherlands last night and was eventually able to reach someone at the Royal and Diplomatic Protection Service division of the Dutch National Police Corps. In the Netherlands, they are usually referred to by their Dutch language acronym, DKDB. Jan Wellers, an investigator with the DKDB, is on his way over now and should arrive later today."

"That sounds great, Lars," I said. "There is a meeting of those involved tomorrow at two in the afternoon at the police station in Niagara Falls, New York, and it looks like all the different interests will be represented by one police agency or another. If you like, I could ask Michael Simone to pick up both you and Jan Wellers to give you a ride to the meeting."

"That would be good, Billy," Lars replied. "We will probably be renting a car anyway, but it would be easier and safer for us to have Michael pick us up for the meeting to make sure we don't get lost."

"I'll phone Michael and ask him to do that. I will suggest that he should be at your hotel by about one thirty to give you lots of time to get to the police station by two," I said.

We both said "Goodbye, see you tomorrow" and hung up.

My next call was to Michael Simone. I dialed, and he picked up right away and answered, "Good morning, Billy. How are things going so far this morning?"

"Michael, I have been busy making phone calls all morning," I answered. "Chief Polowski has planned a meeting for tomorrow at two at his police station to review the situation. He would like to have all interested parties represented at the meeting. We, Canadians, will be well represented by Paul Browne, Ram Delvechio, and me. We will also have a member of CSIS with us, but we don't know just yet who that will be. Ram is arranging for someone to join us.

"I also talked with Lars Hogeboom this morning, and he said he has arranged for a police service guy from the Netherlands's DKDB division to come over to help with the investigation. His name is Jan Wellers. He will be arriving this afternoon and staying at the Brockton Inn, where Lars is staying. I apologize, but I volunteered that you will pick them up at their hotel at about one thirty tomorrow and take them to the meeting at the police station. We will already have four in our car, so it would be better if you could do that."

"I'll be happy to do that, Billy," said Michael. "Maria would rather not come, if you think that is OK. She is still very upset about the situation, and going to that meeting would probably make it worse."

"That's fine, Michael," I said. "There will be a fairly large gathering of various police agencies and House of Owls people, so it is probably best that Maria stay at home this time."

"See you tomorrow at two," he said, and we both said goodbye for now.

Chapter 47
Meeting at the Scaglione Agency in Albany
Saturday, May 11

Anthony Scaglione had heard all the news about the shootings at the library in Niagara Falls on Friday night and was a little concerned about the possibility of it being traced back to the agency and himself. He phoned both Bat and Gunner early Saturday morning and asked them to come in to his office for a review of their projects.

Tony wanted to dispose of any possible evidence from the shootings, so he asked both Bat and Gunner to break their rifles into as many pieces as possible, put them in small suitcases, and bring them in to the meeting that morning so he could dispose of them later today. He asked them both to be at his office at one o'clock that same afternoon.

As the hour approached one, Bat and Gunner arrived at the agency's office with their small suitcases in hand and were shown in to Tony's office right away. They both handed their suitcases over to The Man and waited for him to begin his questioning.

The Man said, "Thanks for coming in on short notice and for bringing these with you. Just so you know, I will be taking these over to our good friend Hubert Radek at the HR Metals Recycling Company to be put into an automobile that is about to go into the compactor."

Hubert was known as Hub by almost everyone who knew him. Maybe it was just an abbreviation of his name, or it might have been because he salvaged a lot of automobile hubcaps from his scrapyard and sold them to auto repair shops at inflated prices.

"As I have mentioned to you before, the metal from the crushed cars and anything in them is sold to Remelt Steel Company, a large US steel manufacturing company that uses only reprocessed scrap metal to make new steel. After being reprocessed, your rifles will never have existed. Within a few days, they could be the steel in part of a new road, a new bridge, a new building, or anywhere steel is needed—just like some people speculate how Jimmy Hoffa was put into the cement columns of the new Silverdome in Pontiac, Michigan, as it was being constructed. So they say.

"Can you be certain that nobody saw you when you left the library last night? Please tell me some of the details of how it went."

Bat spoke up and said, "We scouted out the best spot to shoot from on Friday morning. The spot we picked was about 150 yards away and well covered by some small trees and scrubs. We made sure that we could get out in a hurry without being seen from the library.

"We knew that the meeting would start at about seven thirty and probably finish in one to two hours. The parking lot for the library is in the back, so we knew that people would be coming out that way. When the first four people came out the back door, we fired two shots each, jumped in the pickup, and took off. We didn't turn on the truck's headlights until we were out of the laneway and on the street, well out of sight from anyone at the library."

"It sounds like you did things the right way," said Tony. "But I will get rid of the rifles just to keep us on the safe side.

"Another issue that we need to discuss is Harvey Goldsmith. I understand that you were able to arrange for his death, which will allow our client to collect on the $2-million life-insurance policy that he purchased from the deceased two years ago for $1.3 million. Our client will pay us well for this one, and you will both get a bonus for your efforts in making this happen. I will let you know when the bonus money becomes available."

That was the end of their discussions for that day, and they departed. After they left, Tony wondered if things had actually gone as well and as easy as Bat and Gunner had suggested. They did tend to oversimplify situations sometimes. He also wondered what more he needed to do to get the House of Owls group to stop their movement to promote Direct Democracy and disband the group. Maybe the shootings and the three dead men would do it, or maybe not. Time will tell.

Chapter 48
The Meeting at the Niagara Falls Police Station
Sunday, May 12

I drove my red Corvette over to Ram's hotel to meet with Paul Browne, Ram, and whoever he had arranged to join us from the CSIS. The three of them were standing out in front of the hotel as I arrived. After I parked my car and joined them, I was quickly introduced to Agent Gordon Harris from the CSIS, based in Toronto, who Ram had known during his three years with that organization.

Gordon was tallish with a full head of middle-brown-colored hair and looked very fit, as a CSIS agent probably should. He was well-dressed in what was often called smart casual clothing, much like us three.

Ram drove the four of us to the police station in Niagara Falls, New York, and we parked in what seemed like a very full parking lot. Ram knew the way to the police station because it was on Main Street, only two buildings north of the library where he was wounded on Friday night. We went into the station together and were directed to the station boardroom. The others had all arrived, and the room seemed quite full.

Chief Polowski was taking charge of the meeting and directed us to seats that had our names on place cards for each of us on the table in front of our chairs. The boardroom was smallish and sparsely decorated but was large enough to accommodate eleven of us reasonably well. The boardroom had windows covering nearly the whole wall on one side. The walls were all painted a light blue-gray color that blended nicely with the gray mottled carpet, which looked almost like tweed.

The chief introduced everyone around the table by name and who they represented. Two of the names that were new to me were Special Agent Vincent Mauro of the FBI and Agent Robert Brewer of the CIA. Both agents were tallish and fit-looking men with the modern facial-hair appearance of not having shaved for the past five days. The main difference between them was that Agent Mauro had nearly black hair and Agent Brewer had nearly blond hair. Both were neatly coiffed.

After everyone was introduced, Chief Polowski decided to get the meeting started. Since Ram was the only eyewitness to the shootings, the chief asked him to describe what happened. The chief also asked Ram if his wound was healing OK. Ram told his story again, and everyone around the table seemed puzzled as to how the shooting could happen so easily without anyone seeing anybody.

Agent Brewer asked, "Mr. Delvechio, could you tell which direction the shots came from?"

Ram answered, "Well, it all happened so fast that it was hard to know for certain, but I think the shots probably came from straight out, which would be from an easterly direction. The back door of the library faces east and leads to the parking lot. So the shooters probably knew that we would all be coming out that way eventually."

Agent Mauro asked Ram, "Did you see any sign of people or vehicles over in that direction?"

"No, I didn't see anyone or anything over in that direction or even off to the northeast and southeast. They must have driven away with the vehicle's headlights off," answered Ram.

The questions directed to Ram by the various police agencies continued for some time but were eventually exhausted. It was Ram's turn, and he asked Chief Polowski, "Were any of the bullets recovered?"

The chief said, "Yes, Mr. Delvechio. We recovered all four slugs. The one that grazed your shoulder was embedded in the doorframe, and we were able to dig it out. The other three were recovered during the autopsies. The slugs are quite large and appear to be about .50 caliber. From the markings on the slugs, it looks like there were two different guns used in the shootings. Two of the slugs have one set of markings, and the other two have a different set."

"A .50 caliber is an unusually large size," Ram noted. "It's probably too big for a pistol, so they were probably shot from rifles. I have heard of a relatively new business in Detroit, Michigan, that goes by the name of Straight Path Rifle Company, which makes .50-caliber sharpshooter rifles. Their main product is called the SP-50. One of the promises they made to the policing community when they started their business is that when they test each new rifle, they would keep a record of the ballistics markings and also the name of the dealer that each rifle was sold to."

Special Agent Vincent Mauro of the FBI spoke up and said, "That sounds like something that I could follow up on as part of my help with this project. I will be happy to take that on and get back to everybody through Chief Polowski with my findings."

At this point in our discussions, I thought that I should mention who Ram and I thought the shooters were and why. I began, "Ram Delvechio and I think we know who the shooters were. We think the two guys were Gary Masterson, known as Bat, and Harold Remington, known as Gunner, who both work for Anthony Scaglione, known as Tony the Man. He runs the Scaglione Agency in Albany, New York. The agency is primarily a political lobbying business, but it also does some types of what you might call enforcement activities for a number of nefarious businessmen. We have no hard evidence or solid proof, but we have had run-ins with these guys in the recent past."

I recited the story of them barging into my office on Thursday, April 18, with a bribe of two hundred thousand dollars, trying to stop the meeting of the House of Owls group on Friday, April 19. I also mentioned other events such as how they gave Ram a beating after the Friday night meeting in the parking lot of the Chateau des Chutes Winery; how nearly everyone who attended the Friday night meeting had damage done to their cars on Friday night, April 27; and that Ram and I had our cars blown up in the middle of the night on May 2.

"We could easily recognize them from our two face-to-face meetings, but we have no real proof of the last two events. Having said that, however, we are both very confident that they did do the car damage and the two car explosions that I mentioned. I strongly suspect that they did these shootings as well," I explained.

Michael Simone spoke up and added, "I'm sure you will remember, Chief Polowski, when I came to you about all the House of Owls people who had damage done to their cars that night. The damage to peoples' cars happened on both sides of the border. Billy and Ram feel certain that Mr. Masterson and Mr. Remington were the guys who did it, working as agents for the Scaglione Agency."

"Ram or Billy, why do you think it was these guys who did the damage to all the cars that night?" asked the CIA guy, Robert Brewer.

I responded with "Each of the cars that had some damage done that night had a small business-card type of notice with the words *No House of Owls* written on it, and nothing else. The only opposition we have had to our House of Owls movement thus far has been from these people, so we think they are guilty in this case as well."

Ram added, "I totally agree with Billy on this. These two guys should be investigated. It might help your investigation if you knew that they are both members of the Albany Gun Club and the US Army Reserve. The practice rifle ranges at both places may well have some old targets that these guys used for shooting practice that could still have some of their slugs in them. If they do, you could check the ballistics markings against the ones that were retrieved from the Friday night shootings. This could be proof that they are the guilty parties."

"That seems like a very good suggestion, Mr. Delvechio," said Chief Polowski. "Perhaps Detective Kendrick or some of his associates with the New York State Police could check out the Albany Gun Club, and maybe Agent Brewer could use his influence to check out the US Army Reserve in the Albany area."

Detective Kendrick and Agent Brewer both agreed to do as the chief had suggested. Both Jan Wellers and Gordon Harris thought that there wasn't much that they could contribute at this point in the investigation. They thought it would be best to leave it up to the American police agencies, which seemed appropriate since all the problems happened in the United States.

Both Jan Wellers and Gordon Harris had already received notice from senior officials of each of their governments that they needed to find some answers to the shootings because the media in both their countries was raising many questions and looking for some answers. The pressure was on to find out what really happened and who did it.

"I don't think that there is much more that we can do today," said the chief. "We should probably meet again in about a week to review our progress. I would suggest next Friday at, let's say, two o'clock here in our boardroom. I hope that's OK for everybody?"

Everyone agreed, except Jan Wellers and Gordon Harris, who both asked if they could join the meeting by telephone conference since their roles were quite passive, at least for the present moment.

The meeting adjourned. Jan Wellers, Gordon Harris, and the four of us from the House of Owls group stood together in the parking lot after the meeting was over, discussing our dissatisfaction with the general progress of the investigation.

After several minutes and a mood of discontent, we all went our separate ways. I was able to make it home in time to join my family for our usual Sunday evening family dinner.

Chapter 49
The Week Ahead
Monday, May 13

I knew that Monday would be a busy day at work for me since I had been missing from the job doing other things quite often as of late.

After the meeting on Sunday afternoon, Lars Hogeboom and Jan Wellers thought they should head back to the Netherlands as soon as they could get a flight. They were in luck and were able to fly out on a Sunday-night overnight flight. They had both concluded that there was little they could do to help with the investigation at this point by staying here in Niagara Falls. They also knew that they could contact the various American policing agencies for any information that they might want after they were back home.

Ram's friend, Gordon Harris from CSIS, also headed back home to Toronto, leaving the investigations to the Niagara Falls Police, the New York State Police, the FBI, and the CIA. The shootings happened in their country, and he thought that they should be the ones to lead the investigations and, hopefully, solve the crimes.

I thought that I should phone Ram that day to see if he had any new thoughts about the shootings. I dialed his cell phone, and he answered, "Hello, Billy. What's new?"

"I thought that I should call you to see if you had any new information or thoughts about the shootings or about our hooligan friends Bat and Gunner," I responded inquisitively.

"No, I don't, Billy," said Ram. "I'm as certain as I can be that they are the guilty guys, but I think that the policing groups in the US will probably never be able to prove it to their satisfaction. It seems to me that these criminals may never get their just rewards. Gordon Harris, my CSIS friend, has gone back to Toronto. He also thinks that it will be tough to ever prove anything."

"I understand what you're thinking, Ram, and I am inclined to agree with you. However, I hope you will be able to join us on Friday at two o'clock for the review meeting at the police station in Niagara Falls to see if the policing agencies have made any progress at all with their investigations. It should be interesting," I said.

"Yes, I will be happy to join you for that meeting, Billy. Why don't I pick you up at, say, one thirty?" Ram offered.

"That's great, Ram. See you then," I said, and we each hung up.

I thought that I should call Michael Simone to see if he had heard anything new from the American policing agencies. After a quick, short phone call, I learned that there was no new information and that he was looking forward to the Friday meeting at two at the police station. Both Michael and I hoped that the policing groups would have made some significant progress by then, but somehow it seemed unlikely.

Chapter 50
Good News for the House of Owls
Tuesday, May 14

Tuesday was not usually as busy a day as Monday in our office, but I still had a little catching up to do to make up for the time I had been absent recently while working on various things for the House of Owls. My phone rang, and I answered, "Good morning, it's Billy Jones here. How may I help you?"

The voice on the other end of the phone line said, "Good morning, Billy. It's Nigel Bromley calling. How are you doing this morning?"

"I'm fine, Nigel," I said. "What's new with you this morning? I guess you must have recovered by now from the frightening time we all had at our HOO meeting at the library a week ago last Friday. The shootings were very distressing for our House of Owls group and everyone else who was at the meeting. It has been a fairly hot news and media topic on both sides of the border since it happened."

"Yes, since I was there, I have followed the story in the media more closely than I might have otherwise," he said. "But I think my news today will be more to your liking. The good news is that our town council voted yesterday, six to three in favor of holding a referendum on the real estate development project in the northeast part of Niagara-on-the-Lake. I owe you a lot of thanks for helping to make this happen. Your speech to the council was very effective and won the day for us. I believe that when we put the referendum to all the people in our town, the vote will be strongly against the development project."

"That's very good news indeed, Nigel," I responded. "Now you and all of us who do not want the development to go ahead will need to get our message out to all the people in Niagara-on-the-Lake. Those of us who are opposed to the project need to actively promote our cause to ensure that we win the referendum vote."

"I wanted to get the referendum vote done before the council breaks for the summer," Nigel added. "We have scheduled the vote for Monday, June 17. That should be enough time to get our message out to all the people and to organize the structuring of the referendum."

"That sounds very interesting," I said. "I will send you copies of the speech that Michael Simone gave to our group just over a month ago and also the speeches by Wim Vanderdonk and Lars Hogeboom from our meeting at the library on the night of the shootings. Please feel free to send copies to as many people as you like and to any media people who you think could help the cause."

Nigel responded with "Thanks for your kind offer, Billy. I might need to call on you for support some time during the campaign."

"That would be fine. I would be happy to help the cause in any way that I can. Just let me know what I can do," I said.

It seemed like we had finished our conversation for that day, so we both said our goodbyes for now, fully expecting to be talking with each other again very soon.

Chapter 51
A Special Date with Maria
Wednesday, May 15

My father came into my office at about ten thirty on Wednesday morning and told me that he had a pair of tickets for the Saturday matinee, May 18, for the fantasy musical *Brigadoon* at the Shaw Festival Theatre that he and my mother would not be able to use. He thought that I might like to take Maria. He was right, and I gladly accepted his offer. Maria and I had already planned on going out for dinner together on Saturday night, so now our date would be several hours longer—a matinee musical with dinner to follow.

Our company had been a sponsor of the Shaw Festival for many years now because it is an established tradition in Niagara-on-the-Lake and it is a strong contributor to the local economy. The Shaw Festival draws many thousands of tourists to our town each year. I think our company donates something like $40,000 a year to help them out. Because we are considered a good donor, we can get tickets to almost any of their productions on short notice. This year, the Shaw is doing a total of thirteen different productions at four different venues.

The Shaw Festival was started back in 1962 by a lawyer and playwright Brian Doherty and friends to produce plays by George Bernard Shaw—the great Irish playwright, critic, polemicist, and political activist who died in 1950 at the age of ninety-four. In its first year, the Shaw Festival ran for eight weekends in the summer. Later, the group decided to go beyond just Shaw plays to include plays by other playwrights of the same era and plays written at other times but with subject matter that's in the Shaw era. The expanded playbill had proven to be very popular and very successful. The not-for-profit Shaw Festival Theatre now usually ran from early April right up to late December each year.

Early Wednesday evening, I phoned Maria to talk with her about the Shaw Festival and *Brigadoon*.

"Hi, Maria, how was your day?" I asked in a friendly and caring way.

"Hi, Billy. It was a fairly normal Wednesday for me," she replied. "I didn't have any new problems to deal with today, and that always makes my day go better."

"Maria, I had some good fortune today. My father offered me a pair of tickets to the matinee production of *Brigadoon* at the Shaw Festival Theatre for this Saturday, and I accepted. You probably already know that *Brigadoon* is a feel-good musical by Lerner and Loewe that was a smash hit on Broadway in the late 1940s. I hope you are OK with extending our Saturday date to include theater in the afternoon as well as the dinner that we had already planned for Saturday evening. I'm sure you will enjoy it," I explained.

"That sounds really great, Billy," she said. "As you know, I enjoy going to see live theater productions as often as good ones are available. I know that Shaw Festival productions are usually very good. Samantha Weldon and I have gone to see plays at the Shaw Festival several times in the past, but neither of us have been to one for a few years. I am sure you and I will both enjoy *Brigadoon*, and thank you for being so thoughtful."

Chapter 52
Another Meeting at the Police Station
Friday, May 17

Ram was as good as his word and was at the front door of our office building at one thirty sharp on Friday afternoon to take us over to the meeting at the police station across the river. According to my short discussions with Chief Polowski during the week, the group at the meeting would be much smaller than the last time. There would be three of us from the House of Owls group—Ram, Michael, and me—and the same representatives from the four American policing agencies: Chief Polowski from the Niagara Falls Police, Gordon Kendrick for the New York State Police, Vincent Mauro from the FBI, and Robert Brewer from the CIA. Gordon Harris of CSIS and Jan Wellers of DKDB would also be attending the meeting by phone.

Ram and I arrived at the police station, and as we entered, we saw Michael in the lobby, waiting for us. He had also just arrived. The three of us were ushered into the meeting room, where all the police service people were already seated and waiting for us. Everyone said hello to one another and shook hands to get things underway in a friendly fashion.

Chief Polowski spoke up, welcomed everybody again, and got the meeting underway. His first request was for Vincent Mauro, the FBI guy, to report to the group on his investigations into the ballistics.

"As I promised, I went to Detroit, Michigan, to check out the Straight Path Rifle Company," Special Agent Mauro said. "Mr. Delvechio was right. The four slugs that were recovered from the shootings were fired from SP-50 sharpshooter rifles manufactured by the Straight Path Rifle Company.

"Mr. Delvechio was also right in saying that Straight Path test-fires every rifle before shipping them out. From the test-firings, they keep ballistics records of each gun that they sell and which dealer or agent they sold the gun to. As we already knew, there were two different rifles involved in the shootings, and they were both the same SP-50 model.

"The company showed me the purchase invoice for the two rifles, which listed each rifle's serial number along with the model number and other information. The invoice was dated about a year ago, confirming that both rifles were sold to a retail gun shop with the name Schenectady Arms Company of Schenectady, New York, a smaller city about twenty miles north of Albany.

"I followed up my investigation by going to the gun shop in Schenectady to check their records. They were eager to cooperate with the FBI, so they let me see their sales invoices, which showed that both guns were sold on the same day to two different farmers who lived in the Stoodley Corners area near Schenectady. The names on the invoices were Wilfred Smith and Arnold Johnson. When I checked out the two names and addresses that the gun shop provided, I found that they were both totally fictitious.

"That was the end of my investigation, and that's all that I have to report for now. It looks like we have reached a dead-end in this line of searching, unless anyone else has any ideas that I could follow up."

"Thank you, Special Agent Mauro," said the chief. "It does seem like you have reached a dead-end. Next, I would like Detective Kendrick to report on his investigations."

"Thank you, Chief Polowski," Detective Kendrick started. "I contacted the Albany office of the New York State Police to ask for their help, and they were very obliging. My associate, Detective Raymond Scofield in Albany, visited the Albany Gun Club and was able to confirm that the two men who Mr. Delvechio mentioned, Gary Masterson and Harold Remington, are both members of the club and practice target shooting there quite often.

"Officials at the gun club were not certain what kind of rifles the two men used for practice. But they did tell us that the targets used by members for practice shooting were renewed at least once a week and more often if the club was busy. They also told Detective Scofield that any targets used by Mr. Masterson or Mr. Remington would be gone by now. So you see, their investigations have also led to a dead-end."

"Thank you, Detective Kendrick. It's a little disturbing that our investigations seem to be stalled like this," said Chief Polowski. "Agent Brewer, have you had any better luck?"

"No, not really, Chief," said the CIA Agent. "I checked out the Army Reserve activities of Masterson and Remington, with little success. Their commitment to the reserve is one weekend per month. They spend a good portion of that time at target practice with sniper-type rifles, but they use army-supplied military rifles, not their own. So this investigation was really not much help at all for us. However, we at least know that both Masterson and Remington have had a lot of practice with sniper rifles and would certainly know how to use them."

Detective Kendrick spoke up and said, "I also did some investigation into the activities of Masterson and Remington and the man who they supposedly work for, Mr. Anthony Scaglione. They do appear to work for his company, the Scaglione Agency, as Administrative Assistants, whatever that means.

"The business of the company appears to be political lobbying and possibly some other less savory activities as well, but there are no criminal records that I could find anywhere on the company or Mr. Scaglione. However, both Masterson and Remington have long lists of criminal charges from their younger days, but nothing recent."

I spoke up with "It seems like your investigations have been very thorough even though they produced no significant results thus far. I am not sure what this leaves us with or where we go from here, but the murder of the three men should not go unresolved. I hope there are other avenues to be explored that could produce some better results."

"Thank you for speaking up, Billy. I, too, hope that our four police agencies can continue the investigations and eventually come up with better information," said Chief Polowski. "The four of us will continue to investigate, and we will be in contact with one another frequently to discuss the situation and review our progress."

Both Jan Weller in the Netherlands, and Gordon Harris in Toronto were not pleased with the investigation results to date and were quite vociferous in expressing their dissatisfaction to the group. It's not every day that people from Canada or the Netherlands get shot in the United States.

The meeting appeared to be coming to a close now, so the chief said, "Thank you all for coming today. We will be keeping in touch with each of you from time to time to let you know what's happening."

Chapter 53
Brigadoon
Saturday, May 18

I had always enjoyed going to live theatrical productions, especially some of the old musicals from the 1940s, 1950s, and 1960s. In various conversations with Maria, I realized that her tastes were much the same as mine. I was very pleased that my father thought of me when he found out that he and my mother would not be able to use the two tickets to this Saturday's two o'clock matinee production of *Brigadoon* at the Shaw Festival Theatre.

When I chatted with Maria on Wednesday evening about going to the *Brigadoon* matinee on Saturday, she was very enthusiastic. I drove my red Corvette over to her house and picked her up, and we were back at the theater at about one thirty, in time to have a glass of wine at the theater bar before the show started.

The show was great as expected. Shaw Festival productions were usually of the highest professional quality. The music was memorable, and Maria and I were singing some of our favorite tunes, such as "Almost Like Being in Love" and "I'll Go Home with Bonnie Jean" while we drove over to the Orchard Inn for dinner after the theater and again while we were driving back to Maria's house after dinner.

Driving home alone after leaving Maria, I realized, not for the first time, that she was probably the person who I would like to spend the rest of my life with and that I should think seriously of doing something about it sometime very soon. I guess the next step was for me to go and buy an engagement ring and ask her to marry me. I really hoped she would say yes.

Chapter 54
A Meeting with Tony the
Man, Bat, and Gunner
Saturday, May 18

Tony the Man had called for Bat and Gunner to come to his office for a meeting on Saturday at 1:00 p.m. to review their progress with various projects and for new instructions.

"First of all, here is your bonus money for the Harvey Goldsmith deal. Our client was very pleased with our work and may have some more business for us in the future," said Tony.

They both smiled and happily took the money.

Tony continued, "You should both go for a visit to Syracuse to see if the Downtown Medical Clinic is writing enough prescriptions for oxycodone and fentanyl to satisfy our clients. While you're there, you could encourage doctors to push up the volume a little. More is better.

"There are a couple of new activities that also need your attention. Billy Jones, one of the leaders of the House of Owls group, will be in a seventy-five-kilometer bike ride for charity on Monday. Part of the ride goes along the Niagara River, on the Canadian side, from Fort Erie to Niagara Falls. You should get some of your Blue Cobra Club friends to give him another warning about the House of Owls and rough him up a little, but they should make sure they don't get caught.

"The other one is that our owly friends are holding meetings again next Friday. There will be two meetings this time—one in Niagara-on-the-Lake and one in Niagara Falls, New York. The one in Canada will be at the Chateau des Chutes Winery again. You know where that is because you've been there before. The one in Niagara Falls will be in a function room, the back room, at an Italian restaurant called Trattoria Brunelli. I will give you that address later. It should be very easy for some of your local Blue Cobra friends to find.

"Things are different this time. You can't do these jobs on your own because some of the people at each of the meetings would probably recognize you right away and you could be in a lot of trouble. You might even end up in jail. You will need to hire some of your beefy Blue Cobra buddies for each of the two meetings. I would suggest maybe four people for each meeting, and you could follow them from a distance to see how they are doing. Bat, you could take one of the meetings, and Gunner, you could take the other one. Whatever you do, don't let any of them see you and don't get caught."

Chapter 55
Billy Does a 75K Bike Ride for Charity
Monday, May 20

The Jones family had always been supportive of several charitable organizations, especially the health-related ones. I had followed family tradition, and I had supported charities whenever I could. One event that I had supported for several years now was the annual seventy-five-kilometer bike ride for the Multiple Sclerosis Society that goes through various parts of the Niagara Peninsula, starting and ending at Kingsbridge Park in Chippawa, a suburb in the southeastern part of Niagara Falls.

This ride was very popular for fairly casual bike riders like me, who were not supercompetitive athletes, because this part of the Niagara Peninsula was quite flat, which made it relatively easy for us wimpy bike riders. This ride usually attracted three thousand to four thousand bikers who each raised money in sponsorships supporting their bike-riding efforts.

The MS Society held the bike ride each year in the Niagara region on Victoria Day, a holiday that has been special to Canadians since at least 1845, which honors the late Queen Victoria. The holiday was originally held on May 24, the actual date Queen Victoria was born in 1819. But the date of the holiday has been changed to be celebrated on the last Monday before May 25 each year, which is always the penultimate Monday in May. This year, the May 24 holiday was on Monday, May 20.

The MS Society Bike Ride went from Chippawa, which was only about a kilometer along the river, above the falls before the swiftly flowing Niagara River drops a little more than fifty meters over the falls, and continues on to flow out into Lake Ontario.

I was at the park and ready to go by nine in the morning, dressed in my colorful green biker's helmet, my white New Balance jogging shoes, my black padded Lycra biking shorts, my beige-colored biking gloves with padded palms, and my red MS Bike Ride T-shirt with my rider number 2211 attached. I also had my black leather fanny pack belted around my waist for my cell phone, some cash, and other stuff.

I set off on the cross-country ride, moving along steadily at about twenty-five kilometers an hour as I had done in previous years. I knew that at this pace, I could finish in about three and a half hours or so even after allowing for stopping for refreshments and snacks at some of the rest stops and a fifteen-to-twenty-minute stop for a light lunch break and rest at the halfway point.

Even though the organizers gave each rider a paper map of the route, each turn was well marked as to which way riders should go. I made the cross-country ride to the halfway stop in just over an hour and a half after a couple of brief rest and refreshment stops along the way.

The halfway stop was at the Waverly Beach Park, which fronts on Lake Erie, just southwest of the town of Fort Erie where the Lake Erie flows into the Niagara River. Fort Erie is on the Canadian end of the Peace Bridge opposite Buffalo, New York, on the other side.

After my break at the halfway stop, I got back on my bike and rode through the town of Fort Erie and out onto the Niagara Parkway. The parkway was a very scenic ride, with many attractive, large private residences on the left and the river, which was only about thirty meters from the road, on the right. The parkway would eventually lead me all the way back to Kingsbridge Park in Chippawa, where I started.

The traffic on the parkway tended to be fairly light, which made it a good venue for bike riders. I was only a few kilometers out of Fort Erie when I heard two motorcycles coming up behind me. As they pulled up beside me. one of the riders shouted out, "Your number is 2211. Are you Billy Jones?"

As I responded with a yes, the nearest rider came closer, lifted his heavily booted right foot, and gave me a thundering kick that knocked both my bike and me sideways into the roadside ditch. It was grassy and dry, so it didn't hurt too much when I landed on my side. The two bikers both stopped quickly and came over to me. They tromped on the spokes of both the back and front wheels of my bike and broke most of them. They also slammed their heavy boots in the wheel frames and bent them badly out of shape.

As they started to move toward me, I thought they might be looking to do as much damage to me as they had already done to my bike. They told me they thought I must be the House of Owls guy and that we should not hold any more meetings ever again. They also said that we should break up the organization and quit all activities.

They were ready to convince me physically, but I got lucky. Just as they came nearer to me and seemed ready to do more damage, a group of about a dozen or more cyclists was rapidly approaching and was now less than one hundred meters away. Seeing the group rapidly approaching, the two troublemakers seemed to change their minds about doing more damage to me. They jumped on their Harley Hogs and took off, faster than a cheetah chasing down its lunch, before the friendly cyclists arrived. As they were rapidly speeding out of sight, I looked up and noticed a logo on the back of their leather jackets that looked like a blue snake of some kind, maybe a cobra.

Several of the friendly cyclists stopped to see if I was hurt. I told them I wasn't and thanked them for stopping. I stood up and looked at my bike, and I knew right away that it was in no condition to help me win the yellow jersey of the Tour de France bike race or even finish that day's MS Bike Ride. Fortunately, I had brought my cell phone in my fanny pack and was able to call for a van to come and pick me up. The ride was over for me.

While my broken bike and I were waiting to be picked up by the van, I didn't need to think very long why those thuggish bikers wanted to do damage to my bike and me. It now seemed obvious that they must have been directly or indirectly on the payroll of the Scaglione Agency and that this was yet another attempt to disrupt the activities of our House of Owls group. It was too nice of a day to be thinking only negative thoughts, but it seemed like that was the answer.

They kept coming after us, but someday we'd get even.

Chapter 56
Billy Chats with His Mother
Tuesday, May 21

I was up earlier than usual that morning because I wanted to chat with my mother before she went off to Brock University to give her Tuesday morning history lectures. I had finished my breakfast and was sitting at the kitchen island that served as our breakfast table, sipping my coffee, when she came in. All she wanted for her breakfast that day was a power bar and a coffee, so I poured her a cup, gave it to her, and asked if she had time for us to chat for a minute.

"I need to ask for your advice and opinion on some matters that are important to me," I blurted out.

"That's fine, Billy. I have a few minutes. What is it?" she asked.

"I think I am in love with Maria. Actually, I know that I am in love with Maria, and I would like to ask her to marry me. From what you know of Maria, do you think she might be in love with me too, and do you think Maria would be a good life partner for me? That's really two different questions," I asked her haltingly.

"I'm pleased to know that you are serious about a permanent relationship with someone as extra special as Maria. I have only met Maria once, but I did have the opportunity to chat with her alone for a short while the day that she and her father joined us for our Sunday dinner. From our time chatting together, I thought that she seemed like a very good person. She seemed very intelligent and very friendly. She is also very attractive. She is working hard as a full-time high school teacher, and she is interested in politics as you are.

"Those all seem like the right kind of qualities that you should be considering when you're looking for a life partner. There are many other things that you need to consider, but these characteristics are some of the most important ones. On the other part of the question, I don't know if she loves you or not, but she did seem quite caring, and that's a good sign," my mother offered.

"My other question is about buying a diamond engagement ring for Maria. Do you think I should go to some of those better diamond shops in Toronto, or do you think I could find what I want at one of the local jewelry stores?" I asked.

"Several of the local jewelry shops are very good, but you would obviously get a much larger selection to choose from if you go to the diamond shops in Toronto. The area around the intersection of Yonge and Bloor Streets has several good stores. Or you might want to go a block north to Hazelton Lanes as well. There are also some very good stores in that area that could be worth a visit," my mother advised.

"Thanks for the good advice. I think I will take a day off work tomorrow and go to Toronto," I decided.

Chapter 57
Arranging for the Next House
of Owls Meetings
Tuesday, May 21

As we left the meeting at the Niagara Falls police station last Friday, Michael Simone and I briefly discussed and agreed that we should expand the activities of our House of Owls group by setting up several functional committees on both sides of the border. The committees that we decided on were municipal, state or provincial, federal, and media relations, one of each of these for Canada and another one of each of them for the United States.

Late Tuesday morning, I phoned Michael to see if he had arranged a meeting with the US members of the HOO for this coming Friday evening as we had planned. Michael confirmed that he had arranged for the meeting. He expected to have at least twenty-five people attending who would all be interested in working on a committee. The meeting for the US group was scheduled for seven thirty on Friday evening in the function room at the Trattoria Brunelli restaurant, with the compliments of Michael's good friend Marco Brunelli.

I told Michael that I had arranged for a meeting with the Canadian group for seven thirty on Friday evening at the Chateau des Chutes Winery, compliments of my friends Henri and Jeanne Renault. We also expected to have about twenty-five people who were interested in working on a committee.

The purpose of both meetings was to set up four committees on each side of the border to help the House of Owls promote the cause of Direct Democracy more aggressively and more thoroughly at all levels of government and in the media. Michael and I were both very pleased that so many of our members showed a willingness to work on the various committees.

It seemed like every meeting that we have had for our House of Owls group had been disrupted in some way or another by someone trying to stop our progress. Thanks to Ram, we knew who they were, but there wasn't much that we had been able to do about it thus far.

Maybe they will leave us alone now, or if they don't, maybe we will be able to do something about it. Someday we'll get even.

Chapter 58
Billy Buys a Diamond Engagement Ring
Wednesday, May 22

Just before I left work on Tuesday, I went to my father's office to ask if it was OK for me to take Wednesday off from work to go to Toronto to look for a diamond engagement ring for Maria. I told him my plan to ask Maria to marry me. This startled him a little at first, but he quickly recovered and said that he was very happy for me. I told him that I had already discussed the matter with Mother and that she thought it was a good idea. He readily agreed to my being absent on Wednesday.

I actually slept in a little on Wednesday morning because I didn't want to hit the QEW (Queen Elizabeth Way) that would take me the 125 kilometers to downtown Toronto, too early to be in the middle of the rush-hour traffic. Rush hour for the QEW was something of a misnomer. It was neither a rush nor an hour. The usual pattern was that traffic crept along bumper-to-bumper virtually all the way to Toronto, starting as early as six in the morning and lasting until after nine. Coming back from Toronto was just as bad. Heavy rush-hour traffic usually started to build up before three in the afternoon and continued until after seven in the evening.

By starting out at just after nine, I was hoping to be behind the heaviest flow of traffic, and for the most part, I was. It took me about an hour and a half to drive to the Yonge Street exit, which I took and parked in a large parking lot just south of the railway tracks. I thought it would be much easier to take the subway up Yonge Street to Bloor Street than to try to drive through the city traffic and find a place to park up there.

I went into the subway at Union Station to go north on Yonge Street. I exited the subway on the south side of Bloor Street and noticed that there were many shops of various kinds going west along Bloor from the subway station. I visited three jewelry stores along the street, asking as many questions about diamond engagement rings as I could think of, and I quickly learned that the most important four Cs for judging diamonds are color, cut, clarity, and carats.

The next store that I went into had the elegant and appropriate name of Vive la Coeur. Diamonds are a thing of the heart, and we are told that diamonds are forever. From my own basic knowledge and the tidbits that I had picked up so far that day, I had decided on the color that I wanted, bright white, and the clarity, flawless—meaning no inclusions and no blemishes visible under a microscope that can magnify ten-fold.

I needed to learn more about the other two Cs—cut and carats. I began my questions to the jeweler at Vive la Coeur by asking about various cuts. He showed me several different rings with diamonds of different shapes. I liked the round cut and the emerald cut the best until he showed me one called the Asscher cut. It really caught my interest.

The jeweler told me that the Asscher cut was first introduced into the diamond world in 1902 by the Asscher brothers in the Netherlands. He explained that the Asscher cut diamond is similar to the emerald cut, but its square shape has larger step facets, a higher crown, and a smaller table. I didn't know what all that meant, but I could see the difference between the two rings that he showed me to demonstrate these features. And I liked the Asscher cut better.

The last C that I need to consider was carats. I had been thinking that a three-carat ring would be nice, but when the jeweler told me that good quality diamonds, which I might be interested in, were usually priced at seven thousand to eight thousand dollars per carat depending on various other features. The pricing changed my mind, and I decided to limit the size of the diamond to two carats. I asked the jeweler if he could show me a ring with my four chosen Cs, and he said that he had several that I should consider.

One of the other features that I wanted was that the diamond should be from a Canadian diamond mine, if possible. I had learned a little about diamonds from studying Canadian diamond-mining companies as possible investments for our company and our clients. Canada was one of the largest, diamond-producing countries in the world, along with Russia and Botswana.

The Canadamark is a registered trademark of Canadian diamond producers that ensures quality and gives buyers confidence in a diamond's origin and history. Some of Canada's best diamonds come from the Ekati Diamond Mine in the Northwest Territories. The mine is located on an island in Lac de Gras, about three hundred kilometers north of Yellowknife, the territorial capital. The name Ekati is from a Tlicho word meaning "fat lake." The Tlicho people are the First Nations group in that part of the Athabaskan region of Canada's Northwest Territories.

The jeweler showed me a two-carat, Asscher-cut Canadian diamond from Canadamark. It looked like the one I wanted. I asked the price and winced a bit when I heard $14,400. I asked if there was any way to get a reduction on that price, and the jeweler said, "Maybe. I'll go and ask my manager." When he returned, he explained, "My manager said that if you purchase the ring right now, today, we can offer it to you at a price of $13,600."

That seemed like the best deal that I could get here, so I decided to bite the bullet and go for it. I would get an extra 1 percent cash back on my Visa card, which would help a little. Before I started out on this buying trip, I had made sure that I had enough room on my Visa card to buy a ring at any price up to $15,000. The deal was done. I had the ring that I wanted and was finished shopping for the day. I walked over to the Yonge Street subway and headed back to my car to get on the highway to go home.

On the drive along the QEW heading back to Niagara-on-the-Lake, I felt quite self-satisfied that I was able to buy a diamond engagement ring of top quality that I really liked. I was hoping that Maria would accept my marriage proposal and that she would like the ring that I had chosen as much as I did.

Chapter 59
More Meetings for the House of Owls
Friday, May 24

Michael Simone and I had arranged for two separate meetings on Friday evening, one for each of the respective US and Canadian House of Owls groups. The purpose of the meetings was to set up four operating committees on each side of the border.

Michael had arranged for the US group to meet in one of the functions rooms in the back part of the Trattoria Brunelli restaurant owned by his good friend Marco Brunelli. I had arranged with my good friends Henri and Jeanne Renault for the Canadian group to meet at their Chateau des Chutes Winery in the visitor's presentation area, where we met before. Both meetings were planned for the same time to start at seven thirty so that Michael and I could discuss our progress, by phone, later that evening after the meetings.

The meeting of the Canadian group started on time at seven thirty at the Chateau des Chutes Winery. There were twenty-five people there who were all members and had been to previous House of Owls meetings. After considering many factors, the choices for committee leaders was made.

Henri Renault volunteered to chair the Provincial Relations Committee. Paul Browne agreed to chair the National Relations Committee. Emily Peters would chair the Municipal Relations Committee, and Sarah Wortzer would chair the Media Relations Committee.

I thought that I would not chair any of the functional committees, but I would be available to work with any of them from time to time, as might be helpful or necessary. I thought that I could be particularly helpful with the Municipal Relations Committee since it would be easy for me to work closely with my good friend Nigel Bromley, our lord mayor of Niagara-on-the-Lake.

Sarah Wortzer was a natural to lead the Media Relations Committee since she was a well-known and highly regarded journalist and investigative reporter with *The Penn*, a small but prominent tabloid newspaper covering the whole Niagara Peninsula region. Its masthead read "THE PENN is mightier than the sword." And it often was.

Newspapers, in general, had been losing readership in recent years because the news was readily available online on various forms of electronic media. Although newspapers weren't as popular as they once were as a means of promoting ideas, there weren't many swords around these days either. Sarah had been a reporter with *The Penn* for more than three years and recently took on more responsibility for covering local news in the Niagara region since the shooting of her friend and colleague Mitesh Partook at our meeting on Friday, May 10.

Paul Browne was a local lawyer, but several of his clients had operations across Canada and in other countries. This meant that he was often in touch with business executives and government leaders from different areas, and that gave him the opportunity to spread the Direct Democracy word in different areas. Ram wanted to work with Paul on the National Relations Committee because his business activities also took him to many parts of the country and sometimes beyond.

Emily Peters was an architect and an artist. She and her husband, Franklin Peters, owned a building on the main street in the downtown part of Niagara-on-the-Lake, which had their art gallery on the street level and their architectural business offices on the second floor. Both their businesses had been very successful for many years.

As leader of the meeting, I announced the names of the four chairpersons to the group at large and asked for volunteers for each of the four committees. Earlier, when I had phoned all our Canadian members asking for committee volunteers to come to this meeting, everyone who said they would come to the meeting also said they would like to volunteer to be on one of the committees. Gratefully, we seemed to have a solid core of people who were ready, willing, and able to take an active role in the House of Owls campaign for Direct Democracy.

Each of the committee chairpersons separately asked for volunteers, and the larger group was quickly divided up into groups with three or four people on each committee. Each group went to a different corner of the room to organize and discuss their strategies going forward. Things seemed to be working the way that I had hoped.

About half an hour after our committees began their separate meetings and discussions, four thuggish-looking men walked into the winery and started shouting and pushing things around, like a crash of rhinoceroses in a Swarovski Crystal store. I went over to the gang of four and asked them if I could help them. I recognized two of them as the thugs who knocked me off my bike on Monday. Now I know for sure what the trouble on Monday was all about. Before I could make a move, one of the thugs gave me a hard fist to my eye, and I staggered backward. It looked like these goons wanted to fight or disrupt our meeting any way they could.

Some of the other House of Owls members saw what was happening and came to my aid. Ram was the first one there and gave one of the toughs a very hard, fast fist to the nose. He went down heavily and stayed there while Ram went looking for another one. He grabbed another guy by the neck and wrestled him to the floor with a very hard landing that knocked the wind out of the guy.

While Ram was fighting off two of the bad guys, Jeanne Renault grabbed a bottle of wine from the counter and whacked one of the guys over the head. He went down in a daze with the wine from the broken bottle dripping all over him. He stayed down in a purple daze while Jeanne called 911 and asked for a quick response by the police. She thought that she had wasted a good bottle of their Cabernet Sauvignon, but then again, maybe it wasn't such a waste.

While all this was happening, I quickly recovered from the punch to my face, and I was ready to take my best shot at the guy who had hit me. He seemed surprised that I was still standing and ready to fight back. I swung with all my might, and my fist landed full in his face. He went down in a bundle of rubble on the floor, looking like he might stay there. I was not the strongest guy in the world nor the toughest, but I did land a very solid punch this time.

Between Ram's handiwork, Jeanne's ability to swing a bottle of wine, and my lucky punch, we had all four of them under control. Moments later, four police officers arrived, quickly surveyed the situation, holstered their guns, and came to our aid.

Sergeant Donald Forsythe and Officer Myron Brooks said hello again to Ram and me. They were two of the police officers we had met before on the night our cars were blown up. Sergeant Forsythe said, "Billy, it seems like you and Ram are magnets for trouble. Tell me what happened here."

"We were simply having a meeting of our House of Owls group when these guys came in, uninvited, and started causing trouble. They were about as welcome at our meeting as an Oh Henry! chocolate bar floating in the deep end of a swimming pool.

"One of them punched me in the face, and then our people responded. What you see here is the result. There seems to be someone or some group out there that is strongly opposed to our group's efforts to organize and promote Direct Democracy. We are forging ahead in spite of them, and we will keep on doing our thing," I offered.

"All four of these guys are familiar to us, and they each have a long list of past offenses. We have seen them causing trouble many times before. They are associated with the Blue Cobra Club, an organized gang of hoodlums that has associated groups in many different cities in both Canada and the United States. They must have been paid by someone to attack your group tonight and disrupt your meeting. We'll take them down to the station and hold them overnight while you think about pressing charges," Sergeant Forsythe explained.

After the four policemen left the winery with the four disrupters in tow, our four committees went back to their respective corners to continue their discussions and planning.

Since I wasn't a part of any of the committees, I thought that I should call Michael to see if he had any difficulties with his meeting.

He answered his cell phone on the first ring. I told him it was me and about the trouble we had had at our meeting.

Michael said, "We had a similar experience here, but we were very fortunate that I had invited Chief Polowski to our meeting as an observer. When the trouble started, he took charge very quickly and jumped into action. With his leadership and some help from a few others, the scuffle was over in minutes. The four guys here were also members of the Blue Cobra Club and were well-known to the local police. A backup police team arrived very quickly and hauled the thugs away to jail. We need to consider if we should press charges or not. I think we should."

"I think so too, Michael. We can't let these people, whoever they are, get away with their continuing harassment of our House of Owls members and our meetings," I said.

The four Blue Cobra troublemakers who had disrupted our meeting had been taken away to jail, and our four committees had finished their separate meetings and departed. Paul Browne, Ram, Henri, Jeanne, and I sat at the bar, each sipping a glass of wine. Our conversation was about our House of Owls group, the progress we had made, and the troubles that we had at all our meetings.

Ram said, "I know from my earlier investigations that both Bat and Gunner are members of the Blue Cobra Club in Albany, and I am sure that they and the Scaglione Agency are behind the attacks tonight at both of our HOO meetings. They are almost certainly behind the attack on you, Billy, during your MS Bike Ride on Monday."

We all agreed that he was probably right, but none of us knew what we should do about it. Ram suggested that he, Michael Simone, and I should go back to police chief John Polowski and ask him to arrange another meeting with all the various police agencies that were looking into the shootings at the House of Owls meeting at the library. We all agreed that this was a good next step. We needed to be updated on the progress that has been made in the investigations of the three murders.

Chapter 60
The Day after the Meetings
Saturday, May 25

That day, Saturday, was a very important day for me, and I was suffering from a high level of anxiety that was not common for me. It was the day that I was going to ask Maria to marry me, and I would give her the diamond ring that I selected. In my heart, I knew that we were right for each other and that she would say yes. However, in my mind, I had all kind of doubts. I supposed that this confused state of mind was common to most men when they put themselves in this situation. But I would get through it.

About nine thirty in the morning, I phoned Maria because I wanted to confirm that I would be joining her and Michael for dinner that evening at their home. She answered with her usual cheerfulness and a chuckle, "Hi, Billy, how was the fight last night at your House of Owls meeting?"

Michael must had told her that our meeting had the same type of disruption by thugs that their meeting had. "I'm fine," I said. "But you may not recognize me. I'm wearing a mask or, at least, half a mask. I look like a raccoon that has wiped away the mascara mask from only one eye with cold cream. Actually, I took one fairly hard punch to the eye from one of the thugs before I landed a lucky-but-very-hard punch to his nose that took him down."

"Are you hurt badly?" she asked.

"No. Other than the black eye and my pride, I think I'll be fine," I said. "I was just phoning to see if Michael will be going down to the police station this morning to press charges against the Blue Cobra Club guys who messed with your meeting last night and to make sure that it is still OK for me to join you and Michael for dinner tonight at your house. I hope the mess at our two meetings didn't change our schedule."

"Yes, Billy. My father is down at the police station right now filing charges against those thugs. And no, Billy, we're still on for dinner. We're both looking forward to having you join us," she replied.

"That's great, Maria. I'll be there around five thirty for the dinner at about six, as you suggested. I'll see you then."

Chapter 61
Blue Cobra's Thugs Get Out of Jail
Saturday, May 25

Before we left the meeting Friday night, Ram, Paul Browne, and I agreed to meet at the police station at ten thirty on the next morning to press charges against the Blue Cobra thugs who had disrupted our meeting the night before and started a fight.

The appointed time was drawing near, so I thought I should leave now to get to the station for the meeting. As I pulled into the parking lot, Paul and Ram were already there standing beside their cars, chatting. I parked my car, got out, and said hello to both of them as we went into the police station.

We asked to speak with Chief Ian Fraser because he knew us from previous meetings and he might understand our cause a little better than someone else might. He came to the front desk, said hello to each of us, and ushered us into a meeting room. He knew that we were there about the Blue Cobra guys and asked if we wanted to press charges.

Paul Browne was a lawyer and thought like one. He asked the chief, "Is there any reason why we should not press charges?"

The chief responded with "No, not really. But the charges they face are not very severe, and if you press charges, it could lead to more harassment from the Blue Cobra Club people in the future. And there are quite a lot of them out there."

"We appreciate your comments, but we think we should go ahead with the charges," Paul said. "The Blue Cobras will probably harass us in the future anyway whether we press charges now or not. So we think we will go ahead. What do we need to do today to set the wheels in motion?"

"I'll get one of my officers to come in and walk you through the paperwork. Once it's all completed, we'll gets things moving along. I expect that some lawyer for the Blue Cobra Club will be in today to post bail and arrange for the release of those guys. It's possible that they could choose to skip town on these charges, but it's not very likely. They have been down this road more than once in the past," said Chief Fraser.

While they were dealing with the paperwork, a man came into the station asking about the Blue Cobra Club members who had been locked up. He said, "My name is Myron Shystok. I am a lawyer from Buffalo, and I am registered as a lawyer to do business in both Canada and the United States. I'm here to arrange for the release of the four men you arrested last night on frivolous charges. They are Raul Chavez, Rota Galadhu, George Small, and Sam Ferroni."

The desk sergeant said, "Yes, you called earlier this morning, Mr. Shyster. Your clients are in the cells at the back part of the jail."

"My name is Shystok. That's s-h-y-s-t-o-k, ending in *o-k*, not *e-r*. Get it right, OK! You know my name, copper. I've been here before," he said in a very loud voice. "What have these men been charged with? I'm sure that it's nothing important. I want to arrange for their release right away."

"They have been charged with illegally entering a private meeting, disturbing the peace, and assaulting people," said the desk sergeant. "And they are being held, pending bail," he added.

"I'll post the bail for all four of them," said the lawyer. "Those charges are very minor and are probably bogus anyway."

Paul, Ram, and I watched with interest as lawyer Shystok went through his various activities to get the four thugs released. The lawyer paid the bail, and the four jailbirds were turned over to him. As they left, the lawyer promised that they would be available to attend a court hearing when the time came.

The three of us wondered if they would be coming back for the court hearing or if they might skip town well before that time. We did remember to ask for the names and addresses of the four gentlemen before we left the station, and they were given to us as requested.

What we didn't know, until later, was that a similar scene had taken place about half an hour ago at the police station across the river in Niagara Falls, New York. The four thugs who disrupted the House of Owls meeting in the US had been bailed out by the same lawyer, Myron Shystok. When we learned about this information later, Ram and I both reached the natural conclusion that he must be on a retainer from the Scaglione Agency.

Chapter 62
Another Meeting at the Scaglione Agency
Saturday, May 25

Tony Scaglione wanted to talk with his Administrative Assistants, Gary Masterson and Harold Remington, about the lack of success their Blue Cobra Club buddies had had at the two House of Owls meetings the previous night. He phoned them both early on Saturday morning and asked them to come in for a meeting at ten o'clock.

When Bat and Gunner arrived, they were quickly shown into his office, and the discussions began.

Tony said, "Bat, you were keeping an eye on the meeting at the Chateau des Chutes Winery. Tell me what happened there."

Bat said, "I was about half a block away in a place where I was hidden by trees and shrubs. Nobody from the winery could see me, but I could see real good, with my binoculars, what was going on. I was watching, along with my four Blue Cobra Club friends, when the meeting started at seven thirty. I sent them in at about eight fifteen. They were supposed to disrupt the meeting for a few minutes and then leave. A few minutes after they went into the building, I heard police sirens coming my way, so I left before they could find out that I was there. I don't like dealing with the police."

Toni asked, "Gunner, what happened to your group of heroes?"

Gunner went through his litany. The activities that he described were almost the same as the activities that Bat had done. Gunner said he also took off right away when he heard the cops coming.

"Neither one of your two groups did what they were supposed to do last night, and now all eight of those guys are in jail. I will need to send a lawyer to bail them out. I will call Mr. Shystok after we're done here and get the wheels rolling," said Toni. "These owly guys are starting to be a major problem for us. We'll have to come up with something more convincing than what we have done so far. I'll have to think for a while about what the next step should be, and I'll let you know what I need you guys to do."

Chapter 63
Dinner with Maria and Michael
Saturday, May 25

I left home on Saturday afternoon at about five to head over the river to the Simone house. I arrived at about five thirty, as I had hoped. The front door was opened as I was about to tap on it, and Maria was there with a big hug, a long kiss, and a very friendly "Hi, Billy."

As I stepped inside the front door, I whispered to Maria, "Can we talk for a minute before we go in to chat with Michael?"

She said, "Yes, of course, Billy," and she waited for me to start to say something.

Now was the time for the big question. As I was getting down on one knee, I reached into my pocket for the ring box with my nervous hands shaking noticeably. I looked up into her gorgeous brown eyes and said, "Maria, I love you with all my heart, and I am certain that I would like to spend the rest of my life with you. Will you marry me?" And I put the ring on her finger.

She seemed a little surprised at first, but not for long. As I moved to stand up, she came to me with tighter hugs and many kisses, and somewhere in there, she said yes several times. It was great for me to see that she was so very happy and enthusiastic about my proposal. I didn't know what I would have done if she said no or rejected me in any way.

After we both recovered slightly from the happiness and joy of the moment, we thought we should go in to see Michael and let him in on our good news. He was sitting in his at-home office, relaxing and reading the latest issue of *The Economist*.

He looked up at our smiling faces as we entered his office, and he said, "Hi, Billy. What's up with you two? Why are you both looking so happy?"

As Maria stuck out her left hand to show off her ring, she blurted out, "Billy asked me to marry him, and of course, I said yes. Isn't that wonderful news?"

Michael smiled as he rose from his chair and came over to shake my hand and hug Maria and give his wholehearted approval of our engagement and our future marriage.

When he spoke, he said, "It seemed like only a matter of time before you two would discover what everybody else already knows. You are very good for each other, and you should be together. However, I would suggest, Billy, that you decide to wait at least a few weeks for the wedding to let your black eye heal. You wouldn't want your wedding pictures to show you looking like the Lone Ranger with half his mask missing."

"Thank you for showing your confidence in us, Michael. Maria and I are both very happy to have your good wishes," I said. "We have not talked about when our wedding date will be just yet, but it will probably be sometime after my black eye has healed."

Maria spoke up with "Dinner is almost ready. Why don't we make that a topic for discussion during our meal? Let's all go to the table now, and we can start with a salad before I serve up the main course, my veal parmigiana with asparagus and roasted potatoes."

As we were enjoying Maria's wonderful cooking, the topic quickly turned to planning the wedding date. Maria mentioned that a June wedding would be nice. But the time was too short for June this year, and June next year was too far away. She also said that the same reasoning applied to the month of September. July and August were usually too hot to really enjoy a wedding, and they didn't seem like very good options.

I volunteered, "A guy who I knew at university, Mark Hinkley, and his wife, Mari, chose to get married on New Year's Eve—December 31—last year. That might be an option for us to consider."

"That seems quite different, but it does sound interesting," said Maria. "A New Year's Eve wedding would certainly make it very easy for everyone to remember our anniversary date and would also be a good reason to have an anniversary party every year."

Michael said, "We don't need to decide on the date today, but New Year's Eve would give you both plenty of time to give a lot of thought to all the many details that you may want to consider in planning for your wedding."

The discussion on wedding plans continued right through Maria's great dinner, with lots of ideas considered but no final conclusions made. We did have plenty of time to decide on things if we were going to go with December 31 as the wedding date. Right now, it seemed like we probably would.

After dinner, Michael and I started to chat about each of our episodes at the two police stations earlier that morning. We both learned that things had gone almost the same at both places. We both also had questions in our minds about whether any of these guys would show up for the court hearings when their times came.

The three of us discussed our continuing problems with whoever it was who was attacking us in various ways at all our meetings. Whoever it was, was very persistent in not wanting the House of Owls group to succeed in spreading the word about Direct Democracy.

I mentioned to Maria and Michael, "Ram is virtually certain that it is coming from agents of the Scaglione Agency. The agency is a highly paid lobbying organization, and someone or perhaps several groups do not want to lose the political control they have through their lobbying activities, paying 'special' politicians to vote the *right way*."

I told Michael that I had a list of the names and addresses of the four thugs who barged into our meeting, and I told him that I would send him a copy by email as an attachment. And I asked him if he had a list of the guys from his meeting. He said he did and that he would email a copy of his list to me.

The three of us chatted at some length about the various things for organizing our wedding. We continued our discussion about New Year's Eve as the possible date for our wedding. We also considered what church we should use for the wedding and where we should hold the reception. But we weren't ready to make any final decisions on any of these items just yet.

The three of us agreed that we were making good progress with the development of our House of Owls group and Direct Democracy. We were all quite proud of ourselves since we played a significant role in getting everything started. This was a very happy evening, especially for Maria and me, but Michael was also very pleased for us both.

The time had come for me to head back across the river to home.

Chapter 64
More Trouble for the Scaglione Agency
Monday, May 27

Tony Scaglione thought that he had been followed a few times recently by someone who seemed to know what he was doing. Tony didn't like to be followed by anyone because he never knew what they might be up to. He was able to get a picture of the man from the security cameras of his office building. Through his many sources, he was able to find out that the man following him was Raymond Scofield, a detective with the New York State Police based in Albany.

He wasn't sure why Detective Scofield would be following him, but it didn't matter. He didn't like it. He knew that various police agencies, including the New York State Police, were continuing to investigate the shooting of the three men at the House of Owls meeting on Friday night, May 10. He thought the man following him might have something to do with that.

Tony was not very happy about being followed by a cop on a regular basis and decided to do something about it. He developed a plan and called in Bat and Gunner to carry it out for him. Tony knew that neither Bat nor Gunner could do the deed themselves because they were too well-known to the police in the Albany area. A plan involving them could easily go wrong. He wanted Bat and Gunner to make an arrangement with some of their Blue Cobra Club buddies to carry out the plan, but they would be directed and watched by Bat and Gunner.

At a meeting in Tony's office, Bat suggested that two of their club members from Puerto Rico could do the job. Bat and Gunner had both decided that they would recommend Juan Rodriguez and Javier Martinez. Juan had the nickname J-Rod. This came simply from giving him a nickname similar to the great New York Yankees third baseman, Alex Rodriguez, who was known as A-Rod. Javier's nickname was Gin. This unusual nickname came from the fact that many of the Blue Cobra Club members were white rednecks who couldn't tell the difference between Martinez and martinis. This led to the nickname Gin.

Tony explained his plan to Bat and Gunner on how to stop Raymond Scofield from following him. He had developed his plan after having another one of his lesser-known Administrative Assistants follow Scofield for a few days to see if he had any regular patterns to his daily movements. He did. Almost every day, usually between ten thirty and eleven, he stopped at the Dunkin Donuts shop on East Riverside Drive for a midmorning coffee and whatever. He usually stayed between fifteen to twenty minutes. Regular movement patterns like this made Tony's plans a lot easier.

Chapter 65
J-Rod and Gin Go to Work
Wednesday, May 29

Bat and Gunner arranged with J-Rod and Gin for the project to get rid of Detective Scofield and made sure that they understood the plan. All four of them monitored the movements of the New York state detective for a part of the day on Monday and all day on Tuesday. They were confident that their plan would work and were ready to put it into action on Wednesday.

As expected, Detective Scofield went into his usual Dunkin Donuts shop at about ten thirty on Wednesday morning under the distant but watchful eyes of the four bad guys. J-Rod and Gin drove their pickup truck into the Dunkin Donuts parking lot and stayed in their vehicle, waiting for the policeman to finish his coffee and return to his unmarked police car.

As Scofield exited the coffee shop and began walking toward his car, J-Rod was coming toward him across the parking lot, waving his hands and shouting hello. As J-Rod came closer, he said, "Officer, I need your help." At the same instant, he rammed a hypodermic needle into Scofield's arm and shot the lethal cyanide poison into his body. As Scofield's body went limp, J-Rod moved him into the police car on the passenger side, ran around to the driver's side, jumped in, and quickly drove off. Gin was following in his pickup truck.

They drove over to the East Riverside Mall parking lot, where they were supposed to meet Bat and Gunner to take over for them. All went well for them, and Bat took over driving the police car while J-Rod and Gin disappeared. Bat drove the police car over to HR Metals Recycling Company and talked with Hub Radek about the special delivery they had for him that day for his automobile compactor. They were very specific that this time, the hubcaps should be left on the car because they didn't want any of it left for someone to find.

Hub processed the car through the compactor with the passenger on board. The very compact block of scrap that came out the other end was loaded onto a truck, along with other scrap metal, and sent on its way to the Remelt Steel Company in Pittsburgh.

When scrap is used to make new steel, it is heated in a furnace to above the 2,500 degrees Fahrenheit melting point of steel. The old scrap steel becomes purified, and all the other parts of the scrap are either burned off or separated into different components for resale. There would never be any trace of the human body or the police car that were sent to the scrapyard that day.

Chapter 66
Ram's Motorcycle Repairs
Wednesday, June 5

Ram thought that he would like to give a little payback to get even with the four guys who tried to break up the Friday night meeting of the House of Owls group at the winery. Billy had given him a copy of the list of names of the four Blue Cobra thugs and their addresses, so he knew how to get to them. Billy had received a copy of the list from Niagara Falls Police Chief Ian Fraser. Ram thought these goons should be taught a lesson in some way, but not excessively damaging.

Ram knew that all four of them had Harley-Davidson motorcycles, and he was thinking of various ways that he could mess with their bikes to cause a little damage. He had learned long ago from an old myth that putting sugar in the gas tank of a car or motorcycle to cause the gas to solidify didn't work. Sugar actually had the same effect as beach sand and would simply sink to the bottom of the tank and clog up the works.

He knew enough about mechanics to know that if he simply put water in the gas tanks, then that would do the trick. Water is easier to work with than sand, and water is also heavier than gasoline. The gas would float to the top and leave the water at the bottom of the tank. The fuel lines go from the bottom of the tank and would soon be delivering water to the engine. Since water does not burn very well in a gasoline engine, it would stall, and the line would be blocked with the water.

Ram thought, *Water it is. Raul Chavez, Sam Ferroni, Rota Galadhu, and George Small, I'm coming after you.*

At four in the morning on Thursday, June 6, Ram was out and about and ready to do some watering. He had the list of names and addresses in hand and a case of twenty-four bottles of water sitting on the seat beside him in his Jeep Grand Cherokee.

It didn't take Ram long to do the rounds and see that all four of the Harleys were properly watered. He also used his can of black spray paint to write *I-4-I* in big letters on the windshield of each bike. That was his payback message. In a small city like Niagara Falls, it didn't take long to get from one place to the next. Ram finished his little task in less than an hour. He was done for the night.

Chapter 67
No News about the Shootings
Friday, June 7

I was in my office working away diligently on Friday morning when my phone rang unexpectedly. It was Lars Hogeboom calling from the Netherlands.

He said, "Good morning, Billy. How are you doing today? We haven't chatted for a while. I thought I should get in touch with you to see if you have some better updates on the shooting event than what I have received from the various police agencies in America. They don't seem to be making any progress at all, according to the reports that we have received over here."

"Thanks for calling, Lars. It's good to hear from you. Yes, you're right. They seem to be at a standstill," I said. "We have been pushing them from our side too. Don't forget there was also a Canadian journalist killed in that shooting and my very good friend Ram Delvechio was wounded. We, Canadians, also have a keen interest in making progress at getting somebody arrested and charged.

"I think I mentioned to you before that Ram and I are both fairly certain who the shooters are. We think that the two guys who came to my office offering me a bribe and demanding that we disband our House of Owls group are the guilty ones. These were the same two goons who punched out Ram in the winery parking lot on April 10. They are both Americans living in Albany, New York. We reported those incidents to the US police agencies, but they keep telling us that they have been unable to find any reliable evidence that they could use to file charges against them."

Lars pointed out, "Our government has been pushing the Dutch ambassador to the US for answers, and the DKDB are having conversations with the CIA on a regular basis. Even though our politicians and our police agency have been trying to put pressure on their American counterparts, it's been to no avail thus far."

"As you probably know, Lars, since I am a Canadian, I am not really in any position to put pressure on the American police agencies. However, my very good friend Ram was a former member of CSIS, the Canadian version of the CIA, and might be able to help us in some way through his many connections there. I'll have a chat with him later today to see what he thinks we might be able to do now. I'll send you an email after I talk with Ram and let you know what we plan to do," I said.

"Thanks, Billy. That would be helpful. I hope you can come up with some way to move forward with this," said Lars.

"I hope we can too, Lars. I will let you know as soon as I have something worth passing on," I said.

After we said our goodbyes and hung up, I thought that it would be a good time for me to phone Ram then. So I did.

Ram answered on the first ring with "Good morning, Billy. You must be psychic. I was about to give you a call. I was thinking that it is about time we had some results from the investigations into the shootings. Maybe we should phone Chief Polowski and ask about their progress."

"Ram, I just had a call from Lars Hogeboom from the Netherlands. He is quite upset about the lack of progress that the American police agencies have made. He seems to be thinking the same as you are. We need to understand where they're at with their investigations and what results they have achieved so far. Is there anything in particular that you think we could do right now?" I asked.

"That's why I called, Billy. Maybe one of us should phone Chief Polowski and ask him to arrange another meeting with the US police group. I could make the call if you like," said Ram.

"That seems like a good idea, Ram. Let me make the call, and I'll let you know. I hope you'll join us at the meeting. Is the morning or afternoon usually better for you to go over for a meeting?" I asked.

Ram answered, "I am generally available for the next few days. I have a bunch of office work that I need to catch up on. I could stop working almost anytime to go to a meeting."

We both said, "Goodbye for now."

I phoned for Chief Polowski and was fortunate to find him in and available. After he said hello, I said, "Good morning, Chief Polowski. It's Billy Jones here. I am calling to see if you can tell me where you're at with the investigation into the shootings last Friday at the library. I had a call from Lars Hogeboom from the Netherlands this morning. He is very concerned about the apparent lack of progress that you and the other police agencies are having with finding the guilty parties. Do you have an update that I could pass along to Lars and to my associates with the House of Owls group?"

The chief responded with "There isn't much new that I can tell you about, Billy. The only good news that we have had recently is that an Albany-based New York State Police detective Raymond Scofield has been tracking the activities of a Mr. Anthony Scaglione. According to his latest verbal report back to Howard Kendrick, the state police representative here, Mr. Scaglione seems to be involved in many activities that are on the wrong side of the law.

"Unfortunately, Scofield did not file a written report, and he has been missing for several days now. The speculation is that Mr. Scaglione became aware that he was being followed and did something about it. The Albany City Police and the Albany office of the State Police have some history of Mr. Scaglione's dealings. His reputation is that he can be unscrupulous and brutal and will resort to any kind of criminal activity to protect his interests and his ventures."

"I'm not surprised that he is known for his work," I said. "We have had nothing but bad experiences with him and his associates. Do you think the Albany police would be prepared to bring him in for questioning?"

"That's a good idea, Billy. I'll send a request to them and see how they respond," said the chief. "They tell me that Mr. Scaglione is known to be a slippery character and would likely be able to weasel his way through questioning by the local police without providing any worthwhile information."

"You should probably make the request anyway just to let him know that he is under consideration as a person of interest for the shootings," I pointed out. "Lars, Ram, and I were thinking that it is time to have another meeting so that you and the other police agencies could give us a more complete update on what has been done and what is planned to be done going forward."

"You're probably right, Billy," agreed the chief. "I will get in touch with the other agencies to arrange a meeting, and I will let you know. How is your timing for a meeting over the next few days?"

"Ram and I are available most days next week. For Lars, it's better to have the meeting in the morning since they are six hours earlier than us over there in the Netherlands," I answered.

"Thanks for pointing out the time difference. I'll check with the others, arrange a time, and let you know," said Chief Polowski.

He phoned me back early Friday afternoon and said that he had arranged for a meeting of the four police groups at his office for ten in the morning on Tuesday, June 11. He asked if that would work for our group, and I told him it would be fine. I also told him that I would send an email to Lars Hogeboom in the Netherland to ask him to join us on the speakerphone in the police station meeting room. Everything was set up for a meeting.

I phoned Paul Browne to tell him about the meeting and to ask if he could make it. After checking his schedule, he said that he could not because of other unchangeable commitments, but he wanted me to be sure to give him an update as soon as possible after the meeting.

I phoned Ram to make sure that he would be available. He said he was. We agreed to meet at his place and go over to the meeting together. I suggested that we should be on our way by about nine o'clock to make sure we got there in time. Crossing the border at morning rush hour could be slow.

I thought of phoning Michael Simone, but I decided that it would be better to tell him in person since Maria and I had planned to go out to dinner that evening.

Chapter 68
Another Meeting with the Police Groups
Tuesday, June 11

Ram and I arrived at the Niagara Falls Police Station at about eight forty-five on Tuesday morning, and Michael was already there waiting for us. The three of us went into the station together. We were expected and were ushered in to the meeting room where all the others were already seated around the table and having a friendly chat with Lars on the speakerphone.

After we arrived and were settled in, Chief Polowski reintroduced everybody in the room and Lars on the phone. We had all met before, but the reintroduction was helpful. The chief began with "We have checked every conceivable person in the Niagara Falls area who might have done the shooting, and we have been unable to find any worthwhile evidence or any potential persons of interest.

"We did check all the local members of the Blue Cobra Club but could not find any connection between them and the shooting. We knew that it was four members of the Blue Cobras who disrupted the House of Owls meeting on May 24, but that is all we could charge them with. We had to let them go because we had nothing more to hold them for.

"I am convinced that the shooters were not from this area. It may well be that the Scaglione team from Albany is the guilty group. These are the guys that Mr. Delvechio and Mr. Jones suggested might be the ones who did it. Our state police have been investigating them, and I would like to ask Detective Howard Kendrick to tell us more about that investigation."

Detective Kendrick began with "Thank you, Chief. Yes, I asked my associate, Detective Raymond Scofield, with the Albany office of the New York State Police to investigate Mr. Scaglione and his operations. He delved into their history and followed that up with tailing him at a safe distance to check on his daily activities. Detective Scofield phoned me a week ago with a verbal report that Scaglione was indeed involved in some very unsavory businesses.

"Before he could put his report in writing and send it to me, he went missing. I have not heard from him for more than a week now. He has not reported in to his office, and they have not heard anything from him for over a week as well. He has not contacted me, so I assume he has met with foul play. We have no proof of what happened or who might have done something. It's a very easy guess that Mr. Scaglione or some of his associates are guilty of orchestrating Detective Scofield's disappearance, but we have no evidence at all to prove anything."

The chief spoke up and asked, "Mr. Delvechio and Mr. Jones, could you please tell the group what you know about Mr. Scaglione?"

I thought that I should answer first, so I said, "Yes, Chief. I have never met Mr. Scaglione, but I have met two of his bullyboys who he calls Administrative Assistants. Two guys barged into my office on Thursday, April 18, demanding that I cancel the House of Owls meeting on that Friday night and all future meetings as well. They also offered me a cash bribe of two hundred thousand dollars if I would promise to do what they asked. I said no and demanded that they leave my office right away or I would call the police. That seemed to scare them off. At that point in time, I had no idea who they were, where they were from, or who they worked for."

Ram began to talk just as I was finishing and said, "I first saw the same two guys the next night. That would be Friday, April 19. Billy, Mr. Jones, had asked me if I would keep an eye on the parking lot at the Chateau des Chutes Winery while the meeting of the House of Owls was going on. I parked my SUV off in a corner and watched these two large, scraggly guys wander around the parking lot, writing down license plate numbers. I went over to them to ask what they were doing, and their response was to pummel me with punches, followed by a few kicks in the ribs after I went down.

"As you can tell from our encounters with these two thugs, Billy and I have seen their faces quite clearly and could easily identify them even though we didn't know who they were.

"As Chief Polowski may have mentioned, I am a private investigator. My credentials are that I am a registered CPA and a lawyer with an active membership in the Ontario Bar Association. I also learned many valuable investigative techniques during the three years that I was a member of CSIS.

"Using my experience and the contacts that I have developed over the years, I was able to track down the two goons who threatened Billy and attacked me. They are Gary 'Bat' Masterson and Harold 'Gunner' Remington. I was able to get pictures of them and showed them to Billy, who confirmed their identities. I was also able to find out who they work for. It's the Scaglione Agency, owned and managed by Anthony 'Tony the Man' Scaglione. The business of the agency is political lobbying and a host of other ventures that are usually considered criminal activities."

Chief Polowski asked, "Mr. Delvechio, you seem quite certain about these guys, but you don't seem to have any hard evidence?

"You're right, Chief. The only evidence that we have is the two face-to-face meetings that Billy and I had with these guys. I know what you're saying that neither of the incidents that we suffered is worth much in court to aid a prosecutor," Ram explained, frustrated.

To everyone around the table, the chief said, "Is there some way we can bring these guys in for questioning without charging them with anything?"

Detective Kendrick responded by saying, "I could probably arrange to bring each of them in separately to our Albany office for a discussion since they all seem to live in Albany. We could do the interviews in a regular police meeting room with a one-way mirror so that all of you could watch if you would like to join in these sessions."

I suggested, "This seems like a good idea," and all the heads around the table nodded in agreement.

Chief Polowski said, "Detective Kendrick and I will work together to set this up. We will let everyone know what the interview schedule is and the location."

Lars commented, "I hope these interviews in Albany produce some results. Our FvD party and our police agencies are very unhappy with the lack of anything to date. Please keep me informed going forward."

Chapter 69
Preparing for the Niagara-on-the-Lake Referendum
Thursday, June 13

I had promised my good friend Nigel Bromley, the lord mayor, that the House of Owls and I would help in any way that we could to ensure that the upcoming referendum vote on the proposed lakefront property development would be negative.

I had asked Sarah Wortzer, a HOO member and a senior reporter for *The Penn*, if she could help us out. She said she would. She had already arranged to have several articles published in *The Penn*, including reprints of Michael Simone's speech to HOO from our meeting at the winery on April 19, my speech to the Niagara-on-the-Lake town council on May 7, and the FvD speeches by Wim Vanderdonk and Lars Hogeboom to the HOO meeting at the library on May 10. She also wrote several other articles, including a longer one condemning the shooting of her colleague, Mitesh Partook, and the three others on the night of the HOO meeting at the library.

In addition to these articles, Sarah also volunteered to write an editorial about the referendum on the lakefront property development in Niagara-on-the-Lake. In the article, she wanted to emphasize the fact that the decision was to be made by a referendum of all the residents of the community and not just by their elected town council members.

This was the first time that a political decision like this would be made by the people and represented real progress in the development of Direct Democracy.

Sarah was personally opposed to the development, the same as the lord mayor and me. However, like us, she said she would be ready to accept and support the results of the referendum, pointing out that the process was the important thing even though she hoped for a negative vote. This is Direct Democracy at work.

I had given a speech to the local Chamber of Commerce last week about Direct Democracy and the upcoming referendum. In my speech, I emphasized that everyone should get out to vote even if they disagreed with me. My contributions to the cause also included several luncheon meetings with the lord mayor and local business leaders on a one-on-one basis.

The referendum date was getting very close. It was scheduled for next Monday, June 17. The lord mayor and I both thought that we had done enough to achieve our desired result. The pollsters were agreeing with us, and we were predicting we would get about 64 percent of the vote going our way. But considering how fickle voters can be, at times, you can never be sure of victory until all the votes are counted.

I sent an email to all my friends at HOO encouraging them to make sure they got out to vote on Monday to help us all to let people know that Direct Democracy was a good thing and that it worked.

Chapter 70
Maria and Bill Make More Wedding Plans
Friday, June 14

June was often the best month of the year in our corner of the world. It's like Goldilocks when she ate the baby bear's porridge; the temperature was usually not too hot, not too cold, but just right. This year, the traditional month of April showers extended through to the early part of June. But now, the rainy days were gone, and the sun was shining brightly. The warm, sunshiny days of June were welcomed and appreciated by everybody.

Maria and I frequently talked about our wedding plans. After a lot of thought and consideration, we both agreed and decided that the date should be December 31, New Year's Eve. This would give us a good reason for a double celebration every year. We both liked that.

There were still many things to consider and plans to be made for our wedding. Our first step of choosing the date was done. Having our wedding on a Tuesday seemed unusual, but New Year's Eve was when it was. We couldn't change that.

The next step was choosing a church. This was a little bit problematic since Maria was Roman Catholic and our family was Anglican. Maria and Michael didn't go to church very often, unless going to mass at Christmas and Easter was considered regular churchgoing. On the other hand, my family and I usually went to church every Sunday and supported our church on a regular basis.

Our church, Saint Marks, was built in 1790 and is one of the oldest Anglican churches in Canada. The church has a classic design from that era, with old-fashioned, stained-glass windows; a bell tower; and more. The location of the church is also very attractive, sitting on more than three acres of land at the mouth of the Niagara River as it flows into Lake Ontario. We both decided that Saint Marks would be a good place for our wedding.

All four of Maria's grandparents were still living, and we wanted them to come to at least some part of our wedding. Since they were older, somewhat infirm, and didn't travel well, we knew we should have our wedding reception on the US side of the border. That's why we had earlier booked the Niagara Gorge Mansion on Center Street in Lewiston, New York. It's a grand old mansion and was exactly what we wanted.

Choosing the church and the place for our reception were the most important things for us to finalize, but now we had to work on the thousands of little things.

Chapter 71
Troubles at the Scaglione Agency
Friday, June 14

Chief Polowski and Detective Kendrick worked with the Albany office of the New York State Police to arrange to have Anthony Scaglione, Gary Masterson, and Harold Remington come in for "discussions." The agreement was that they would come in separately on Monday, June 17. Scaglione would come at two o'clock, Masterson at three, and Remington at four. The police wanted to talk with each of them independently to see if their stories jibed.

Tony the Man knew that he needed to talk about what they would say to the police. He impressed on both of them that the first and most important point was that they would not admit to anything they might be accused of. Deny everything.

The second point was that they should not volunteer any information and answer all questions with as little information as possible. Simple yes or no answers would be preferable. If they were asked why they went into Canada on several occasions over the past few months, they would say that they went to visit some Blue Cobra Club friends in Hamilton and Toronto. "Whatever you decide, make sure that you both have the same answers."

The Man told them that he would be going in for discussions at two, Bat should go at three, and Gunner at four. He reconfirmed to them that there was no evidence of anything that they had done anywhere. If the police tried to say that there was, they should just deny it and ask for proof.

The Man told them that he was not sure which ones of the police agencies or which individuals would be there, but it really didn't matter. The questioning would probably be done by one man from the New York State Police, or it might also include Chief Polowski from Niagara Falls. Whoever was doing the questioning would probably be backed up by others behind a one-way mirror. This group would likely include someone from the CIA and the FBI and possibly some other agencies as well.

The Man also told them that they should get together again late Monday afternoon to review how everything went and to see if there were any actions they needed to take to follow up on these meetings.

Chapter 72
Police Interviews with Scaglione and His Bullyboys
Monday, June 17

Ram and I agreed to meet at our polling station for the referendum on Monday. We met, and we both voted against the project. We were very hopeful that the majority of the people in our town would vote the same way as we did. After we cast our votes, we headed off to Albany to watch the interviews with Mr. Scaglione and his bullyboys from behind the one-way mirror. We were both very interested in watching the interviews, and we wanted to be there.

We left for the four-and-a-half-hour drive to Albany right after we voted, when the polls first opened at nine o'clock. We wanted to be sure that we arrived in time for the first meeting with Tony the Man, or Mr. Scaglione. We arrived at ten minutes before two and were shown right into the private viewing room.

The interviews were being conducted jointly by Agent Vincent Mauro of the FBI and Henk Laufenberg, chief of the New York State Police based in Albany. After a half hour of relatively innocuous questions about what his business was, who worked for him, if he has been to Canada that year, and several other soft lobs, they were finished with Tony and allowed him to leave.

We had about half an hour before Bat was due for his interview. We took the time to talk with the two police officers about their discussions with Tony and if they planned on changing their approach for the other two. We knew that if Bat or Gunner saw us, it would cause problems since they had seen both of us before. We had to make sure that we stayed out of sight from those two guys while they were coming or going.

Bat arrived a few minutes ahead of his scheduled three o'clock appointment time and was directed straight to the interview room. Mauro and Laufenberg followed him into the room and began their questioning. First, they thanked him for coming in even though he wasn't legally compelled to. They explained that these were simply fact-finding meetings and he could refuse to answer any questions that were too uncomfortable for him.

After a series of easy questions like "What's your full name?" "Where do you live?" "Where do you work?" and so on, the fun began. When asked if he went to Canada often, he told the interviewers, "I seldom go to Canada, and I haven't been there this year. Whenever I go there, it's usually to go to a baseball game in Toronto to watch the New York Yankees beat the Toronto Blue Jays or to visit with my Blue Cobra Club friends at either the Hamilton or Toronto Clubs."

When asked if he had been to Niagara Falls, in either Canada or the US that year, he answered, "No." When asked if he had been to Niagara-on-the-Lake that year, he answered, "No, I've never heard of that place, so I wouldn't have gone there." They were finished with Mr. Masterson and allowed him to leave.

When Mauro and Laufenberg came in to talk with Ram and me, we told them that Bat had lied to them about going to Niagara-on-the-Lake and to Canada. We knew because we had both seen them face to face. Ram suggested that they should contact both the US Customs and Immigration and the Canada Customs to ask them to check their records for border crossings for the big black Ram pickup truck that Bat drove. Ram had done this before, and he knew what the result would be.

When Gunner came in at four o'clock, they went through the same routines as they had done with Bat. Since the answers were basically the same, it was apparent that they had both been well prepared and coached by their boss. We all knew that the next move should be to check the Customs records for these two guys.

Ram and I were very pleased that we had taken the time to come to Albany for the interviews. We hoped that the obvious lies told by both Bat and Gunner would help to encourage Mauro, Laufenberg, and the other police agencies to turn up the heat on their investigation on the shootings at our meeting.

Chapter 73
Referendum Day at Niagara-on-the-Lake
Monday, June 17

Ram and I drove back from Albany in just over four hours, arriving home at about nine o'clock. We went to the town hall, where we hoped the lord mayor and others would be gathered to celebrate the referendum victory. When we arrived, the counting of the votes was not yet complete, but returns from the early polls showed that those of us who were opposed to the development had a big lead. As the night wore on, the lead even grew larger, and we knew that at the end of the night, we would win.

Once the victory seemed secure, we chatted with the lord mayor about the success in stopping the development and the political process that got him there. He was very happy with the results from the day's voting and was now even more convinced than ever that Direct Democracy was the right way to go for all democracies. Referenda were important for everybody.

The lord mayor raised the possibility of moving our town to a full-scale Direct Democracy and establish rule by referenda for all our municipal legislation and political decisions. Naturally, I agreed. That's what the House of Owls was all about and what we had been working for since we started.

I asked the lord mayor if he would help us with our push to get Direct Democracy moving in some of the other nearby municipalities.

He said he would. I knew that Michael Simone had been trying to get the opportunity to speak to his city council in Niagara Falls. If Nigel would help us, we might be able to get there a lot faster.

Niagara Falls currently had an acting mayor, Robert Geller, whom Nigel had met on several occasions. He was the temporary replacement for the last elected mayor of Niagara Falls, Bruce Benson, who was one of the people shot and killed at our meeting at the library.

Chapter 74
Tony, Bat, and Gunner
Discuss Their Interviews
Tuesday, June 18

After their interviews with the police, Tony thought he should call his two henchmen in for a meeting to review what happened. Their meeting was scheduled for eleven in the morning, and both bullyboys arrived on time.

Tony began their get-together by telling the other two how his meeting with the police had gone. He told them that the questions they asked him were quite easy, and he was able to answer all of them truthfully without having to make up any fictitious answers. There was nothing that they knew about that he had to hide from.

Toni asked Bat how his meeting went. Bat replied, "It was good. When they asked me if I ever went to Canada, I told them that I did for baseball games in Toronto and to visit my Blue Cobra Club friends at the Niagara Falls, Hamilton, and Toronto clubs. When they asked me if I was in Canada this year, I told them no, just like you said we should."

When Tony asked Gunner how his meeting went, his answers were the same as Bat's. "You coached us real good so we wouldn't get into no trouble, and we didn't."

Tony had to warn them about possible future meetings with the police and said, "If they want to talk with either of you again, we should get together first to make sure you know what to say so that you don't get yourselves into any trouble. The police would probably call me first to arrange meetings with you guys, but if they don't and they contact you directly, you have to tell me about it so I can help you to be ready for your meeting."

Bat and Gunner both said that they understood and would call Tony right away to let him know about any meeting arranged by the police.

The discussions about their meetings with the police were finished for now. Tony took the rest of the morning to review some of the other ongoing projects that Bat and Gunner were working on.

Chapter 75
More Progress for Direct Democracy
Wednesday, June 26

My good friend, our lord mayor Nigel Bromley, phoned me at about ten that morning to ask for my help. He wanted Niagara-on-the-Lake to be the first town or city in Canada to convert to Direct Democracy on a full-scale basis. He asked if we could meet for lunch that day to discuss the situation. After checking my appointment schedule on my computer, I found that I did have some free time that day. He suggested, and I agreed, that the Orchard Inn at twelve thirty would be a good time and place for us to get together.

When I arrived at the Orchard Inn for lunch, I noticed that Nigel's car was already there. I went straight in and told the hostess that I was meeting with the lord mayor, and she walked me over to his table, which was in a nice, quiet corner of the dining room.

After our usual friendly greetings, he reiterated what it was he wanted to discuss. He started by explaining to me what he thought he needed to do to make a change in how our local municipal government worked.

"One of the first things that I need to do is to prepare a resolution proposing a change to Direct Democracy for our town's system of government for our council to discuss and debate. After ample time for full consideration, I will then propose a vote by council members. I hope the council will agree since they have previously agreed to the referendum on the real estate project development. It worked out very well, and this one should also be successful even though it is much more complicated," said Nigel.

"If I can get our council to agree, then we would ask for a referendum of all the residents of our town to vote on the issue. I think that this is something our town would like and will approve, but you never know," he added.

Since I had long been a strong proponent of Direct Democracy, I was very pleased to know that a solid politician such as our lord mayor was eager to go in that direction. He asked, "I hope it's OK for me to circulate copies of the various speeches that the House of Owls has done to my council members. I have copies of the talks, including the one by Michael Simone at your House of Owls meeting on April 19, your comments to our city council members on May 7, and the very impressive speeches by Lars Hogeboom and the late Wim Vanderdonk of the FvD on May 10."

I added, "Sarah Wortzer has written several articles for *The Penn* about the House of Owls and Direct Democracy, and I will get copies of these for you to circulate to the council members. These articles indicate that the level of interest in Direct Democracy is very strong among the residents of Niagara-on-the-Lake."

As we finished our lunch and were ready to leave, I told Nigel I would like to help in any way that I could in getting the referendum process established in our town.

Chapter 76
The CIA and the FBI Get Serious
Monday, July 8

Robert Brewer of the CIA and Vincent Mauro of the FBI told Chief Polowski that they would work closely together in trying to solve the mystery of the shootings at the library on May 10. It was very unusual for the two agencies to help each other, but the investigations into the mystery of the three shootings was not making any progress at all. Something new was required. If you keep doing the same things, you will keep getting the same results. Nothing!

On Monday, the week after the July 4 holiday celebrations, Brewer and Mauro drove together to Albany from Niagara Falls to start their search from the only meager lead they had. Ram Delvechio and Billy Jones were quite convinced that Tony Scaglione and two of his henchmen, Masterson and Remington, were the guilty parties. Brewer and Mauro would start their search with this group.

When they arrived in Albany, they checked into the Hilton in the downtown area and were ready for a long stay, if necessary. After they were settled away, their next stop was to go to the Albany City Police Office and get as much information as they could about Scaglione, Masterson, and Remington—their primary targets.

They had phoned ahead and were able to meet with a local police detective at two o'clock just after lunch on Monday. From their discussions with the local police, they learned that Mr. Scaglione had never been convicted of any criminal offense. Many of his shady activities had been investigated at one time or another, but nothing had led the police to attempt an arrest or prosecution.

When they checked the police files on Masterson and Remington, they learned that each of them had a long list of relatively minor criminal offenses in the past, but nothing very recent. They had both been convicted and had spent short stints in jail several times, but again, nothing recent. The records showed that the last time the two were put away, their defense lawyer was Anthony Scaglione, and now they both worked for the Scaglione Agency. It seemed very suspicious.

To try to move their investigation along, they thought that it might be worthwhile to monitor the day-to-day activities of these three guys for a few days to see if that might lead them somewhere. That was the general plan, but the devil was in the details. However, nothing ventured, nothing gained. They would give it a try.

Chapter 77
The Scaglione Agency Is Being Watched
Thursday, July 11

Bat and Gunner had phoned The Man on Wednesday to tell him that they thought they were being watched and followed. Tony asked them to come in to his office that morning at eleven so that the three of them could review the situation together.

As usual, Bat and Gunner arrived on schedule. Over time, Tony had taught them that it is very important to be on time for meetings. He began by saying, "Thanks for letting me know that you've been watched and followed. I have also been watched and followed, and it's probably the same two agents My informants tell me that they are Robert Brewer of the CIA and Vincent Mauro of the FBI.

"This puts us in a very uncomfortable position, and we need to do something about it. Have both of you used tranquilizer pellet guns before?" he asked.

They both said, "Ya, we have."

Tony continued with "I have a plan to eliminate these two cops. You will need to get some help from one of your friends from the Blue Cobra Club. You should get him to follow the cops while they are following you."

Bat said, "Our friend the Hat would be a good one for that. I'll ask him if he will do the job for us. I hope you could pay him something for his work. He won't want much."

The Hat was Thomas Hattenburg, sometimes known as Tom but usually called the Hat or just plain Hat. The sobriquet was not only an obvious diminutive of his surname but also referred to his large, weird, and wonderful collection of hats of all kinds, shapes, and colors.

Tony responded with "That seems fine. You can make an arrangement with Hat to tail the men from the FBI and the CIA. I will pay him after the job has been done. The main problem will likely be trying to find a time and place to use the darts without anybody knowing what you're doing. You will need to have Hat track their habits for a few days to see if there could be a good time and a place where you can execute our plan without anyone watching.

"You will probably find that the best time to catch the two cops off guard is first thing in the morning when they are starting out. They might not be as alert as they are later in the day. You could shoot them both with tranquilizer darts, dump them into their car, and take the car over to Hub Radek at HR Metals Recycling Company. Once you get them over to him, Hub knows what to do to make them disappear without leaving any trace. Do you understand the situation OK?"

In unison, they both said, "Ya."

Tony said, "OK then. That's it for today. Keep in touch to let me know how it's going."

Chapter 78
Follow the Leader
Friday, July 12, to Thursday, July 25

Brewer and Mauro followed the two thugs every day for the better part of two uneventful weeks. But nothing happened. Each morning, by seven thirty at the latest, they parked their car in a spot outside the condo where Bat and Gunner lived and where they could see the front door of the condo and the exit from the underground garage but not be easily seen by anyone coming out.

On a typical day, Bat and Gunner would come out of the building together in one of their vehicles. Occasionally, they came out separately, each one driving alone. Bat had his pickup truck, and Gunner had his SUV. They never seemed to walk anywhere. During the time that Brewer and Mauro had them under scrutiny, they never left home before nine o'clock in the morning. Sometimes it was much later. They seemed to be a lazy pair.

While Brewer and Mauro followed Bat and Gunner every day, they seemed to be oblivious to the fact that they, too, were being followed. Hat was doing his job. In a meeting with Bat and Gunner, Hat told them about the patterns that Brewer and Mauro were following. It was particularly interesting for them to learn that the two policemen usually left the downtown Hilton hotel by seven fifteen or earlier to go over to begin their tracking for the day.

In a conversation with Tony, Bat and Gunner told him that it looked like the best time to get these guys was first thing in the morning. They usually parked their car in the Hilton parking lot behind the hotel and went to their car to begin their days.

That was the plan. On Thursday morning, Bat and Gunner were up at six and arrived at the Hilton parking lot by 6:45 a.m. They saw the two policemen coming out the back door of the hotel at about seven fifteen, as expected. As Brewer and Mauro approached their police car, Bat and Gunner each fired their air pistols, and the two cops started to crumble on the spot. The two assailants rushed over to them and quickly dumped them into the back seat of the police car.

Bat drove the police car, with the two unconscious men in the back seat, over to HR Metals Recycling Company and asked Hub Radek to do his job for Tony. Gunner had followed along in his SUV, picked up Bat after he had given instructions to Hub, and away they went. Hub did his usual good job of making things disappear.

Chapter 79
The Investigators Are Missing
Monday, July 29

The manager of the Hilton hotel in Albany phoned the local police to let them know that agents Brewer and Mauro had not been to their rooms since last Thursday but had not checked out. The Albany police went to the hotel to investigate but found nothing. The local police knew that Brewer and Mauro were with the FBI and CIA, so they called their local offices to let them know that their agents had been missing since last Thursday.

The Albany local police and the offices of the FBI and the CIA each phoned Chief Polowski in Niagara Falls to let him know that the agents were missing, without any trace of where they might have gone or what might have happened to them. These were courtesy calls. It was, after all, Chief Polowski who had made the request to have the two police agencies investigate the Scaglione Agency in Albany and anyone else they wanted to about the shootings at the library.

Chief Polowski was saddened and very frustrated with the news, but he knew that he needed to tell the House of Owls people. He phoned Michael Simone to tell him about the two agents disappearing and was not surprised that Michel was quite upset. Michael knew that he needed to call his fellow leaders of the House of Owls group and also Lars Hogeboom of the FvD in the Netherlands.

Michael phoned Billy just before noon on Monday. In a serious tone, he said, "Good morning, Billy. We have more bad news about the police agencies that are investigating the shootings at the library. Both Brewer of the FBI and Mauro of the CIA have been missing since last Thursday, and apparently, there is no trace of them anywhere. I just had a call from Chief Polowski with the bad news."

"That really is bad news, Michael. What do you think we should do now?" I asked.

"I can't think of any other police agency or authority that could help us. At two different times now, investigators have gone to Albany to look into the situation, and each time, they seem to disappear. That's not very good," said Michael.

"It seems like we have a problem. As you know, Michael, my good friend Ram is a private investigator and is very good at what he does. It wouldn't hurt for me to ask him for his advice on this. He may have some new ideas. You remember that it was Ram who found out about the Scaglione Agency for us in the first place. It's possible that he may be able to help us again now with this situation," I said.

"I can't think of any other possible solution right now, so why don't you talk to Ram and see what he says?" inquired Michael.

I told Michael that I would talk with Ram and explain our problem. I phoned Ram right after I hung up with Michael. Fortunately, he was in, and I was able to explain our problem to him. He, too, was very concerned but said he would look into the situation as soon as he could, but it might be in a day or two.

Chapter 80
The Niagara-in-the-Lake Referendum
Tuesday, July 30

The lord mayor called Billy on Tuesday morning in a very happy mood to tell about the progress he had made with getting the town council to vote in favor of the referendum process. After the council had debated his resolution very thoroughly for several days, the vote was five to four in favor of moving to Direct Democracy.

The council also voted to hold a referendum of all the residents of Niagara-on-the-Lake to let them decide if their town should be run on a Direct Democracy basis. The vote by all residents on the issue would take place on Tuesday, September 10.

"Nigel, it looks like you have done a great job," I said. "I'll be very happy to help the cause in any way that I can, and so will all my associates in the House of Owls group.

"I will ask Sarah Wortzer to write as much as she can about Direct Democracy and the upcoming referendum in *The Penn*. I will also ask her to push many of her fellow media types to support our cause. This should help," I said.

"I knew you would be interested in the results of our council's vote. I thought I should let you know right away so that you could start some of the wheels in motion," the lord mayor added.

"Thank you for letting me know, Nigel. It's much appreciated by me. All our House of Owls associates will also be very happy to see that we're truly making some real progress with our cause," I said in parting.

Reaching a certain level of success with a project like this was always very self-satisfying. This good news from the lord mayor gave me that feeling. I felt confident that this success would likely be the first of many for Direct Democracy, and I look forward to the future of our cause in a happy frame of mind.

Chapter 81
Ram Investigates
Thursday, August 1

Ram began thinking about the problem of the missing FBI and CIA agents soon after he heard about the situation from Billy. He also remembered that a detective from the New York State Police had gone missing under similar circumstances about a month ago. He thought that whatever it was or whoever was responsible, it could be the same kind of activity going on again this time.

He thought that it was highly probable that the Scaglione Agency was behind all these in some way. But to be sure, he needed to investigate the situation in a lot more depth to see if he could find out what was really going on.

Ram was puzzled about how items as large as two police cars and three policemen could go missing without a trace. If it was Scaglione, he must have a means of disposing large items like cars and human bodies that leaves no trail of any kind. There are a number of fairly simplistic ways of getting rid of bodies, such as crematoriums, landfill sites, or cement coffins, but cars are much more difficult.

The most obvious ways to get rid of cars would be to drive them a long way away and abandon them, dump them into a river or a lake, or chop them up or shred them in some way and sell the scrap metal. It could be any of these, but because the third choice would be the most probable and the easiest one for Ram to start his investigations, he thought that he would try that.

The disappearance of the three policemen happened in Albany, so Ram thought he would start there. On his laptop, he searched for Albany on Google Earth and zoomed in to the maximum. Then he scrolled carefully across the city in a grid pattern looking for scrapyards or scrap-metal dealers. He was able to identify three of them and decided to go to Albany and snoop around to see what he could find. Ram went to Albany for the weekend to follow his logic and investigate the three businesses. The first one that he came to as he approached the city from the northwest was Albany Metals Recycling Company. He stopped by their yard and looked in to see many piles of different types of scrap and a half dozen automobiles in various states of being torn apart. Each of the autoskeletons had various fenders, doors, and other parts missing—probably sold to auto repair shops. It looked like the business was closed as there was no one around to talk to about the business operations, and the doors were locked.

As Ram drove all the way through the city, he came to Larry's Iron and Metal Trading Company on the northeastern perimeter. He stopped his Jeep out front to have a look at the scrapyard from outside their fence. It was almost the same as the previous one except there were no autoskeletons in this one and, like the previous one, there was no one around to talk to.

He left Larry's and drove in a southerly direction along the outskirts of the city. He soon arrived at the HR Metals Recycling Company scrapyard. The company was also not open that Saturday and had only a security guard on duty protecting the yard from metals thieves. Ram stopped nearby. He could see firsthand that the yard was large, and he saw what he thought was a huge automobile compacting machine. He remembered the great James Bond movie *Goldfinger* where a car with a body inside was put through an automobile compactor and came out the other side as a crushed block of metal, ready for recycling. The body had vanished.

This could be it, he thought. The next chore was to think up a way to investigate the place someday when it was in operation and chat with the owner without letting on what he really wanted. Ram was satisfied with the progress of his investigations and decided to return home for now and come back another day to complete his work.

Chapter 82
Direct Democracy Is Moving Forward
Tuesday, August 27

The lord mayor had called me and asked me to join him for lunch again that day, at one of his favorite places, the Orchard Inn. When I arrived, I was taken to his usual quiet table off in a corner of the restaurant. After we exchanged greetings, our server came, and we both ordered a glass of wine. Nigel seemed very excited that day. I quickly learned that his agitated state was because he was eager to talk about the upcoming referendum for our town on September 10, his current favorite subject.

"Billy, I am very happy and excited that the polls are showing that we could win the referendum. The pollster that I use tells me that his latest reading shows that 64 percent of the people in our town are in favor of moving to our proposed system of government by referendum," said the lord mayor.

"That's great," I said. "Niagara-on-the-Lake could go down in history as the first modern democratic government to move to Direct Democracy. I think I am even happier and more excited than you are. This is why we started the House of Owls movement in the first place, and this would be major success number 1 for our group."

Nigel said, "Thank you for your kind thoughts, Billy. Much of our success will be because of all the help that you and your associates have given us along the way. Our town will owe you a debt of gratitude for getting things going."

"There is nothing better than keeping the ball rolling once it gets started," I said. "My good friend and future father-in-law, Michael Simone, would like to organize a presentation on Direct Democracy to the city council of Niagara Falls, New York. When I last spoke with him, I suggested that our referendum vote here looked like it could be successful.

"This led to him asking if you would consider being the featured speaker on Direct Democracy at a meeting of their city council. Local members of the US federal government and the New York State legislature would also be invited to the meeting. Michael thinks that he might also be able to convince New York State governor Bruno Martinetti to attend."

"That sounds very interesting," Nigel replied. "Yes, I would like to do that, but it will depend on the date of the meeting."

"Michael was thinking of Friday evening, September 27, at, say, seven o'clock. His thought was that you would still be fresh from your victory with the referendum here and would be able to speak with a winner's enthusiasm on our favorite subject. I'm assuming that you will win, of course," I said.

"That sounds good, Billy. I could do that to help your cause. I will need to check my calendar, but I'm fairly certain that I am clear for that date and time," he said. "I will let you know later today, and you can pass it on to Michael."

After they finished their lunch, they parted and went their separate ways.

Chapter 83
Arrangements for the City Council Meeting
Saturday, August 31

I had chatted briefly with Michael by phone earlier in the week after my meeting with the lord mayor. A longer discussion seemed necessary, so we planned on getting together on Saturday at his home. He suggested that Maria would prepare one of her great dinners for the three of us and we could continue our discussions about the city council meeting right through dinner and beyond.

Michael had already started to put the wheels in motion. He had spoken with the new acting mayor of Niagara Falls, Robert Geller (The former mayor, Bruce Benson, was shot and killed at our meeting at the library on May 10, and a new permanent mayor had not yet been elected or appointed.) Geller was strongly in favor of what Michael wanted to do and was willing to support our cause in any way that he could. He and Michael had agreed to a meeting at the City Hall Council Chamber at seven o'clock on Friday, September 27.

As we were enjoying Maria's dinner of homemade cannelloni and a fresh garden salad, Michael commented, "Billy, I have been in contact with our New York state governor, Bruno Martinetti, and he has agreed to join us for the meeting. He will probably bring one or two of his aides with him. I expect we will be able to attract several of the local federal members as well."

"That sounds very good, Michael," I chipped in. "The lord mayor, our featured speaker, will probably bring one or two of his council members with him, and there will be several of us from the Canadian side of the House of Owls group. Sarah Wortzer, a member of HOO and a senior reporter for one of our local newspapers, *The Penn*, will join us so that she will be able to report back to everyone on our side of the border."

"We should have a pretty good attendance, Billy," noted Michael. "I wonder if I should ask Chief Polowski if he would attend and perhaps bring one or two of his police officers with him."

"That seems like a good idea," I said. "I hope we won't have any trouble, but you never know. That was great cannelloni, Maria. I really enjoyed your dinner again."

"Thanks, Billy. I do like to cook. I am told that people who enjoy what they're doing usually do it better," she said, "There will be quite a few of us from the US House of Owls group at the meeting, so we could have a full house."

"That's great. Nigel would be very pleased to be able to speak to a full house," I said. "It would probably be a good idea if both of you came over to help the lord mayor and Niagara-on-the-Lake celebrate the referendum victory on the evening of September 10. Nigel has done some advance polling, and it seems fairly certain that the referendum will vote to move to a government system of Direct Democracy for our town. A historic first."

Chapter 84
Referendum Night at Niagara-on-the-Lake
Tuesday, September 10

We were all there, ready to celebrate—Paul Browne, the Renaults, Ram, Sarah Wortzer, and the other members from the Canadian side of the House of Owls group. Naturally, all the local politicians were also there, milling around and waiting to get the final results of what now seemed inevitable.

Michael and Maria arrived just before the polls closed at nine o'clock. As the results started to come in from the various precincts, the early results were as expected, strongly in favor of our town moving to Direct Democracy. The continuing flow of returns showed more of the same. Direct Democracy was winning by a large margin. By the end of the night, the vote was 66.4 percent in favor. Very decisive!

The lord mayor wanted to say a few words to the crowd gathered at our town hall. He began with "Thank you all for coming out tonight to help celebrate the dawn of a new era. Our local government of Niagara-on-the-Lake will be the first one anywhere to make the move to Direct Democracy. But I know we won't be the last. People in every democracy everywhere will look at our model and see just how well it works and how much better it is than the old system of representative democracy." The lord mayor was interrupted by loud and long cheers from the crowd.

When they quieted down a little, he continued with "Our push to Direct Democracy was started by our friends in a local group known as the House of Owls. They are making good progress here and across the border in Niagara Falls. I have agreed to help them with their cause because they have helped me here. I will be the featured speaker at a meeting in the City Council Chamber there on the evening of Friday, September 27.

"By explaining how we have done so well here, I hope that they will be the second jurisdiction to hold a referendum on Direct Democracy and the second one to move in that direction. Again, thank you all for coming out to help us celebrate tonight, and please enjoy the rest of the evening."

Chapter 85
The Scheming Scaglione
Wednesday, September 18

Tony Scaglione was very upset when he heard about the Direct Democracy victory in Niagara-on-the-Lake and the plans for a major meeting at Niagara Falls on his side of the border. He thought that his clients would want to do something about it. After discussions with several of them, he knew that he needed to take some action.

He knew that it would be difficult or even impossible to stop the meeting, but some kind of disruption might be possible. Disruption it would be, but how exactly?

He had learned from his usual clandestine sources that the meeting would be on Friday, September 27, at seven in the evening. The meeting was scheduled to be held at the Niagara Falls City Council Chambers, a very large room on the top floor of the city hall building on Main Street. It would be a very hard place to get at to disrupt the meeting.

After considerable refection on the matter, he came up with the idea of using a drone in some way. He thought about loading a drone with twenty to thirty pounds of explosive material and crashing it through one of the windows of the Council Chamber. The problem with that approach was that the drone operator would need to be nearby and might be easily caught. He needed a better idea.

Next, he thought of landing the drone and carrying the explosives on the roof of the Council Chamber in the darkness of the night before the meeting. By putting it in place in the middle of the night, no one would be aware that the drone was on the roof. Then while the meeting was in progress on Friday evening, he could trigger the explosion by some remote device such as a cell phone. A large explosion during the meeting would definitely be a major disruption. In his mind, he thought this would work.

As he continued to develop his plan, he realized that he could probably trigger the explosion by a long-distance telephone call while he sat in his office in Albany. That would keep him safely away from the scene when the explosion went off. This plan seemed good, and there appeared to be very little risk that he could be caught.

He realized that he would need to enlist the help of his two chief henchmen, Bat and Gunner, in arranging the purchase of a suitable drone and the right amount of explosive material. He knew that they had at least one set of false identification that they could use to make these purchases. They had used false IDs when they purchased the SP-50 sharpshooter rifles, and they could use the same set again.

He decided he would ask for their help in acquiring the goods but would do the final placement of the drone with the explosives himself. This way, Bat and Gunner could swear honestly that they were in Albany at the time and had no part in the event.

Chapter 86
The Meeting at Niagara Falls
City Council Chambers
Friday, September 27

The big meeting had gathered extensive publicity from all the media players in the area on both sides of the border. All the local TV and radio stations as well as the newspapers had been running features on Direct Democracy, referenda, and the House of Owls for the past several weeks. The meeting at the city hall was a well-promoted and highly anticipated event. Everybody in the region was engaged in discussing the ramifications of possibly moving to a new form of democracy.

The day of the meeting had finally arrived. Ram, Billy, and the lord mayor drove over to the meeting in Ram's Jeep. They parked behind the city hall, in the large parking lot, and went into the city hall building looking for the Council Chamber.

The parking lot was filling up rapidly with a steady stream of people arriving for the meeting. All the Canadian House of Owls founders would be attending the meeting. Paul Browne wanted to drive on his own as he thought he might be a few minutes late. Henri and Jeanne Renault drove over separately from their winery. Sarah Wortzer was also there and was currently in an animated discussion with some of her media associates.

Michael and Maria were in the lobby of the Council Chamber in a discussion with Maria's good friend Samantha Weldon and her husband, John. They were part of the large crowd that had gathered in the lobby.

It was now approaching seven o'clock and nearing time for the meeting to start. Robert Geller, the acting mayor of Niagara Falls, was asking everyone to move into the gallery of the Council Chamber so the meeting could begin. He was the organizer, host, and master of ceremonies for tonight's meeting.

Acting mayor Geller called for order to start the meeting. His nine council members were all in their places around the semicircular table that faced toward the mayor's desk or podium that was at the front of the room, facing out.

He began by thanking everyone for coming out to this very important meeting, with special thanks to Michael Simone and all his associates with the House of Owls group. He referred to the successful referendum on Direct Democracy at Niagara-on-the-Lake and that the lord mayor would be speaking to the meeting in a few minutes. But first, he wanted to introduce Mr. Bruno Martinetti, the governor of New York state, and ask him to say a few words.

Chapter 87
Scaglione Carries Out His Plans
Friday, September 27

Tony Scaglione's plan to disrupt the big meeting was to put an explosive device on the roof and trigger an explosion while the meeting was in progress. He needed to set this up in advance with utmost secrecy. For this highly sensitive project, he would do it himself and not rely on his usual assistants.

He asked Bat and Gunner to arrange for the purchase of the drone and the C-4 explosives. It would be his job to get to Niagara Falls and put the explosives in place without anyone knowing that he had been there to set his plan in progress.

He did have one set of false-identity papers that he used occasionally, and he thought he needed to use them this time. The phony driver's license showed him with a long-haired black wig and a matching fluffy black beard. He also had a credit card to go along with this identity.

On Thursday, he drove to the city of Syracuse about halfway between Albany and Niagara Falls and parked his car a few blocks away from an Enterprise car rental location. He put on his disguise, walked over to the car rental shop, and rented a car using his false-identity papers. He did not want to take any chances that someone might recognize his car, and he did not want to have any record that he or his car were ever in Niagara Falls that day.

He drove the rented car to Niagara Falls and went to the city hall on a scouting mission. It was only midafternoon. In broad daylight, it was easy for him to see that the deep corner of the city hall parking lot would be a good place for him to work. It was obscure, and he thought he could park his car for a few minutes in the middle of the night to launch his drone as he had planned.

He waited until four in the morning, when all was quiet and very few people were out and about in the city, and drove back over to the city hall parking lot. He checked to see that no one was around, and he was ready for action. He set it all up and launched the drone with the explosives duct-taped to it and landed it on the roof behind an air duct, where it was less likely to be seen.

The deed was done. He headed the rental car back toward Syracuse to pick up his own car before returning home. The drive to Syracuse took just over two hours. It was still only six fifteen on Friday morning, and he needed to waste some time until the Enterprise shop opened at eight.

He parked the rental car in a shopping mall parking lot for a few hours' sleep to wait for the eight o'clock opening. He awoke at eight fifteen, slightly refreshed from his short nap, and returned the rented car. After settling everything with his false identification, he walked back to his own car and headed for home.

As he traveled along the New York State Thruway, the I-90, he stopped in the Montezuma Wildlife range—where the highway crosses the northern end of Cayuga Lake, one of New York state's famous Finger Lakes—and threw the drone control unit out as far as he could into the water. He wanted the toss to put the control unit out into the deepest part of the lake, and he thought he made it. He watched the control unit sink like a rock and felt confident that it would never be found.

Tony arrived back at his office in Albany shortly after eleven on Friday morning. He was still quite tired and decided to have another short nap on the sofa in his office.

As evening approached, he grew increasingly apprehensive. He knew that the meeting at the Niagara Falls City Hall was scheduled to start at seven. He anticipated that it would probably start at least five or ten minutes late, as most political meetings do.

He had decided that the best time to set off the explosion would be at about 7:25 p.m. There was a cheap, throwaway cell phone, often called a burner, attached to the triggering device on the package of explosives. Tony had a similar burner with him in his office to use to make the call. Neither of the burners could be traced.

The time had now arrived. Tony made the call. He was very confident that arranging the burners the way he had done would make it virtually impossible to trace the source of the explosion back to him. The explosion should now have happened, but he had no way of knowing if it worked right or not. Time and any follow-up news reports would soon tell him how things went.

After he made the call, Tony went over to a walkway along the Hudson River. He strolled along until he could see no one around and then threw his burner out into the river as far as he could. He watched it land and sink and thought that he was now safe.

Chapter 88
A Massive Explosion at City Hall
Friday, September 27

The host, acting mayor Robert Geller, was in the midst of introducing New York state governor Bruno Martinetti when the explosion hit. The massive blast was like a tsunami or the Mount Vesuvius volcano erupting again. All of a sudden, there was a monstrous hole in the roof, and dust and debris were flying around everywhere. Bits of plaster, wood, steel, and other materials were hitting most of the people. Everyone was scurrying about like rats on a sinking ship, looking for a safe place to hide, but there was none.

Many people had shards of wood or chunks of metal sticking out of various parts of their bodies, which the blast had thrown at them. Some of them had wounds that looked like they could be lethal, while others did not seem to be too serious.

I had a small piece of metal sticking out of my right forearm. I took off my suit jacket, rolled up my shirtsleeve, and saw that it had not penetrated very far. I pulled out the offending object and wrapped my clean handkerchief around the wounded spot on my arm to help stop any flow of blood. There was already too much blood in the room. Many people were bleeding, dead, or dying.

I went looking for my friends and to see if I could help anyone. Maria and Michael were close by as were Samantha and John Weldon. It was very comforting to see that none of them appeared to have been hit. Ram, Henri and Jeanne Renault, and Nigel Bromley also looked like they had escaped the blast with no personal physical injuries.

Many others were not so fortunate. Paul Browne was lying on the floor with a large piece of shrapnel buried deep into his chest. He looked like he was not breathing and was probably dead, murdered by whoever caused this terrible disaster. I could guess who it was.

Looking around the room, there appeared to be many like me with small wounds that would probably heal fairly quickly. There were also many bodies lying motionless on the floor with serious or even fatal wounds. Governor Martinetti, acting mayor Robert Geller, and several of the city council members were among those who seemed lifeless and would later be declared dead.

Immediately after the explosion had hit, Chief Polowski phoned for reinforcements and for as many ambulances and other first responders as could be rounded up in a hurry. A large group of paramedics, police officers, and firefighters arrived very quickly and were now searching through the room, looking for anyone they might be able to help. Too many were beyond help.

Chief Polowski had a wound similar to mine. He had a six-inch piece of shredded wood sticking out of his shoulder. He asked one of his fellow police officers to pull out the oversized sliver from his shoulder so he could take off his jacket and see how bad his wound might be. On quick inspection, he was able to see that the bleeding had stopped and that his wound wasn't too bad. He was still mobile and was able to take charge of the aftermath of the explosion.

The chief had brought two of his fellow Niagara Falls police officers with him for the meeting. One of them appeared to have no injuries at all while the other was on the list of those who didn't survive. The unwounded officer was able to help the chief with directing people and avoiding total panic by the crowd. This was a scene of total pandemonium and could easily have led to a massive panic. Fortunately, the quick responses by the chief; his helpful, unwounded officer; and all other first responders kept the situation more or less under control. When it was all over, no one was hurt or injured by panicking crowd actions after the blast.

This was a sad night for the city of Niagara Falls, the Niagara Falls Police, for Direct Democracy, and for the House of Owls.

The investigators would spend all of the next week carefully searching through the rubble in the City Hall Council Chamber for any possible clues as to how this deadly explosion could have happened. In their careful search, they found small bits and pieces that could be part of a cell phone and other small bits and pieces that could have come from a drone.

Unfortunately, the investigation team was not able to find any evidence or clues as to who might be responsible for this terrible tragedy. Their conclusion was that whoever planned the explosion was very careful in covering their tracks and left no useful traces of anything that could indicate who they were or why they did what they did.

Chapter 89
The Aftermath
Saturday, September 28

As might be expected, the aftermath of the explosion at the Niagara Falls City Hall was a loud and long media circus. There was national coverage by news teams from all the major TV networks. ABC, CBS, CNN, Fox, and NBC were all there, along with major local, statewide, and national newspaper reporters. There was even media coverage from Canada since it was well-known that a number of Canadians had crossed the border to attend the meeting.

All the reporters were looking for a different angle on which to focus their stories. They were also trying to find out if there were any leads as to who was responsible for this vicious mass murder.

It wasn't just the reporters who were circling like frenzied, feeding sharks looking for more food. Local, state, and federal politicians of all colors were also making rash accusations and demanding answers, but getting none.

Chief Polowski was heavily under the gun but didn't know where to turn. One of his first moves was to ask his police department friends in Albany to set up another round of interviews with Anthony Scaglione and two of his associates, Gary Masterson and Harold Remington. As before, these meetings proved to be of no value in the investigations. All three of them had strong alibis as to their whereabouts on the evening of Friday, September 27. They were all in Albany, each minding their own business.

As might be expected, all the other police agencies had the case forced on them. The New York State Police, the FBI, and the CIA all got involved in the investigations, but none of them had any more success than Chief Polowski and his city of Niagara Falls police force. Whoever planned and executed the explosion appeared to have been very careful to not leave any clues or a trail of any kind for investigators to discover.

After a week or so of being the major headline in the local and national media, the story faded from view, mainly due to the lack of any change to the narrative or any progress in the investigations.

Gone, but not forgotten. Ram and many of the members of the House of Owls group believed that the explosion and the murder of twenty-three innocent people at the Niagara Falls City Council Chamber was done somehow by the Scaglione Agency through one of its many tentacles.

Ram had a vindictive temperament and promised himself that someday he would act for the whole group and get even with whoever it was who caused all this damage and death. The traditional system did not produce any results. Justice would have to be achieved in some other way.

Chapter 90
Maria and Billy Get Married
Tuesday, December 31

Maria and I spent most of the summer and fall planning our wedding. The first decision we made was to choose December 31, the day for New Year's Eve, as the date. Choosing the date was one of our most difficult decisions but, as it happened, was one of our best. It gave us lots of time to plan all the other details, and we thought all our friends would be in a good party mood over the Christmas–New Year's holiday season.

When planning everything for a wedding celebration, it's very helpful if the bride and groom are easily amenable to some give-and-take with the many decisions they need to make. Maria and I were able to do the give-and-take part without much difficulty since we easily agreed on most things. Our planning was actually fun, not a chore, as some couples seem to make it.

Maria's matron of honor was her best friend, Samantha Weldon. Her two bridesmaids were Lori Beaumont and her cousin, Sophia Simone. Lori was one of her favorite teacher friends from Saint Mary's High School, where they both taught in Niagara Falls. Her cousin Sophia still lived in Aloquin, in the Finger Lakes district of New York state, where the Simone family originally settled when they immigrated to America.

On my side, Ram agreed to be the best man, with Henri Renault and Nigel Bromley as my two groomsmen. These selections were fairly easy to make since all three of them were very good friends.

One of the next steps was choosing a church. This was a little bit problematic since Maria was a Roman Catholic and our family was Anglican. Selecting the church was a concern. After some discussion, we agreed to have the wedding ceremony at my family's church, Saint Marks Anglican here in Niagara-on-the-Lake.

As part of the give-and-take process, we had already decided that our wedding reception and dinner would be on the US side of the border. After some searching and reviewing several options, we chose the Niagara Gorge Mansion on Center Street in Lewiston, New York. It's a grand old mansion and was exactly what we wanted.

The western border of the town of Lewiston is the Niagara River, down river from the falls. Lewiston is just across the river from Niagara-on-the-Lake. It is a small town with a population of just over sixteen thousand, soon to be increased by two since Maria and I will be living there after our wedding and honeymoon.

At 2,800 square feet, our new house was not large, but it had plenty of space for the two of us. The building was quite attractive and well located. We were very fortunate to have our new home in the upscale area of Lewiston Heights, a neighborhood built on top of the Niagara Escarpment. Our new home was a wedding gift from my family.

The location suited both Maria and I very well since her commute to Saint Mary's High School will be less than twenty minutes. My commute might be even shorter. All I will need to do was zip across the Queenston–Lewiston Bridge back into Canada using my NEXUS pass to go through the border, crossing smoothly and quickly. From there, it was only a short drive to our company office in Niagara-on-the-Lake.

As our wedding day drew closer, both Maria and I became a little more anxious. The wedding rehearsal on Monday evening went exceptionally smoothly, which helped to put both of us more at ease. Reverend Reginald Hinchcliffe of Saint Marks was an older man and had many years of experience at doing weddings. It showed up in how smoothly the process went for us.

Our wedding ceremony on Tuesday, December 31, proceeded on schedule at four o'clock in the afternoon. With the help of Reverend Hinchcliffe, the wedding ceremony went smoothly, according to plan and on schedule.

The reception began at seven. Maria and I headed the receiving line as we ushered our guests into the reception area. The dinner was planned for eight thirty, and it actually started on time. Most of our guests were probably more accustomed to having dinner a little earlier and were now more than ready to eat.

Everything went well. The various dinner speeches were mostly short and lighthearted and therefore well received. The after-dinner party was a rather typical after-a-wedding dinner dance but also took on the flavor of a New Year's Eve party. That was exactly what we had hoped would happen when we planned the event. Now it was time for all of us to dance and celebrate both our wedding and the happy new year ahead.

The DJ that we hired for the evening came well recommended, and the recommendation was quite valid. He seemed to have a million different songs to choose from and was able to satisfy every request that people made.

Maria and I were able to have a few dances, but I think we both danced with every one of our guests of the opposite gender who was there. I noticed that Ram had quite a few dances with Maria's cousin Sophia. They seemed to be getting to know each other quite well.

As Father Time faded away during the evening and the Baby New Year got closer, the wedding celebration seemed to morph into more of a New Year's Eve party. Everyone seemed to be enjoying themselves as the New Year's gong was sounded amid kisses all around. Happy New Year!

Chapter 91
Ram Visits Albany
Tuesday, April 14 the Next Year

The police investigations into the explosion at the Niagara Falls City Hall Council Chamber had discovered absolutely nothing. The investigations had been going on for more than six months now and seemed to be going nowhere. None of the police agencies had found any useful clues that could lead them anywhere.

Ram was tired of waiting for their activities to produce even some modest results. Nothing was forthcoming. He knew that if the bad guys were to be caught and put out of business, he would need to take some action himself. He was ready to be the one who would deliver the appropriate retribution to Tony Scaglione and friends.

Ram had been through a lot. He was punched out after the House of Owls meeting at the Chateau Des Chutes Winery on April 19. His SUV was blown up on May 6. He was shot in the shoulder after the meeting at the library on May 10. He somehow miraculously escaped without injury after the explosion at the Niagara Falls City Council Chamber on September 27, but he could have been badly wounded or even killed as twenty-three others were.

Enough was too much. Now it was the time to get even.

Ram followed the same routine that he had followed in previous vengeful visits to Albany. He drove his Jeep across the river to the Buffalo–Niagara International Airport, parked in the airport's long-stay parking area, and went to the Enterprise car rental station. He rented a Toyota Camry and hit the road. He didn't want to have any trace of his Jeep being in Albany while he did what he had to do.

Ram had left home at around noon and arrived in Albany at about four thirty, right on his schedule. He knew where Tony Scaglione lived and went there. He parked the Camry about two blocks away, walked back to Tony's house, broke into his garage, and waited for him to come home from his office.

From his earlier research, Ram knew that Tony lived alone because his wife had left him a few years ago after she found out what kind of business he was in. She had successfully filed for divorce, took half his ill-gotten wealth, and left him the house.

When Tony arrived home from his office and drove his Jaguar XJ50 into his garage, he didn't notice Ram hiding just inside the door. As Tony got out of his car to go into the house, Ram shot him with a tranquilizer dart. Tony faded rapidly, but Ram caught him before he hit the floor and carried him into the house, using Tony's keys to get in. Ram put him on a sofa and waited for him to wake up from the milder-than-usual dose he had used in the tranquilizer this time.

About forty-five minutes later, Tony began to stir. Ram had tied his hands and feet together so that he wouldn't be making a run for it anytime soon. As he woke up, Tony almost yelled, in a garbled sort of way, "This is my house. Who are you, and what are you doing here?"

Sitting in a chair opposite the sofa, Ram responded with "My name is Jeramiah Delvechio. Your thugs beat me up once, blew up my SUV, shot me in the arm another time, and murdered twenty-three people at the Niagara Falls City Council Chamber last September. You have broken the sixth commandment too many times. You have murdered too many people. You don't deserve to keep on living"

Tony answered, "I have heard about those events, but as I told the police inquiry, I had nothing to do with any of them."

"I really don't believe you," said Ram. "But I do know how to make you speak more truthfully. This syringe with sodium pentothal or truth serum, as it is sometimes called, should help your memory a little bit."

Ram walked over to him, rolled up a sleeve, and did the injection the way he had learned while he was with CSIS. The response time for the drug to take effect varied from one person to another, so Ram allowed a full half hour before he got down to serious questioning. He didn't want any wrong answers.

Ram's first question was "Are you a doctor?"

Tony answered, "No."

"Are you a banker?"

"No."

"Are you a lawyer?"

"Yes."

"Do Gary Masterson and Harold Remington work for you?"

"Yes" was the mumbled response from Tony.

"Have you ever told them to do things that are illegal, such as intimidating, beating up, or shooting people?" Ram asked.

Tony answered, "Sometimes."

Tony seemed to be answering truthfully, so Ram continued with "I know that it was Masterson and Remington who beat me up in the parking lot at the Chateau Des Chutes Winery in Niagara-on-the-Lake on April 19. I saw their faces, and I learned later who they are. Were they also the ones who blew up my SUV on May 11?"

"Yes," he said.

Ram followed with "Did they do the shooting at the library in Niagara Falls on May 10?"

Tony gurgled a yes.

Ram's next question was "Did Masterson and Remington plant the explosives at the Niagara Falls City Hall Council Chamber on September 27?"

Tony was still a little groggy, but his answer was no.

Ram was a little puzzled but continued on with "Did you plant the explosives yourself?"

Tony murmured a muffled yes.

Ram's last question was "Have you ever used HR Metals Recycling to dispose of dead bodies"

Another yes from Tony.

Ram had been fairly confident in his own mind about the guilt of Tony, Bat, and Gunner before this little session. He was also fairly certain that they were responsible for all the abusive activities that he was asking about. Now he had the "a la mode on the apple pie of certainty" about who was responsible for all these malicious things that happened to him and his friends.

Ram's next move would be to keep Tony in an unconscious state, put him in the trunk of his Jaguar, and drive it over to HR Metals Recycling Company to visit his good friend Hub Radek. He couldn't do it today because it was too late in the evening. Hub Radek would have already closed up shop and gone home for the day.

Ram gave Tony another shot with the tranquilizer gun—with a heavier dose, this time—so he wouldn't wake up for at least twelve hours, but probably longer.

He slept in Tony's car for the night because he didn't want to leave any trace of being at his house in case his disappearance might eventually be investigated. Ram tried to be as careful as possible. From the time he first arrived at Tony's house, he had been wearing latex gloves to make sure he wouldn't leave any fingerprints.

Ram was awake and up and about by six thirty on Wednesday morning. He had checked earlier and knew that the scrapyard was scheduled to open at eight. As planned, Toni was still unconscious. Ram put him in the trunk of the Jaguar and was off to see Hub Radek.

When he arrived at HR Metals Recycling, it was open for business. Ram parked the car out front and went in to see the proprietor. Hub was there, having a morning coffee and reading his daily paper. "That looks like Mr. Scaglione's car," said Hub.

"You're right. It is," Ram replied. "He asked me to bring it over to you to put through your compactor. It has some stuff inside that he didn't want anyone to see."

"I understand," said Hub. "I've done things for him before. I guess he will be over to see me later today with the five thousand dollars."

"Yes, of course, he will. Is Mr. Scaglione a good customer of yours?" asked Ram.

"Well, yes, he is. We have been doing business together for several years now," Hub answered. "Just park the car over in front of the compactor. I can move it in with the automated controls that I have in here," he added.

Ram parked the car where he was told and came back into the control room to see how things worked. Hub pushed a big red button, and the car was moved into the compactor. When it was in position, he pushed another big button—a green one, this time. The compactor started into its slow-squeezing motion, like a boa constrictor swallowing a goat or a lamb.

When the block of crushed scrap metal came out of the other end of the compactor, Hub said, "I should give that block a strong wash with sulfuric acid to make sure that no unusual stains are showing, then a good drenching with water to clean off the acid." Hub proceeded to do as he had suggested.

As Ram was about to leave, he said to Hub, "Toni may have another car for me to bring over to you later today." He left the scrapyard, walked a few blocks to a local convenience store, and then used his cell phone to call for an Uber ride. When the Uber driver arrived, Ram directed the driver to an address that was about five blocks from the condo where Bat and Gunner lived. They were next on his list.

It was almost nine o'clock as he walked up to the condo and broke into the underground parking garage. He waited in the underground garage in the area near where both Bat and Gunner parked their vehicles.

Bat was the first to arrive. Ram shot him with a tranquilizer dart then ran over to catch him before he hit the cement. Ram carried Bat to his black Ram pickup truck, unlocked the doors with Bat's keys, and tossed him into the back seat of the quad cab with no concern for his comfort or how he landed. He looked like a small pile of rubbish ready for a landfill site.

A few minutes later, Gunner appeared. Ram shot him with another tranquilizer dart and dumped him into the back seat along with his good friend and buddy in a lumpy pile. It was now time for another trip to see Hub Radek at the HR Metals scrapyard.

When Ram drove the pickup truck into the scrapyard, he pulled it up into position to go right into the compactor. He got out of the pickup and went into the shop to talk to Hub. Ram said, "I've got another vehicle for you from our friend Mr. Scaglione. There is nothing in this one. He just wants to get rid of the truck. Check it out if you like. You'll see."

Hub said, "I think I would like to do that, like you said." They both walked out to the pickup parked at the front of the compactor. As Hub opened the back door to the quad cab, Ram shot him with a tranquilizer dart and pushed him into the back seat with the other lumps that were already there.

Two's company, three's a crowd. Everybody liked a good crowd. He also threw in the tranquilizer gun to get rid of it. He didn't want any loose ends anywhere.

Ram went back into the shop, found the big red button, and pushed it. The pickup was moved into position in the compactor. Next, Ram found the big green button, pushed it, and the action started. He waited around for the big block of scrap metal to come out the other end and doused it with a wash of sulfuric acid, followed by a heavy water wash, just like what he had learned the last time he was here.

As he walked away from HR Metals, Ram thought to himself that this should be the end of these brutes and hopefully the end of the tough times they have been giving his friends with the House of Owls group. Their meetings should be much easier in the future.

He walked a few blocks then called for an Uber ride. He stopped several blocks short of where his rental car was parked because he wanted to cover his trail as much as possible. It had been a very difficult two days of tough slugging, but it was now over and done with. He got to his car, jumped in, and headed for home.

To Tony Scaglione and friends, "Beware the ides of April."

Chapter 92
Heading Home
Wednesday, April 15

Ram was on the New York State Thruway, the I-90, heading west back to the Buffalo Airport to retrieve his Jeep and head for home. The four-hour drive left lots of time for reflection.

He was confident that Anthony Scaglione, Gary Masterson, Harold Remington, and Hubert Radek all deserved to be removed from life. He was resigned to the high probability that the many police forces involved in the investigation would not be able to learn who the culprits were or to have them punished in any way.

The police were much too shackled by their own rules and regulations to get the necessary results. He knew that if he didn't deliver justice, it would not be done. He accepted the chore as something he could do that others might not be able to do, and now it was over and done with.

There were some elements of morality associated with removing people from life, but the greater good prevailed in this case. In Ram's mind, the many considerations included talion, an eye for an eye, revenge, retribution, and justice. These were all very important to him.

Talion is the ancient, historic law of letting the punishment match the crime. It was a principle of law, developed in the early part of the ancient Babylonian empire. It was prevalent in biblical times as seen in Deuteronomy, a book in the Old Testament of the Bible. The law of "an eye for an eye, a tooth for a tooth, and a hand for a hand" was the standard practice of the day.

Many societies adopted the talion principle, but it died out in early Roman times. It resurfaced in medieval Germany and again later in the seventeenth and eighteenth centuries in some parts of Scandinavia. Talion is not in modern laws in most countries, but the principle of talion is still in the minds of many people as a way of getting even for wrongs committed against them.

Another element was revenge. It is the act of inflicting hurt or harm on someone for an injury or wrong suffered at their hands. The many people murdered by the Scaglione bunch were gone and not able to exact revenge for themselves. Someone should do it for them, and Ram volunteered for the job. It has been said that revenge is often more satisfying if it is not done immediately.

Retribution may be defined as "punishment inflicted on someone as vengeance for wrong or criminal action committed against them." This was usually the purview of the law, but for the Scaglione gang, that was most likely to ever happen. Ram delivered the retribution.

For some people, the definition of *justice* is simply "the administration of the law." For others, fair play or fair-mindedness are more important than the law in achieving justice. Ram's sense of justice was in the latter group. Fair play or fair-mindedness were more important to him. Removing Scaglione, Masterson, Remington, and Radek from life satisfied his sense of justice.

Many people often take the view that vigilante justice is not much different from no justice at all. Many other people take the view that vigilante justice is useful and even necessary in some situations. In essence, Ram was a vigilante delivering vigilante justice. He was OK with that. This particular circumstance made it necessary since his vigilante actions were probably the only way that justice was likely to be achieved in this situation.

The whole Scaglione gang and their friends in the Blue Cobra Club would probably have continued on their merry way selling illegal drugs, intimidating people with physical violence, and murdering people if they had not been stopped. But now they had been stopped.

Injustice is a way to resolve injustice.

Chapter 93
The House of Owls and Direct Democracy
Thursday, April 16, and the Future

The decision by the residents of Niagara-on-the-Lake to adopt Direct Democracy as the official form of government for the town was a milestone. The new system of democracy had been working very well for their town for more than a year now.

Under the new system, any town councilor can propose a resolution to the council for consideration. A vote by the council takes place to decide if they should go ahead with a referendum on that resolution or not. If the council approves a resolution, a referendum date is set, and a vote is held. Those for or against the subject of the resolution explain their positions to the residents of the town through all forms of media—town hall–type meetings and personal contact. The voting day happens, and the results of the referendum carry the day.

The other approach for initiating a referendum vote is for a private citizen to start the process. The first way is to simply ask one of the councilors to propose their idea to the council for discussion and a vote. If the council approves, the referendum follows the basic procedure. If the resolution is voted down by council, then the private citizen can proceed to demand a referendum on the subject by getting a petition signed by a preestablished number of residents. In our town, a minimum of five hundred names were required. This petition process forced the council to put the subject into the referendum process.

Through the Direct Democracy process, the people of Niagara-on-the-Lake made the changes to the governing rules that they chose to live by. Everyone, collectively, decided what was best. They didn't need to rely on the opinions and ideas of city councilors, whose votes could be influenced by extraneous or inappropriate considerations.

The success of Direct Democracy in Niagara-on-the-Lake soon became the envy of many other towns and cities in the area. The city of Niagara Falls, New York, was next on the list to adopt Direct Democracy, thanks to the continuing efforts of Michael Simone and the US House of Owls group.

Niagara Falls, Ontario, was next and was quickly followed by Buffalo, the largest city to make the change so far. After these early adopters, the Direct Democracy movement spread rapidly as if gasoline was dumped on a wildfire. The movement quickly spread eastward across New York state and westward across Southern Ontario in Canada.

From these early beginnings, Direct Democracy spread to most towns, cities, and states in the United States and to towns, cities, and all provinces in Canada. Direct Democracy, *a mari usque ad Mara*.

Epilogue
Forum voor Democratie, FvD
Moving Forward Rapidly

In this fictional story, the Forum voor Democratie or FvD party is referred to with fictitious names of party members. The names of the people in the story are indeed fictitious, but the party itself is very real, and its ideas are spreading rapidly in the Netherlands.

The real FvD party was founded on September 22, 2016, in the Netherlands by Thierry Baudet as a think tank. Mr. Baudet has continued to be the leader of the party up to the present day and is currently a member of the House of Representatives. Two of the FvD party's major policies are Direct Democracy and balanced budgets—more or less, as they were described in the story.

The FvD first participated in electoral politics in the March 15, 2017, general election in the Netherlands and won 2 of the 150 seats in the House of Representatives.

In the provincial elections held on March 20, 2019, the FvD went from zero votes and zero seats in the 2015 elections to a total of 86 seats out of the 570 seats available. In the 2019 election, the party received 1,057,030 votes, representing 14.53 percent of the popular vote from across the twelve provinces.

While the seat count and the percentage of the popular vote may not seem very high, they were the most for any party. The FvD won seats in every one of the twelve provinces of the Netherlands, but they had the strongest showing in Groningen, a large eastern province.

The country known as the Netherlands is best described as a constitutional monarchy. As such, the government of the Netherlands has a king as the nominal head of government. The Dutch Parliament has the primary legislative power. It is officially known as the States General of the Netherlands and consists of the House of Representatives and the Senate. The House and the Senate are based in The Hague.

Democracy was established in the Netherlands in 1815 as The Kingdom of the Netherlands. The first king of the Netherlands was Willem Frederik, a prince of Orange. He was King Willem I. The royal house of Orange-Nassau is still the ruling royal family today. Princess Beatrix succeeded her mother, Queen Juliana, on April 30, 1980. As Queen Beatrix grew older, she abdicated and allowed her son, the current King Willem-Alexander, to be inducted as the country's new king on April 30, 2013.

The Netherlands is a democratic country where Direct Democracy is rapidly gaining wide acceptance. It seems like Direct Democracy is an old idea whose time has come again.

Printed in the United States
By Bookmasters